1984

A Year in the Life of Nobby Clarke

By Jason Ayres

Text copyright © 2025 Jason Ayres

All Rights Reserved

This is a work of fiction. Names, characters, businesses, places, events and incidents are either the products of the author's imagination or used in a fictitious manner. Any resemblance to actual persons, living or dead, or actual events is purely coincidental.

Contents

December 2023 1

January 1984 28

February 1984 56

March 1984 80

April 1984 106

May 1984 128

June 1984 145

July 1984 158

August 1984 177

September 1984 194

October 1984 211

November 1984 230

December 1984 245

January 2024 265

December 2023

"My name is Robin, and I am a compulsive gambler."

Those were the words that tumbled out of my mouth when I was given the floor at my first, and to date only, visit to a Gamblers Anonymous meeting.

Before I go any further, I should say that I've nothing but respect for what organisations like GA do. Gambling can ruin lives, and for many people, finding a group like that is the lifeline they need. I'm genuinely glad those communities exist. But for me, at least back then, it didn't feel like the right fit. Now, more than twenty years on? I'm not quite so sure.

Why did I attend the meeting? To cut a long story short, it was down to a girl I was smitten with. At the time, I thought she might be 'the one' I had been looking for ever since I had lost the first love of my life, some fifteen years earlier. She wasn't, as it turned out, but I had convinced myself that she was.

The jury is still out on whether I am a problem gambler or not, but the die was long cast when it came to women. I was, and to some extent still am, a hopeless romantic. I've lost count of the number of women I've fallen head over heels for, usually far too quickly before either of us had got to know each other properly. That tendency to fall hard and fast has never gone away, but I am beginning to think that now, at the age of sixty, where affairs of the heart are concerned, the ship has well and truly sailed.

I believe it all stems back to Molly, that first love, whom I lost. After that, I was desperately trying to replace her, and having never fully got over her, it simply didn't work.

Many of my amorous cravings over the years remained unrequited. My love life was one long series of disappointments, punctuated by occasional moments of joy that were just enough to keep me hoping. My brief, tempestuous relationship with Sally, the girl who persuaded me to go to the GA meeting, was one of those rare interludes when the flame burned brightly, alas briefly. She was seemingly as desirous of me as I was of her, and for a few glorious weeks in the summer of 1999, I was so loved up from the hours I spent in her bed that when she suggested I stop betting, I seriously considered it.

Sally didn't like horse racing. She was as anti-racing as it's possible to be anti about anything. I get that – a lot of people don't like it for a variety of reasons, concerns over animal welfare and gambling harm being just two of them. She also wanted us to do things together at the weekend and took a dim view if I so much as hinted that watching the three o'clock at Sandown Park on a sunny afternoon was more important than going for a picnic or driving down to the coast.

Looking back, she was probably right, and at the time I was so enraptured with her that, for the first time in my life, I earnestly contemplated knocking punting on the head. And that was how I ended up sitting in a circle of strangers, confessing my deepest, darkest secrets as well as listening to their sorry tales.

As for my opening statement, I had some issues with it. To begin with, there's my name. Robin is what it says on my birth certificate, but no one has called me that since I was a teenager, other than my mother, and she's long dead now. I don't like it, and haven't ever since I was at school.

Back in those formative years, I got teased that it was a girl's name because some of my friends had seen an American TV show which included a female character called Robin. Also, without fail, every person I met growing up made the Robin Hood connection as soon as they heard my name. They all thought they were being hilarious, as if they were the first person ever to think of it, even though I'd heard the same boring thing hundreds of times before. I had a friend at school called Jason, and he used to get the same nonsense about Jason and the Argonauts. We both concluded it was incredibly irksome, but couldn't do anything about it.

In my case, this went away in the end, because from my teenage years onwards I acquired the nickname Nobby, and it's stuck with me ever since. I can't remember the exact moment it started, and it was a mystery at first. Even people referring to me as Nobby Clarke couldn't tell me why, but I eventually figured it out.

I remember another friend at school telling me that Nobby is short for Norbert, but I've never met anyone called Norbert, so I dismissed that suggestion. Then, a few years later, it came up in conversation in the pub when I discovered that there is a penchant in this country for people with the surname Clark or Clarke to acquire the nickname Nobby. That led to further research and several possible explanations. The most likely relates to a certain type of hat worn by clerks in the City of London hundreds of years ago.

Quite why this archaic tradition should have endured into the modern era, I have no idea, but the name stuck at school in Kentish Town, and I've never shaken it off. It's not the most flattering of nicknames, being not a million miles away from 'knobhead', which has also been cast in my direction on a few occasions. To be fair, that was probably with justification as I was doubtless acting like one at the time.

Even so, I still prefer it to Robin, and at least it stopped people from banging on about Robin Hood all the time. The only reason I used my real name in the GA meeting was that it's supposed to be anonymous, so I went with my birth name, which no one I had met for at least a decade knew me by. Not even Sally.

As for the compulsive gambler bit, I did not consider myself to be one then, and I don't consider myself to be one now. My fascination with betting has always been about the mechanics and the mathematics of it all, not a desperation to pour every spare penny in my pocket into a fruit machine the second I enter a pub. I learned my lesson about those things the hard way, chucking away my pocket money in them as a teenager, and haven't touched them since.

I realised early on that there are two types of gambling. The most common being those where the odds are mathematically and irrevocably stacked against you. Fruit machines, roulette, scratch cards, bingo – they all fall into this category. Of course, anyone can get lucky on a given day, but play any of those games long-term, and in the end, you will certainly lose.

Take a roulette wheel, for example. There are 37 numbers on the wheel, including zero. Bet on a winning number, and the casino will pay you out at odds of 35/1 if you win. The true odds, however, are 36/1. That doesn't sound like much of a margin, less than 3%, or twice that if the wheel also has a double zero. Even so, it's been enough to build places like Las Vegas into glittering metropolises, dripping with wealth.

In the long run, nobody wins, and computer simulations have proved it. Pick any number you like, spin the wheel ten thousand times, and put a quid on the same number each spin. Whichever number you picked, trust me, you'll be showing a loss after that many goes. So, gambling on such things has never interested me.

The only caveat I'd add to the roulette scenario is that there have been cases of rigged and biased wheels in the past. But I've never come across one. So, I'm happy to stick with my conclusion that it's a mug's game.

The forms of gambling that do interest me are the ones where the odds are a matter of judgment and where there is an element of skill involved, not just luck. For me, that boils down to two main areas – poker and racing. In poker, the competition consists of real people, not a machine, and in horse racing, the odds are a matter of opinion, set by bookies, punters, and supply and demand. They also fluctuate, which creates value opportunities. Or at least they did in the old pre-internet days. Things are much harder now.

With superior knowledge or skill, it was possible in the past for a handful of professional punters to thrive. I know because I was one for a while. But I rarely bothered trying to explain the ins and outs of how I went about my business to the average Joe, as they only ever had one of two responses.

The first was 'got any tips?' and the second was blatant disbelief, usually accompanied by that old cliché, 'you never see a poor bookie'. It was pointless wasting energy trying to persuade these people otherwise.

That included Sally. But I was so desperate to hold on to her, believing I had finally found the girl to banish the ghost of Molly after so many failed romances, that I went to the meeting at her insistence. It was all to no avail because less than a week later, she dumped me for an estate agent from Godalming.

Attending the meeting hit me in the pocket too, because it ran late by nearly an hour, which meant I was late getting to the betting shop. When I got there, I discovered I'd missed out on backing a 16/1 winner in the first at Chepstow, so I vowed never again. Going to GA, that was, not betting.

This all happened almost a quarter of a century ago, but for some reason, it still rankles with me. I'm not sure what I'm most annoyed about – losing the girl, not backing a big-priced winner I had carefully picked out that morning, or that I had wasted so much of my life on what was increasingly seeming like an utterly pointless hobby, which was probably the reason I had lost her, and others, in the first place. Had the life I had chosen blinded me to the things that really mattered? Getting married, having children, or some sort of proper career, for example?

And as for racing and betting itself? I'm bored to the back teeth with it now, because the game is not what it was. I can see that right now, as I sit in a local betting shop, looking around the soul-destroying surroundings that these places have become in recent years.

'When the fun stops, stop', they say on the TV adverts. This stopped being fun a long time ago, and that's nothing to do with winning or losing.

Betting shops are unrecognisable from the places they were when I first started going into them in the early 1980s. Nowadays, they open before breakfast and stay open late into the evening, a cacophony of noise and colour, assaulting the senses from all angles.

Walls are plastered with dozens of screens, flashing up odds, races, and sports from all over the world. When there's no real sport, the customers, if there are any, are bombarded with cartoon, arcade-style races going off every couple of minutes. Then there are the FOBTs (fixed odds betting terminals), those vampiric offspring of the old fruit machines, sucking every last penny out of the poor souls unfortunate enough to have become addicted to them. More than anything else, these machines and their online equivalents are responsible for the gambling epidemic that has swept the nation in recent years.

And the big betting companies? They've positively encouraged it, whatever they might claim. They don't want horse racing punters, especially ones who might make a profit over the long term. Their ideal customer is someone who'll pump money into their slot machines and casino games, where the profits are guaranteed. They want to keep those customers, no matter what new guidelines are brought in to protect the vulnerable. It's the old-fashioned punters, the ones with enough knowledge and skill to pose a threat to the balance sheet, who are banned or restricted online, or shown the door marked exit in the betting shop.

I'm amazed there are still so many bookies on the high street, because most of the time, aside from one or two desperadoes hunched over the FOBTs, they're practically empty. They're relics, outdated windows into a world that no longer exists. And as I sit perched on a stool on New Year's Eve in one of these godforsaken places, I'm seriously considering whether to give up betting as my resolution for the year ahead.

I had come in to put a bet on a horse called Big Ange, running in the last race at Uttoxeter. I still had one or two contacts in the racing industry, nowhere near as many as I once had, but this tip came from a very reliable source within a racing stable, whom I only heard from once or twice a year. I once did him a huge favour, years ago, and he's never forgotten.

I had to go into the shop because I can't get a bet on online anymore. All my accounts are restricted. If I try to put twenty quid on a horse on my phone, the app will refuse it, telling me I can only have twenty pence on, or some similar paltry amount. When it comes to online accounts, the companies know every bet you've ever placed with them, and once your card is marked, that's it. In the shops, at least, you've got some chance of getting a bet on, just as you do at the racecourse, but I wasn't trekking all the way to Uttoxeter for one bet. It's not like I was lumping a large wedge on anyway. Those days are over.

I managed to get my twenty quid on in the shop, which wasn't the one I normally use, but even so, they wouldn't let me take a price, only SP – the starting price, which is generally bad value. Other than a gaunt and dishevelled bloke feeding the FOBT rather than himself, I was the only punter there, and when Big Ange won on her debut at odds of 7/2, the sullen, middle-aged female cashier handed over my ninety quid with a scowl.

As I made my way towards the door, I could see on one of the screens that the next cartoon race from the fictional track of Portman Park was about to go off. Even though I had won, I felt little joy at my success, and just wanted to get out of the depressing place as quickly as possible.

Forty years ago, betting shops were very different places. Slightly seedy, edgy, and full of characters who came in to bet and smoke all afternoon when the pubs were closed. They were full of atmosphere, and there were no screens, just a board marker chalking up the results and a tiny crackling speaker giving out the race commentaries in the corner. The humour, the banter, and the camaraderie made for an always enjoyable experience.

From pensioners with their 10p each-way accumulators to dodgy geezers lumping on odds-on favourites with ill-gotten gains from dubious enterprises, there was a real sense of being part of something, even if it was of an unsavoury nature. But that's all gone now, part of a world that exists now only in my memories.

As I tucked my four twenties and a tenner into my wallet and stepped outside, I was seriously debating whether Big Ange was going to be my last bet of all time.

I was reasonably comfortable financially, owning my house outright. My private pension had kicked in when I turned sixty earlier in the year, and I had a fair bit tucked away from when times were good. I didn't need to do this anymore.

What I didn't have is that special someone to share my life with. That was largely my fault. I no longer had any links to my roots, on the border of Kentish Town and Camden Town, where I grew up in the 1970s. I moved out to Oxfordshire in the early 2000s after my mum and dad died. Ostensibly, it was for a job, but really it was for a girl I met on holiday in Greece, whom I was sweet on at the time.

That didn't work out either, but I had been here ever since, and to be honest I quite liked it. There were plenty of worse places I could have ended up. Now, I spend most of my spare time drinking in my local, The Red Lion, in this town where I settled all those years ago, and it is not a bad little boozer, even if some of the regulars get on my nerves. And that's where I was headed tonight to see out 2023, because it's not like I had anything better to do.

I went home, showered, and had a shave. For some years, I had sported an immaculately trimmed beard, but I had shaved it off recently, an act that people said made me look younger. But I felt a little naked without it and was considering growing it back at some point. Next, I picked out a fresh shirt and tie. One thing I've always prided myself on is my appearance. It was something my father impressed upon me, and I've always made the effort, in stark contrast to most people around town, particularly in recent years. It's one thing to dress casually, but slovenly would be a more accurate description of late. I even saw a bloke in Sainsbury's in his dressing gown last week.

With tonight being a special occasion, I had decided to wear a bow tie, even though the regulars in the pub would probably take the piss, especially Andy, the pub's resident alcoholic. Somehow, I always end up lumbered with him. He is nothing like me at all, and can at times be one of the most obnoxious individuals I've ever associated with, but I seem to spend more time with him than anyone else. Perhaps it's because he is there more than anyone else, or maybe it's just my penance for a life badly lived.

I microwaved a supermarket lasagne, another sad routine that brought home the loneliness of my existence, wolfed it down, and headed out for the evening. At least I had lined my stomach, which is more than can be said for Andy, who would doubtless have been on the liquid diet all day. I wondered at times how that man even stayed alive. I don't think I had ever seen him eat anything, not so much as a pork scratching.

It was about a quarter of a mile's walk in the cold from home to the pub on the town's main street, and I was gratified to see the logs piled up on the roaring fire as I opened the front door. I walked across the bare flagstones, worn smooth by the footsteps of generations of drinkers, to where Andy was perched on the same stool he always occupied, clad inevitably in the dirty and faded denim jacket some swore he hadn't been seen without since the late 1980s.

As I approached, I could see he was chatting up Lauren, the young barmaid who had been working here on and off over the past few months. Lauren was pretty and flirty, with a short-cut black bob, and Andy was always trying it on with her despite being at least twenty years her senior. The idea that she might be interested in the likes of him was laughable, but then, as someone who had been no stranger to self-delusion when it came to women myself, I suppose I had no right to judge.

"All I'm saying," said Andy, swaying slightly on his stool, "is that you shouldn't be seeing the New Year in on your own."

"I won't be, will I?" retorted Lauren. "I'm working here all evening. I'll be in a pub full of pissed noisy people when midnight rolls around."

"I mean later, after the pub closes. I've got a bottle of champagne in the fridge at home, I've been saving to share with the right person."

"Yeah, it's been in there since 2003," said Richard Kent, the landlord, who had spotted me approaching and was already pulling me a pint of my preferred beer. "I've lost count of the number of women you've tried to entice back to your sorry abode with that line. Now, if you don't mind, I'd prefer it if you refrained from harassing my bar staff."

"All I'm saying is that I don't think a young woman like her should be walking home on her own," said Andy.

"Who says I'm going home alone?" said Lauren. "My ex-boyfriend is over there by the pool table," she said, gesturing at two lads I vaguely recognised. I think the one she was referring to was called Josh. He was busy racking up the balls in the triangle for the next game.

"Ex being the operative word," said Andy. "Take my advice, never look back. The best cure for getting over the last partner is the next one."

"For goodness' sake, give it a rest, Andy," I said, sidling up next to him at the bar. Was this really the best company I could find? "You're starting to sound seriously creepy. Leave the poor girl alone."

"Nothing poor about me," said Lauren. "I can take care of myself."

"Oh, look at you, all dressed up like a dog's dinner," said Andy, clocking my outfit. "Fancy your chances yourself, do you? Going to pull her with your girlie bow tie?"

"No, because I don't lust after women less than half my age like some old pervert."

"He's just making an effort to look smart for the occasion," said Lauren, taking my side. "Unlike you. When did you last wash your hair?"

"Oi, Kent, can you hear this?" protested Andy. "You want to have a word with your staff about how they talk to your loyal customers. She's casting aspersions on my personal hygiene."

Kent handed me my pint, took the tenner from the bookies I was offering, then let out a deep sigh.

"You know, I'm seriously thinking about trying to attract a better class of clientele to this place in the New Year," he said. "That means reviewing who we do and don't allow in, if you get what I mean."

"Dream on," said Andy, as a large gaggle of women, dressed up to the nines, burst through the front door. "It may be busy in here tonight with all these once-a-year drinkers, but who keeps this place going all year round, eh? People like me, that's who. You're not going to get rid of me, you can't afford to. Enough pubs are closing down as it is. You need my money, just like Craig did before you."

"More accurately, the taxpayer's money," said Kent. "Still claiming incapacity benefit, are we? How is the back these days? You seem to be able to get on and off that stool all right."

"You still talk like a copper, even years after they threw you out," replied Andy, in reference to Kent's previous occupation.

Kent couldn't be bothered to answer, giving me my change before moving along the bar to serve the new arrivals as Andy turned his attention back to Lauren. As she had stated, she could more than take care of herself and always gave him short shrift. I would have found the whole exchange amusing if it weren't for the fact that I had heard variations of it so many times before that it was getting boring.

She'd had enough too, and turned her back to load the dishwasher, so that left me stuck with him, as usual.

"Nobby, can you get me a pint?" he asked, lifting his almost empty glass to his lips. "I'm a bit skint."

"When aren't you?" I replied, but I would probably end up getting him one anyway, even though he didn't deserve it. Then I noticed he was looking past me at another woman who had just come into the pub. I turned to see that she was around my age, sixtyish, and someone I had never seen before. She didn't look dressed for a night out, in jeans and a red hoodie advertising a surf shack in a place called Pencarven, which I had vaguely heard of. It was somewhere in Cornwall, I think.

Strangers wandered in and out all the time, but there was something about this one I found oddly alluring. Not in a sexual way, more a hypnotic one that gave me a strong sense that this woman was important to me in some way. It was irrational, and I couldn't remember feeling quite like this before. She had my complete attention, and as she took the short walk across the floor to the bar, I realised she was making a beeline straight for me. She couldn't avert her gaze from me any more than I could from her. Something extremely odd was going on here.

The woman glanced at her left wrist, where I noticed her sleeve was rolled up, looked back at me, and spoke.

"Excuse me," she asked in her West Country accent. "Is your name Robin?"

"Haha!" said Andy. "Robin? Him? You've got the wrong bloke!"

"Shut up, Andy," I replied, surprised at being called by my long-unused real name. "Yes, that's me."

Andy seized on this right away, jumping in before she had a chance to reply.

"Robin? What is this?" he persisted. "A blind date? An escort? Is that why you've given her a false name? Never tell a prostitute your real name, that's what I always…I mean, a friend always says."

The new arrival looked Andy up and down with all the contempt he deserved, given that he had just more or less called her a hooker.

"Is there anywhere we can go to talk privately?" she said, turning back to me.

"There's a smoking area out back," I replied. "We could go there."

"Good idea!" said Andy. "I could do with a ciggie. I'll join you, and then you can introduce me to your new friend. Do you do a two-for-one offer?"

"For fuck's sake, Andy," I said, realising we weren't going to get a moment's peace with him hanging around. I had no idea who this mysterious new arrival was, but I was certain that whatever she had come to find me for had to be important. The last thing I needed was this irritating twat interfering.

"We could go to your place," she suggested.

"I knew it. She is an escort!" said Andy. "Go on, son, fill your boots."

"That's it. We're getting out of here," I said, furious at Andy and wishing Kent really would bar him, even though I knew he wouldn't. I would be having words later, but for now, all that mattered was getting out of here and finding out what this woman wanted with me.

"Can you get me that pint before you go?" asked Andy, with a pathetic, pleading look in his eyes.

"No," I replied firmly. "You don't deserve it."

We escaped to the sanctity of the street, but I didn't want to go straight home, so I suggested we go for a quiet drink at The Carpenters Arms. This was an old-fashioned, Tudor-built pub just a couple of hundred yards up the road, frequented by an older, more sedate clientele. It didn't have Sky Sports or fruit machines, just open mic nights, folk groups, and other traditional entertainment. It tended to be busier in the day than at night, and I was pleased to see, as we approached, that it was as quiet as usual, even given the date.

Other than a little small talk on the walk up the main street, I hadn't gleaned much about my mysterious visitor beyond the fact that her name was Jenna and where she was from. She told me the sweatshirt was from a surf shack started by her husband and now run by her son in Pencarven, which she confirmed was a seaside village in North Cornwall.

"It's not very busy in here, is it?" she remarked as we entered the old-fashioned building, with its low ceilings and exposed wooden beams. There were about a dozen customers, most of whom were musicians sitting around in a circle near a piano, holding various instruments. As we made our way to the bar, they began an impromptu jamming session, which was all unplugged, so it wasn't in any danger of drowning out our conversation.

"Time was, you could barely get in a pub on New Year's Eve," I said. "They were all ticket-only, and you had to pay. Now they're glad of anyone they can get. Hence why Andy hasn't been barred from The Red Lion."

"Yes, I'm sorry about dragging you away from your friend."

"Friend is pushing it a bit. Acquaintance might be a more apt way to describe him. I think you're being most diplomatic, considering what he said to you. Quite honestly, by dragging me away from him, you've done me a favour."

"Not as big as the one I'm about to do you," she replied, making me more curious than ever. Andy, no doubt, would have seen innuendo in that remark, but I knew she was no escort. She had sought me out for some higher purpose, and as I ordered our drinks, I could not wait to get tucked away in a corner somewhere and find out what all this was about.

"I've got a pub in Pencarven," said Jenna, as we sat down. "I've lived there all my life. This is the first time I've ever been away from it at New Year."

"That makes it all the more mysterious," I replied. "Why have you dragged yourself up here just to see me?"

"Because what I'm about to tell you is going to change your life for the better, just as it changed mine."

"You had better hurry up and tell me, then, because you're being a tad too cryptic for my liking. I think it's time we got to the point."

"OK," she replied. "But first, one more question. I want you to think back forty years to 1984. What was going on in your life at that time?"

This was getting ever more intriguing. Why would she want to know that? I cast my mind back to the life I was living back in London at the time. Some of the people I hung around with in those days made Andy look positively civilised. My gambling habit was well ingrained by then, as I thought about a life that revolved around pubs, bookies and card schools. The latter were unregulated, taking place in backrooms and secret places where we played our illicit games, which were always referred to as 'spielers'.

The rest of the time, I hung around on the fringes of the criminal underworld. Most of the time this was just a world of petty thieves, dodgy second-hand goods, and small-time conmen. It was sordid and sometimes risky, but despite that, there was a strong sense of community and loyalty. The exception was the day my dad was convicted of armed robbery of a bank vault, in which two security guards had been held at gunpoint. Everyone knew he hadn't done it, but because they knew who did, they were too scared to speak out.

I didn't tell Jenna all this because I didn't imagine she would be impressed, given that it hadn't been the most wholesome of lifestyles. It had been late 1983 when my father was convicted, and that was when my life began to spiral downhill. My mother was left in financial difficulties, with the family business in jeopardy, and the accompanying threat of eviction hanging over her. Not long after, I had lost Molly, who probably really had been 'the one'. Sally and the others who came after her, no matter how much I tried to convince myself otherwise, could never hold a candle to her.

I couldn't do anything about my father at the time, but the business, which we eventually lost, and Molly? That was a different matter.

"It wasn't a good time," I replied after a few seconds of awkward silence as I tried to figure out how best to sum all this up. "My father was in prison for a crime he did not commit, I lost the girl I loved, and my family fell on hard times. And if I hadn't been so wrapped up in my selfish pursuits, perhaps I could have done something about at least some of those things."

"Everyone has things in their life they wish they had done differently," said Jenna. "But few get the chance to go back and fix them. Hardly any, in fact. Just one chosen person per year. I was the last, and you are the next. I know that probably sounds mad, but it will all make sense in a moment. Hold out your arm."

She was right, it did sound crazy, but I felt an overwhelming urge to comply and naturally held out my left arm alongside hers across the small round table, trying not to knock over my pint glass in the process. She still had the sleeve of her hoodie rolled up, so I did the same with my suit jacket. Then, I finally found out what this was all about.

An ornate golden bracelet materialised on her arm, fading in over a couple of seconds, rather like Doctor Who's TARDIS. It had a central glowing green jewel in the design, which looked powered, as if there were a battery concealed beneath. As soon as it was fully formed, it uncoiled from her wrist and slithered snake-like across to mine. All the while, I felt no fear. Intuitively, I knew that this was destined to happen.

The bracelet wrapped itself around my wrist and sealed itself into place with a click. As it did, I felt a sense of warmth flowing through me and into my mind, like a soothing, comforting drug. It was relaxing me in a similar way to when I'd been given a sedative for a minor procedure in the local hospital.

"There," she said. "How do you feel?"

"I'm not sure," I admitted. "Different. And still a tad confused."

"It takes a bit of getting used to," she said. "But you've still got a few hours until you go back."

"Back where? To The Red Lion?"

"Hardly," she said, with a smile. "Somewhere far better than that. You're going back to 1984."

Under ordinary circumstances, if anyone had suggested such a thing I would have scoffed at them, but as I watched the bracelet pulse green on my arm, I knew that what she claimed was true. This device, whatever it was, had got inside my head, making everything she said perfectly plausible.

She went on to explain in detail how the bracelet worked, about how I was going back for a year, starting as Big Ben chimed in 1984, with the ability to reshape the timeline. She had done the same in 1983 and told me all about the things she had achieved, setting my mind racing at the possibilities.

I was particularly fascinated when she described how the bracelet would guide me, enabling me to do things I hadn't before. When she told the story of how she had uncovered evidence to expose a corrupt councillor, my thoughts immediately turned to my father and the way he had been framed. With the bracelet to help, perhaps he wouldn't have to rot in prison for the best part of a decade after all.

When I put this to Jenna, she was most encouraging. However, my next suggestion did not go down so well. Given the nature of my lifelong hobby, it didn't take me long to realise one obvious potential benefit.

"I tell you what, this thing could be an absolute goldmine! I'm a racing fan, I've followed it for years. I can remember who won all the big races in 1984, for a start. With that knowledge, I can win millions!"

My excitement was to be short-lived. I could already sense from the disapproving look on her face as I excitedly delivered those lines that the proverbial piss was about to land on my chips.

"I'm sorry, I'm afraid you can't. One of the rules of the bracelet is that you can't use it for personal financial gain."

"But that contradicts what you said earlier about 1983. You said that your life is way better now than before you went back in time."

"Yes, but those were actions that benefitted me more on a personal level, not blatant attempts at financial gain."

"But you are better off financially!" I protested. "You said you were living in a caravan in absolute poverty when the bracelet was first given to you. And now you've got your pub back."

"Yes, I suppose so," she conceded. "But I didn't go out of my way to try and make money. My improved situation is a result of actions I took to help friends, family, and the whole community around me. Any improvement in my lot is just a side benefit."

"Well, that's a little disheartening," I said. "But how are these rules enforced? I mean, if I want to put thousands on Secreto to win the Derby, how's it going to stop me?"

"Oh, it'll find a way, if you're just doing it out of greed," she said. "Remember, it's all about your motivation. I do find it interesting that the bracelet should have chosen a gambler as its next recipient, though, because it must have known that would be the first thing you'd think about."

"So, it mustn't be for personal gain," I ventured, mulling over the possibilities. There was all sorts of ducking and diving going on in Camden in the mid-1980s, and I'd seen plenty of good people lose their shirts in bent card schools, ripped off by conmen, even welshed on by an absconding bookie in one case. These small-time crooks were everywhere – in the pubs, the market, the betting shops. Could the bracelet help turn the tables on some of them? The more I thought about it, the more I began to see the possibilities.

"That's right," she replied. "Better your life, by all means, but not by selfish methods. Help others, right wrongs, and make the world around you a better place. The more you do for others, the more the bracelet will do for you."

A thought struck me, about my real name and the years of ribbing I'd taken because of it. I decided to run it by her.

"Jenna, what's the first thing you think of when you hear the name Robin? Be honest."

"Why, Robin Hood, of course. I bet you get sick of hearing it, don't you?"

"I did, when I was younger. But no one calls me Robin anymore. That's why Andy reacted how he did in the pub. Now, you do remember what Robin Hood was most famous for, don't you?"

"Robbing the rich and giving to the poor?"

"Exactly. Well, on my manor, which is what we used to call our little corner of London, plenty of people acquired their wealth at the expense of others. Maybe it's time that balance was redressed, don't you think?"

As I spoke, I glanced down at the bracelet. It was pulsing green with approval. Already, I felt like I was on the right track, and Jenna seemed to think so too.

"Oh, I like that," she said. "A modern-day Robin Hood, in the cut and thrust of 1980s inner city life. Yes, I think that could work very well."

We talked for a while longer, as she gave me as much detail as she could about how the bracelet worked and what I could expect. Then, at nine o'clock, she rang her husband to come and pick her up, explaining that they were staying up here for the night. I was left alone, waiting for midnight, when the adventure would begin.

I left the pub, went home, and spent the next couple of hours on the internet, cramming as much information into my head as I could about 1984. Winners of sporting events, big news stories, anything that might come in useful. Jenna had warned me against betting for personal gain, but there was no reason some of that knowledge couldn't be put to good use as part of my potential Robin Hood strategy.

She'd told me the bracelet would glow both green and red, depending on the situation, but so far, even while looking up the sports results, all I'd seen was green. It didn't seem to have a problem with what I was doing. Then I remembered my form books.

Back in less technological times, the form book was the serious punter's bible. These thick tomes, as wide as the *Yellow Pages*, were published annually, containing detailed breakdowns of every race during an entire season. That amounted to far more information than could be found in the daily newspapers or even *The Sporting Life*.

I remembered that I had started collecting them in the mid-1980s and had been storing them in the loft for years. I don't know why I bothered keeping them all this time. I mean, what use is a form book for events that happened decades ago? Well, they were going to come in very handy now. Had I subconsciously kept them because I had known somehow that I was destined for this moment?

It had been ages since I had been up in the loft, and it was dark, dusty, and full of cobwebs. When I flicked on the light switch, the bulb flashed briefly then expired, so I had to go back down and get a torch to help me locate the old cardboard box in which my books were stored. The box was dilapidated and chewed, as were the edges of some of the books. I had suspected there had been rats up here for some time, as I had heard some scuttling above my bed at night, but thankfully there were none around now.

I wasn't sure if I had books going back as far as 1984, as I examined the contents of the box by torchlight.

Then I found what I was looking for with its trademark blue spine – *Chaseform Annual 1984-85*. I couldn't find anything older, so this must have been the first one I bought.

By the time I got back downstairs with my prize, it was less than an hour until midnight. My mind was working overtime, trying to process all that was going on, so trying to concentrate on the faded pages of the old book wasn't easy, and I needed my reading glasses to examine the small print. It contained detailed results of every race in the 84-85 jump season, which in those days ran from August to May.

I couldn't take this book into the past with me. Jenna had already explained that it was only my mind going back, not my body. There was no need to pack a suitcase. I already remembered or had looked up online the winners of some of the major races, but what I was after was a single day, one with a set of decent-priced winners I could string together.

Yes, technically it was against the rules, but only if I was doing it for my own benefit, and that wasn't going to be the case. Already, the seed of an idea had planted itself in my mind, and it needed to be near the end of the year, so I flicked through the November and December results until I found a suitable day. Then I memorised the winners of half a dozen key races, saying their names out loud over and over again. As soon as I got back to 1984, I would write them down.

At no point during the process did I ever question whether any of this was real. The bracelet bonding with me had quelled any doubt. All I felt now was excitement, and those last few minutes, sitting watching the clock tick round to midnight, felt like an eternity. Ahead lay an adventure beyond anything I could have imagined.

I would be meeting old friends and revisiting places that no longer existed, and I was going to see Molly again. If I hadn't lost her, perhaps I'd have been spared living through decades of failed relationships, trying and failing to replace her.

Most important of all, my mother and father would be alive once more. I would be arriving at what had been dark times for my family, but if I had anything to do with it, that was all going to change. I was determined to get irrefutable proof about who was behind my father's incarceration, and with the bracelet's help, I was certain I could do it.

As for everyone else, well, I couldn't stop thinking about Robin Hood. Could I emulate my famous fictional namesake?

January 1984

"Nobby? It's your call."

My mind reeled for a moment, the transition back to 1984 leaving me momentarily disoriented. Midnight had struck, and now I was somewhere else. Wherever that was.

It took me a few seconds to come to my senses, but then the familiarity of my new surroundings began to sink in. I was in an upstairs gambling den, perched above The Golden Dragon, a Chinese takeaway nestled down a dimly lit side street off Kentish Town Road.

At street level, it was an establishment like many others, with plastic menus outside, red lanterns in the windows and the wafts of various sizzling oriental dishes drifting out into the street. Upstairs was very different, where the only smell registering was the thick fog of cigar and cigarette smoke, permeating every inch of a room I had frequented many times during my ill-spent younger years.

This was the domain of Raymond and Ken Wong, the two brothers who owned the restaurant and ran the Saturday night card school on the side. The legalities were murky at best. On the surface, it could have been passed off as a friendly gathering of like-minded players, but the reality was somewhat different. Large sums of cash exchanged hands here over a few hours, and the clientele ranged from small-time chancers to serious operators.

Raymond and Ken took a cut from every participant, each of whom was vetted carefully before being allowed entry. There were only two rules – that the games were conducted in the utmost secrecy, and that no trouble was brought to the table. Of course, given the clientele, the latter was easier said than done, and a couple of times I had seen things turn nasty.

I was seated at a circular wooden table, its green baize surface worn down in places, the results of years of play, with Raymond and Ken having been here since the late 1960s. A yellowed fluorescent strip light buzzed faintly overhead, highlighting the wafts of smoke as they drifted slowly, cloud-like, across the table.

The game of choice back in the 1980s was seven-card stud, a more sophisticated and challenging game than Texas Hold'em, which had come to predominate in the internet era. Despite the shock of finding myself here, I was able to compose myself sufficiently to observe that all the dealing in this hand had been done. This was the final round, and the pot in the middle of the table was already swollen with crumpled banknotes. I couldn't tell exactly how much, but it looked like a few hundred, and there were only two players left out of the half dozen around the table. Directly opposite sat my one remaining opponent, a man who had been part of this world long before I was born.

Harry 'Tinker' Bell was a veteran former greyhound trainer from White City, who had enjoyed some success before being kicked out of the sport in disgrace for allegedly fixing races. He had a face that was a crater of deep-set lines highlighting years of late nights, alcohol and nicotine. His hair, what remained of it, was a dishevelled tangle of grey clinging to the edges of his liver-spotted scalp, and his crumpled suit looked as if he had been sleeping in it. A fat King Edward cigar jutted from his lips, the tip glowing red as he took a slow, deliberate drag and fixed his gaze on me.

It hadn't been he who had spoken, but a chap I remembered as Eddie Carter, a local wheeler and dealer sitting next to Harry. It seemed I had arrived at a critical moment. We were facing a showdown, and the ball was in my court.

Harry's bloodshot eyes met mine, his gaze heavy with disdain as he tried to psyche me out. He might have pulled it off if he hadn't immediately let himself down as he became wracked with a deep, rattling coughing fit, culminating in him hacking into a filthy handkerchief which he pulled from his chest pocket with a shaking hand.

Still spluttering, he reached for his glass of scotch and took a long gulp, the amber liquid flowing down his throat to give some temporary respite, before placing the tumbler back on the table and turning his attention back to me. I had never seen a person to whom the phrase 'death warmed up' could be better applied. By the look of him, he wasn't long for this world.

"Come on, kid, don't fuck about," he grunted, his voice seemingly unaffected by his bout of coughing. "What's it going to be?"

With every passing second, the memories of this night were flooding back, and I was confident I remembered how all this had turned out. For months, I had been trying to get into this school, but there seemed to be no place for a new kid on the block like me. The Wong brothers were very choosy about who they let join, and only familiar, trusted faces got a look in. The fact that I had been buying prawn crackers from them since I was knee-high to a grasshopper seemingly didn't count for a lot.

Tonight, my moment had finally arrived. It was New Year's Eve, and most of the usual crowd had better things to do. But it wasn't Chinese New Year, and it was still a Saturday, so as far as Ken and Raymond were concerned, it was business as usual. They always liked to have six players, and for once, a couple of spaces were going begging at the table. I had been badgering them about playing for months, so when they finally gave me the nod, I jumped at the chance.

I'd scraped together enough cash over the year to afford the buy-in, which was £200. That wasn't a fortune by the standards of the bigger underground games around London, but it was still a sizeable sum for a twenty-year-old in 1984, and certainly enough to get the adrenaline flowing.

Unlike many other joints that ran illicit games, Ken and Raymond didn't take a rake. They charged a flat fee of £20 to play, which was a system I preferred. It meant people stuck around longer, determined to get their money's worth. The brothers rarely participated themselves, but there were always one or two family members or friends in the mix, and tonight there were three.

Forty years on, I couldn't possibly recall every detail of every hand that was played that night nor the people who were playing them, but one thing I did remember was this: I had gone up against Harry, and I had beaten him.

And I had loved every second of it, given that he had spent the night belittling me, calling me 'whippersnapper' and 'wet-behind-the-ears'. Taking his money had been an absolute joy. I had walked out of this room with over six hundred quid in my pocket that night, and a sizeable chunk of it had come from him.

But in this instant, I wasn't thinking about that. Right now, I had a decision to make and I couldn't remember how we had got to the current point in this particular hand. All I could see was that it was crunch time and the onus was on me.

As is the nature of seven-card stud, some of my cards were face-up on the table and some were not. The latter, I had to check. I took a peek and was thrilled to see that I was able to make a full house, queens over nines. That was one hell of a hand. No wonder I had managed to wipe the floor with him.

I looked up. Harry was staring at me impatiently. But, having arrived after the last round of betting, I couldn't remember what the stake was.

"Remind me," I said, casually. "How much to see you?"

"A hundred and fifty, if you've got it," he said with irritation.

I glanced at the pile of money in front of me. I had it, alright, plus a good sixty or seventy on top of that. I counted out the ton-fifty and pushed it into the middle with confidence.

"I'll see you."

Then, on my outstretched arm, I caught sight of the bracelet. The jewel was glowing red.

A chill ran through me. Doubt crept in. Then dread. But it was too late. The money was already down.

"Sorry," I blurted out. "I've changed my mind. I meant to fold."

The sharp intakes of breath around the table were almost in unison. I had broken one of the cardinal rules.

"You can't do that," said Eddie, leaning forward and lifting the brim of his trademark pork pie hat slightly. Paired with his off-white suit, crisp but a little too lightweight for the season, he always appeared as if he lived in a perpetual warm climate, unaffected by the damp chill of the London winter.

"I think you need to be more careful who you let in here, Raymond," said Harry to one of the proprietors, who was manning the small unlicensed bar from which he dispensed the whiskies and brandies that sustained the players. It was a nice additional little earner for the brothers. "At least teach them some etiquette before you let them loose at your table."

And with that, he flipped over his hole cards, revealing the devastating truth. He too had a full house, but his contained three kings, making him the winner of the hand.

How could I have been so stupid? It was all coming back to me. The first time I played this hand, years ago, I'd figured out at this point that he probably had another king, going on the cards that had gone before, and I had also picked up on his tell, a slight tapping of his whisky glass when he had a winning hand. I had backed down at this final stage, realising he had me beat.

Perhaps I should have got out sooner, but folding was the right thing to do. I had lost what I'd already put into this hand, but had minimised the damage and went on to clean up later that night.

This time, I'd come in cold, forgotten all the details and blundered right in, forgetting this hadn't been the hand where I'd taken him apart. And the bracelet's warning had come too late, which I wasn't impressed about. It should have warned me before I put the money in. Why wait until I was already committed? Was it trying to teach me a lesson?

I had barely sixty quid left in front of me now. The whole dynamic had shifted.

"You're out of your depth, kid," said Harry. "Maybe it's past your bedtime."

And then I made my second mistake. I let him get to me.

Not letting emotions dictate my decisions was one of my first rules of betting. I had always been cold, calculating, and in control. But tonight? The shock of coming back in time and the injustice of what had happened in the last hand, well, it was all a little overwhelming. Even though the bracelet was still glowing red, warning me not to play anymore, I decided to ignore it. It had not helped me when I had needed it before, and now I had the needle.

I wondered briefly if it might help me out once the cards were dealt, by way of compensation, but no such luck. There were no more red or green lights, and no magic flashes of insight. I should have left there and then because I was like a fish out of water, still, so soon after coming back through time. Continuing was wrong, and I knew as much, yet here I was, desperately trying to outplay an opponent because of a bad beat and making more mistakes as a consequence. In less than an hour, I had barely pennies left to rub together, and I had no choice but to scuttle away, tail between my legs.

"Come back when your balls drop," shouted Harry, as I walked out the door, just to rub salt in the wounds.

I emerged into the cold night air, the drizzle outside only adding to my gloom as I tried to get my bearings. It had been a long time since I had lived around here. The takeaway had now closed for the night, its windows in darkness, but a few New Year's Eve revellers were still about, their laughter and drunken chatter echoing down the street.

As I contemplated events, I thought again about that GA meeting I'd once sat through, convinced that none of it applied to me. Even first time around in 1984, when I'd walked out of this building with my pockets stuffed with cash, my mere presence here tonight had led to problems.

Most people picture someone with gambling issues as some poor sod who's blown his last penny, left with nothing but self-loathing and no money to pay the rent or feed his family. But it's not always about winning or losing. It's about how you choose to spend your time. That night, forty years ago, I had made a choice, and it had cost me – not money on that occasion, but something that money couldn't buy. Winning or losing didn't matter. What mattered was that I'd been there at all.

Participating in the poker game itself wasn't the issue, if you put aside the legalities. The problem was that I had dropped everything at a moment's notice to take part. In the process, I let down Molly, the one girl I should never have lost. And that night was the final nail in the coffin of our dwindling relationship.

By pure coincidence, she had a gambling-related job, working in a casino as a croupier. That wasn't where I'd met her, because casinos are not my thing, though I have played poker in them occasionally. She was someone who had grown up in the same area, who drank in the same pub as me, and had also been to the same school. We'd shared a couple of classes, but I hadn't known her well. It was only a year or two later in the pub that we got talking properly, and by the spring of '83, I'd finally plucked up the courage to ask her out.

We started dating, and it had gone well at first, but recently things had soured, which was all down to me. Tonight's events had been the final straw, bringing things to an abrupt and irreversible end.

I hadn't treated her badly, not in the way some men did. There was no belittling, no cheating, no abuse of any sort. But my neglect and a slow erosion of trust caused by one broken promise after another led to the same inevitable outcome in the long run. My failings were minor at first, like being fifteen minutes late for a date, that sort of thing, but had grown worse just recently.

One Saturday, a week or so before Christmas, we had made plans to go shopping together, pick out some presents, and have a nice day in town visiting Selfridges and all the other big stores. But before meeting her, I popped into the bookies to put a couple of bets on a big meeting at Ascot. Just a quick stop, that was the idea. Then the first horse came in. And then the second. My luck was in, and I wanted to ride it. I lost track of time, leaving Molly standing outside Kentish Town Underground Station at one o'clock, waiting for me to turn up. After an hour, she lost patience and went into Central London alone.

It hadn't been the best of months. At the start of December, I had lost my job at a small local electronics firm, which manufactured small parts for use in the burgeoning home computer market. It didn't sound glamorous, and it wasn't, but it provided a steady income. One Friday morning, I turned up to find the place boarded up, and the owner disappeared with no explanation. I eventually found out he had absconded to Spain, taking a sizeable sum of cash along with him, including the staff wages for that week. This sort of thing happened from time to time in our part of London, where half the people I knew were on the fringes of criminality, bankruptcy, or both.

I'd only been there a couple of months and wasn't cut out for it. I had been drifting from one job to another ever since leaving school, never sticking at anything, because betting always came first.

This left me with no income, but that wasn't the worst thing that happened that week. Just a few days later, my old man was sentenced to ten years in prison for armed robbery.

Once I was out of work I should have thrown myself into the family business, my parents' florist shop, because with Dad inside, it was going to be a struggle. Mum couldn't do it all on her own and needed help, particularly with the books, something which I was more than capable of handling, given my natural aptitude for facts and figures.

To my shame, I hadn't done enough to keep the business afloat due to my own selfish desires, but that was something I could rectify this time around. As for Molly, perhaps it was already too late. That afternoon, when I had left her standing around waiting for me, it had been bad enough. Afterwards, I swore to her I'd never let it happen again. And then, two weeks later, tonight happened.

We had planned a meal, then a trip to The Salisbury Arms, our local pub, to see in the New Year. She was working a day shift at the casino, and the plan was that after she finished, she would go home to get ready. She had a new dress to wear, a late Christmas present I had bought her courtesy of my winnings from lumping on Wayward Lad in the King George at Kempton on Boxing Day.

I was supposed to pick her up at eight, but a couple of hours before, Ken Wong called. A seat at the table I had coveted for so long had become available, and could I step in at short notice? I knew if I turned him down, a second invitation might not be forthcoming, so I felt I had no choice. I had to say yes.

I decided I couldn't tell Molly the truth, so I rang and left messages at her work and home, saying I was ill and that I'd make it up to her. But my lies soon caught up with me.

Mum was staying in that night. Normally, we saw in the New Year at The Salisbury as a family, but she wasn't in the mood for celebrating without Dad. She was in when Molly turned up at the house, armed with a bottle of Lucozade wrapped in orange cellophane. When she discovered there was no illness, and I wasn't there, furious didn't begin to describe her reaction, from what my mother later told me.

The next day, in that original timeline, when I tried to justify myself, including showing off my winnings, it made not one iota of difference. I could have won a million quid, and it wouldn't have changed a thing. She didn't care about the money. She cared that I had put her second again. And that was it. Over. No way back.

And this time around? Now, I had managed to make an even bigger mess of it. This time, I didn't even have the winnings from the game. I was skint. Potless. Boracic. Pick any slang term you like; that was where I was. No money, and very shortly, no girl. So much for the bracelet helping me better my life. Things couldn't have got off to a worse start.

An irrational thought struck me – maybe it wasn't too late. It was only an hour or so after midnight, and the pub would have had an extension. Last time, I hadn't left the poker game until many hours later. Perhaps there was still a chance to salvage something out of the evening.

I dashed along the rain-lashed pavement, marvelling at how fast my newly rejuvenated youthful legs could carry me. It was just down this street, duck through an alley and up to the end of the next street, barely a couple of hundred yards.

The Salisbury stood at the junction where two streets converged, its distinctive wedge shape conforming to the acute angle of the corner plot. The exterior was adorned with the signature maroon glazed tiles and brickwork characteristic of the brewery that owned several similar pubs across the city.

From afar, I could see through the frosted windows that the lights were still on. Might she still be there? But as I neared the door, I realised I was almost certainly too late.

Above the entrance, a sign read: 'Desmond Gittins – Licensed to sell Beers, Wines & Spirits for consumption on and off the premises'. And beneath it stood Desmond himself, known as Des to his 'friends', ushering his last couple of merrymakers out into the night.

I use the word friends in the loosest possible terms, given Des's general demeanour. He was a thickset, barrel-chested man in his fifties with a face set in a permanent scowl, giving off the air of someone who didn't suffer fools gladly, or pretty much anyone come to that. He was consistently rude and sarcastic to everyone. Git by name, git by nature, I had heard some say, but back in the 1980s, when the pubs were packed, he could get away with it. And many of his patrons gave back as good as they got.

As soon as he saw me running up to the door, he was on the offensive.

"What the bleeding hell do you want? I hope you're not thinking of trying to get a drink at this time of night?"

"No, I was looking for Molly. Has she been in?"

Des rarely smiled, but he did now, revealing his yellowed, crumbling teeth. It was the grin of a man who revelled in delivering bad news.

"She's been in, all right! And your name's mud, or I could say, wanker, tosser, and dickhead. Just three of the words she was bandying around about you tonight when you didn't turn up. Still, she shut up after midnight, when she was too busy giving out New Year's kisses."

"I take it she's gone."

"Yeah. Martin walked her home."

"From the garage?"

"That's the one. With the big biceps. They were holding hands. And you're a fucking idiot, mate. It must run in the family, given the way your old man let himself get fitted up. Fancy letting down a tasty bird like that. You ought to be ashamed of yourself. Now fuck off, because I want to go to bed."

That was another thing nobody loved about Des, his foul-mouthed charm. As he slammed the door, and I heard the heavy clunks of the bolts being drawn across, I realised that coming here had been pointless. What could I have said, even if Molly had still been around? It was way too late to mend fences, and with a few drinks inside her, goodness, what level of wrath I would have faced. Dejected, I realised there was only one place I could go now, and that was home.

I lived in the rooms above the florists, in the three-storey building where my family had resided since my paternal grandfather had opened the shop, initially as a greengrocer, in 1938. Everything was in darkness by the time I got there, so I let myself in and instinctively made my way to bed, still remembering every inch of the place, even though I hadn't set foot in it for years. I was exhausted, and all I wanted now was sleep. Perhaps, refreshed, I could put tonight down to experience and start anew in the morning.

My reunion with my mother was an occasion that, despite my overwhelming joy at seeing her alive again, I had to play down. Who wouldn't, having lost their parents, give anything to have a moment with them again – to hold them, tell them how much they were loved, and how much they were missed? But from her perspective this was just another day, and any such sudden display of emotion on my part would have looked decidedly odd.

So I did my utmost to suppress those feelings and avoid showing them as I came down to the kitchen, even though I was filled with bittersweet joy inside. There she was, buzzing away with the radio on, making coffee and listening to Capital Radio. London's local station had the big advantage over Radio One in those days of being on an FM transmitter, while the BBC's flagship music station languished on AM, where the music quality was nowhere near as good.

The song playing on the radio was 'Hold Me Now' by The Thompson Twins, which, more than anything else since I had got here, made me feel like I was well and truly in 1984. I watched my mother slip two eggs into a pan of boiling water on the stove, wondering how long it had been since anyone had last made me a meal, other than in a restaurant.

She was a slim woman with dark hair, set in a perm as was still the fashion in 1984. Her makeup was non-existent, and her clothes were plainer than I remembered, just a simple blue cardigan and a grey skirt. There was a sense of sadness about her that hadn't been there before my father had been sent to prison. This wasn't the Sheila Clarke who had brought me up.

Back then, she had commanded the sort of authority that made people think twice before crossing her. Although kindly and fair, she still had the toughness of a true matriarch, like so many of her generation brought up in tough times during and after the war.

Eggy soldiers and toast had been my preferred breakfast in childhood, and it had lived on into adulthood. She had the uncanny ability to get the eggs just right without using any sort of egg-timer – gooey in the middle without being slimy, and toast dripping with real butter, not margarine.

Recent events had knocked the stuffing out of her though, and I was sure I hadn't helped, which, as her only child, I should have done. I hadn't been back here long, but there were certain things I could see that I had overlooked before, in my youthful naivety. It was time to start putting things right, and now was as good a time as any to declare my intentions.

"Mum, I've been doing a lot of thinking recently and have come to some decisions. Call them New Year's resolutions if you like. Firstly, I'm going to help you out more in the shop. A lot more – in fact, I am going to work there full-time."

"Do you mean it? It has been hard work with your father away. I was hoping to keep the business going until he came out, but it's such a long time, and there is so much to do."

"Yes, I do mean it. And that's another thing. If I have my way, he won't be in there for long. We both know he didn't do it. I'm going to prove his innocence and get him out."

She looked at me, worry lines appearing on her forehead, suggesting she had doubts about this idea, and when she spoke again she made her position clear.

"We talked about this before, remember? I don't want you putting yourself in harm's way. It was armed robbery, not a few dodgy video recorders. What do you think will happen if you try and expose the real culprits? It's been bad enough losing Tommy, but at least I know he's coming home someday. I couldn't bear it if anything happened to you too, Robin."

She was right, we had had this conversation before, more than once. But that was forty years ago, from my perspective, and I didn't have the bracelet then. I wished I could tell her about that, but it was so fantastical she wouldn't believe me. I couldn't even show it to her, because as Jenna had explained, it was invisible to all but the wearer.

"We both know who did it, Mum."

"Yes, and that's why you need to leave well alone. They don't call him Frankie the Fillet for nothing."

Frankie 'the Fillet' Fowler was a notorious local villain who had a fearsome reputation not only for being a hardman, but also for having links to the serious criminal underworld, including the local firm who ran this part of London. His nickname had been acquired because, legend had it, he had once filleted a rival who had grassed him up to the police, with a chef's knife, ripping him open like a fish. 'Nasty piece of work' didn't even begin to describe him.

Whether or not the story was true, I did not know. It could just have been an urban legend put about by

Frankie himself to burnish his reputation, and I didn't know the details. Perhaps I should try to find out more, but, like my mother suggested, I needed to be cautious.

I looked at the bracelet. It was glowing green. Perhaps it wanted to nail Frankie as much as I did. One less villain causing mayhem would be good for the timeline, right? I was certain it was he who had done it because he occasionally drank in The Salisbury and, like most clever villains, liked to let slip just enough to assure you he was a wrong 'un without incriminating himself, all delivered with a hint of menace, of course. And he had said enough to convince me it was also he who had framed my dad.

"Don't worry, Mum," I assured her. "I know what I'm doing."

"Do you? Did you know what you were doing last night? Where were you? I had Molly round here, all concerned because she thought you were ill. When I told her you weren't here, she went ballistic. How could you let her down again like that, after the last time?"

"I had to go somewhere, that's all."

"Where? What was so important? She's a diamond, that girl, and she adores you. Or rather, she did. After last night, I wouldn't be surprised if she never spoke to you again."

"Yeah, well, that's another thing I need to fix," I said, once again looking at the bracelet. It was going to have to be a miracle worker to sort all this lot out. Jenna had said it normally sought out someone down on their luck, and it couldn't have picked a person who was making more of a pig's ear of things than I was right now.

"Have you got any money for me?" she asked.

I knew I hadn't, having blown the lot last night.

"I'm sorry, I'm a bit skint at the moment."

"You always pay me on a Sunday. I don't like having to take money off you, but I need it for the housekeeping. Twenty quid a week we agreed, it's not a lot to ask."

"I know, and I'm sorry," I said. "I'm going to sort it."

"Like you're going to sort things out with Molly? And your father? And the shop? I'm sorry, son, I hear a lot of promises, but you're not exactly delivering, are you?"

Now she was beginning to sound like the old Sheila Clarke, getting firm with me like this.

"Well, from now on, I will be," I insisted. She was completely right about everything, of course, but I couldn't make these things happen overnight. "You just need to give me a little time."

"Time is what we don't have. We need to start bringing in money fast, or not only do we not eat, but we also lose the shop. And if we lose the shop, we lose this flat. Then where will we be?"

We didn't own the flat or the shop. It was rented, and always had been. We might have been here for decades, but that wasn't going to be much defence if we couldn't pay our way.

"Mum, we are going to sort it. Together. I am on the case. When the shop reopens on Tuesday, you'll have my undivided attention. And as for the rest of it, you just need to trust me."

"Never trust a man who says trust me, that's what my father used to say," she said.

For a moment, I felt annoyed. I might have been overjoyed to see her again just a few minutes ago, but she was giving me a remarkably hard time.

But a hard time was better than no time at all, and it was probably a good thing that she was putting me under pressure because, quite frankly, I deserved it. I'd have said the same things in her shoes, and at least it showed she hadn't given up. Now I just had to turn my words into actions.

I went back to my room after breakfast, lay on my bed, and mulled things over. I hated thinking about my father rotting in jail, and I didn't want him to have to be there a moment longer than necessary, but it would be wise to tread carefully at this stage. Even if it took a few weeks or even months, it was better to do this properly, rather than steaming in and potentially making things even worse. I was still confident in the bracelet's ability despite the shaky start. I just needed to figure out the right way to get it to work for me.

The best way forward, at least for the moment, was to spend my time reacquainting myself with the world of 1984 and sorting out my finances. I felt bad about not giving my mother my keep, but as I looked around the room, I noticed a tartan shortbread tin on one of my shelves, next to a row of music tapes. They were my way of listening to music as I did not have a record player, only a cassette radio.

There was plenty I was looking forward to revisiting in this room, everything from my Atari games to my beer mat collection, which I had completely forgotten about. But that could all wait until later, because right now I was hoping, even praying, that there would be some money in the tin.

It was where I used to keep my gambling winnings, but they had been severely depleted thanks to my trip to The Golden Dragon the previous night. There was just a single five-pound note inside. Could I do anything with it?

It was New Year's Day, and that meant there would be racing at Cheltenham, or so I thought. Then I remembered it was Sunday, and betting shops didn't open on Sundays in the 1980s, nor was there any racing. It would all be tomorrow, on the bank holiday Monday. I had followed the horses closely at this time, and although I hadn't possessed a form book going back this far, it was possible I might remember if a well-known horse had won at the meeting.

Then I looked at the bracelet. It was glowing red. Seemingly, it didn't approve.

What if I gave the winnings to Mum? I wondered, imagining that if I placed a bet and gave all the money to her, without keeping a penny of the profit for myself, perhaps it might take a different view. And that's exactly what happened. Now the jewel changed colour, giving me the green seal of approval.

So that's how this was going to work. It was no surprise, because Jenna had told me as much. Now I just needed to pick the horse, but with no way of finding out the runners until the next day's newspaper, I'd have to wait until then. Our telly didn't have Ceefax, which was the only electronic medium by which it was possible to find out such things.

With only a fiver to my name, there wasn't a lot I could do around the local area, other than go for a walk. Apart from the pub, everything would be closed anyway. But why not take a stroll and get a feel for the old neighbourhood?

Bud & Bloom, our florist shop, was part of a small parade of retail outlets on the edge of Kentish Town, which were functional rather than charming. It was far enough from Camden High Street to be away from the tourist trade, but attracted plenty of locals with its vibrant mix of businesses. Ordinarily it was a lively, noisy place, but today was a rare respite, with it being both Sunday and New Year's Day. Even the road, normally busy with noisy, smelly vehicles, was devoid of traffic.

We were in the middle of a row of what had originally been seven establishments, with Reg's café to the far left. It was the most dilapidated of the five, with cracked and peeling paint on the doorframe, greasy windows that never seemed to get washed, and tired lace curtains hung inside, yellowed from years of frying and cigarette smoke. When it was open, you couldn't pass this place without breathing in the smell of bacon fat, but today the air was fresh and clear, a rarity in the London of this time.

Reg's café stood detached, next to a patch of waste ground that had once been a butcher's shop. It had taken a direct hit from a German bomb in the war, leaving a pile of smoking rubble. Beyond repair, it had been abandoned, while the dwellings on either side, although damaged, were renovated. It had been a great place to play as a kid when these bomb sites were still scattered all over London, but by now, as land prices began to soar in the mid-1980s, developers were beginning to realise the value of these empty plots.

After this gap was McGarvey's Turf Accountant, a posh term for a betting shop which bookies liked to adopt to try to sound respectable. We all called it 'Big Mick's'. It was also lifeless today, and there was no point looking through the window, as there wasn't one. By law, it wasn't possible to see inside betting shops at this time, presumably to discourage people from venturing inside. You could not even see through the door when it was open, due to the vertical barrier of plastic strips that you had to push aside to gain entry. These measures hadn't deterred me, merely adding to the mystery during my years growing up next door to the place.

We were in the middle, and on the other side of us was a ladies' hair salon, then a launderette, run by two Greek brothers, Theo and Andreas Georgiou. Finally, at the end was Patel's newsagent, which was the only place open. The Sunday papers were still publishing, despite the holiday, but I didn't need one. Despite being only a few doors away, we got ours delivered, and I had seen it on the kitchen table when I was having breakfast. There was no information in it about the following days' runners, though.

I walked on through a residential area and past some manufacturing businesses, including the boarded-up place I had worked at until recently. Already it was covered in graffiti, with the usual colourful patterns, the anarchy symbol, Debbie + Colin in a heart, and lots of AFC, understandable, given that Arsenal was the nearest first division club to us. I walked up past The Salisbury, where thankfully there was no sign of the ill-disposed Des, and on towards Camden High Street. I had no real route in mind, I was just randomly wandering, drinking in the sights and sounds of how London used to be all these years ago.

I walked as far as Regent's Park, where I sat for a while on a bench, still deep in thought about everything. The tasks I had set myself seemed daunting. Was I up to the challenge? The bracelet must think that I was, or it wouldn't have chosen me. I lost track of time, and when I finally glanced at my fake Cartier watch, which I remembered buying off Eddie in The Salisbury, I saw that it was after 1 o'clock.

I needed to head home because Mum always did a roast on a Sunday, and we ate at 2.30pm, even though it was now just the two of us. My father used to like a drink on Sunday lunchtime, with time called at 2pm, which had become the default time to have the meal on the table.

I was almost home when I was shaken out of my ruminations by a shout from behind me.

"You bastard!"

I wheeled around, already recognising the voice, even though I had not heard it for such a long time. There on the pavement in front of me, on the corner by the newsagent, was my girlfriend, or more accurately now, my ex-girlfriend.

Molly Miller stood with her arms folded, always a bad sign, in a defiant stance, her green eyes fixed on me with an intense glare. Her thick blonde hair, shoulder length, was just as I remembered, flowing down over her burgundy leather jacket. Despite the cold, she wore a knee-length skirt and a pair of heeled ankle boots, looking every inch the woman I had agonised over losing for so many years. What could I do to win her back?

Very little, it seemed, judged by her reply to my feeble, mumbled response, which was, "Molly, I'm so sorry ... I'll make it up to you."

"That's what you said last time. And I said one more strike and you're out. So, you're out."

What could I say that I hadn't said before? She had no way of knowing how dramatically my situation had been altered by my trip back in time overnight. Surely there had to be some way of convincing her, especially given that I'd had forty years to reflect on where I had gone wrong.

"There's no excuse, I know," I said. "But as of now, I've changed. I'm not the same person I was yesterday."

"You expect me to believe that? You haven't even told me where you were last night."

That was a tricky one. I paused because last time I had come clean and confessed, hoping that the fact I had won would mitigate the situation. Now things were worse, as I had lost all my money. How could I tell her? But how could I not tell her? It was agonising, as I was in a no-win situation, but then she took the decision out of my hands. I had hesitated long enough for her to preempt me.

"I'll save you the bother of making some shit up, shall I? I saw Eddie in the pub earlier, and he told me the whole story about how you blew all your money. And to think I was seriously considering it when you talked about us getting a flat together a few weeks ago."

"We still can," I said. "I'm going to turn all this around. I just need a little time."

"You've had more time than you deserved from me already. I should have dropped you last time, but I gave you the benefit of the doubt, given what happened to your dad. But after this, I know I can't ever trust you again, so this is it. We're done."

I didn't know what else I could say, so I just looked sullenly down at my Hush Puppies before blurting out something utterly stupid.

"Is it true you went home with Martin last night?"

"So what if it was? For your information, he walked me home, that's all. Not that it's any of your business. But he has asked me out on a date. Whether I go or not, I haven't decided, but that's nothing to do with you anymore. Now just stay out of my life. Don't phone me, and if you see me in the pub, don't talk to me. Just keep away. Got it?"

"Yes," I mumbled.

"Good. We understand each other, then."

And then she walked past me, off up the street, seemingly out of my life for good. The only vaguely positive thing I could say about the encounter was that it hadn't been any worse than the first time she had dumped me.

Sunday roast with Mum was simply delightful, a roast chicken with stuffing and all the other trimmings. No one else's cooking had ever come close to hers. Afterwards, I didn't feel like doing much, so I retired to my room to listen to the Top 40 with Tommy Vance. It wasn't an ordinary week but a special year-end show, featuring the biggest-selling singles of 1983. It was somewhat therapeutic listening to these classic tunes, with the best-seller of the year turning out to be 'Karma Chameleon' by Culture Club.

After that, Annie Nightingale came on, which I listened to for a bit before going to keep my mum company, watching *The Two Ronnies*. I didn't want to think any further about my woes this evening; I just wanted to enjoy some quality time with her.

I was up early in the morning when the newspaper dropped through the letterbox, keen to peruse the runners in the hope something would leap out at me. I kept my vow in mind, that this was to help my mother, not me, and as luck would have it, there was a very familiar horse running, one I knew would go on to glory at the festival in March. I was almost certain it had won on this day, and the bracelet, seemingly cooperating, given my good intentions, gave me the green light.

I was in the bookies bang on opening time before any of the regulars, when Big Brenda, wife of the proprietor, opened up the door, expressing surprise to see me. It seemed news of my humiliation at the poker table had travelled fast, and she seemed to find me handing over my final fiver to stick on a horse rather amusing. I must have cut a sorry figure under the circumstances, but when the horse came in later that afternoon at odds of 8/1, she paid me out with a little more respect.

I went straight home and handed my mother forty quid, enough to cover this week's keep and the next. Then, the following morning, I was up long before dawn to drive with her in our white Bedford van down to New Covent Garden Market to restock the shop after being closed for two days. This was a job my father had done two or three times a week before he went inside, but now it was down to us.

About half of what we sold came from the market, with the rest delivered by local suppliers. The trip was around five miles, but at that time of the morning, around 5 o'clock, just as the newspapers were being dropped off at Patel's, we could cover it in fifteen minutes.

I loved the market, the earthy dampness underfoot mixing with the rich scent of pollen from the flowers on offer, as traders called out prices and haggled over stock. It was noisy, hectic, and fun – one of the liveliest places I had ever been. Then it was back to the shop to get ready for opening time.

And so, my first few weeks in 1984 passed in a blur of early starts, flower orders, and cautious reintroductions to a world I once knew inside out. I kept my head down, eased back into the rhythm of the old life, and prepared for whatever my second crack at the cherry had in store.

February 1984

"I'm going to get you out, Dad."

"I'm not sure you can, son."

I was sitting in the visiting hall at Pentonville, which was as grim and featureless as I remembered from my visits in the old timeline. The drab grey walls, the heavy scuff marks on the floor, and the wire-meshed, barred windows left no doubt as to the purpose of this institution. Plastic chairs and tables were bolted down in evenly spaced rows, the layout clinical and devoid of comfort.

The uniformed officers, one by the door, two more against the far wall, stood with arms folded, watching the prisoners like hawks to ensure nothing illicit changed hands. All contact, beyond a cursory handshake on my arrival, was strictly off limits.

It had taken nearly a fortnight to arrange this meeting, following my mother's last visit in January. She had wanted me to come with her then, but as I explained, that would have meant closing the shop for the afternoon, which was something I told her we could ill afford. Instead, I suggested we alternate for a while, an arrangement she reluctantly agreed to, though it meant she would no longer see Tommy as often.

The truth was, we probably could have found someone to cover the shop so we could go together, but I needed to see my father alone. Mum had already warned me off poking my nose into his case, afraid of the trouble it might bring our way. Visiting him without her was the only way to speak freely.

My father sat opposite me, a broad-shouldered, solid man in his late forties who had more than held his own in the rough-and-tumble world of the 1950s and 60s. I could see that he was trying to put on a brave face for my benefit, but the slumped shoulders, clad in the standard prison-issue uniform, gave him the look of a defeated man, resigned to his fate.

"We both know you didn't do it," I insisted. "Detective Sergeant Ritchie's case was flimsy at best."

"He had everything he needed for the conviction," said Tommy. "A witness placing me near the scene of the crime, fingerprints in the vehicle, and no alibi."

"All of which were engineered to stitch you up."

"Yes, but not by him. Let me tell you something about Dicky Ritchie. There are two types of bent copper in this world: bent clever and bent stupid. He's one of the latter."

"That's good, then, isn't it? If he's stupid, he's more likely to have made a mistake. Something we can use to overturn the conviction."

"Not necessarily. I'm no better off than if he were one of the clever sorts. Worse, possibly."

"How so?"

"The clever ones are the dishonest ones who have gone over to the dark side. They are bent because they are on the villains' payroll, turning a blind eye for a few backhanders and whatever other perks the job brings. They're the sort that start small, say by letting a fence off with half a dozen dodgy Betamax players in return for a free one, but one thing leads to another. Within a few years, they're as thick as thieves with the local gangsters who've got so much dirt on them, they can never get out of it."

"And Dicky's not one of them?"

"No, he's clean on that front. But he's not very good at his job. Promoted above his abilities, I'd say. That means he's got to get arrests to prove himself, and what makes blokes like him bent is that they'll do anything required, including burying or falsifying evidence. Even if that means nicking the wrong bloke."

"Like you."

"Exactly. He didn't have a cast-iron case, but he had enough. Even though deep down, he probably knows as well as we do that I didn't do it. But he needed a collar. He wasn't smart enough to get the real villains, and I just happened to be a convenient scapegoat."

"Rather too convenient, if you ask me."

"Oh, absolutely. You're right that I was fitted up, but it wasn't by the police. Conveniently for them, all the evidence they needed just fell into their laps. Even then, it wasn't solid by any means, but then there's the jury. They can be got at, you know."

"I know who was behind it. It was Frankie the Fillet. Mum knows it too because I've spoken to her about it."

"Keep your voice down," hissed my father, casting furtive glances to either side. "Frankie's got ears everywhere. It wouldn't do for one of the other prisoners to overhear. How do you know so much about this, anyway? He's not been giving you any aggravation, has he?"

He hadn't, but I couldn't tell Dad the reason I was so clued-up was due to what I'd found out over the years, before coming back in time. So I'd just have to blag it.

"No, it's just stuff I've heard around the manor," I replied.

That was still partially true, because during the past month, as well as throwing myself enthusiastically into the flower business, I'd spent as much time as possible reintegrating myself into the community of 1984, and that had led to some interesting conversations.

"Yes, well, you should be careful who you talk to," warned my father, but I was already a step ahead of him there.

"Oh, I am," I said, though I was beginning to wonder how far it was getting me. I couldn't speak to anyone with serious ties to Frankie because I knew it could come back on me. So a lot of the gossip I'd picked up was just rumour and hearsay, mostly from the harmless old boys in the betting shop who needed something to talk about in between dog races at Monmore and Brough Park.

"I hope so," he added. "Because the last thing we want to do is make things worse."

"What I want to know," I said, "is why Frankie picked on you in particular. I mean, he must have planned to set you up from the start."

"Because we've got history. You could say we go back a long way, as far as the 1950s. Frankie and I are the same age. We were even at school together, did you know that?"

"No," I said, having genuinely not heard this before. Back in the old timeline, we never got around to having this discussion, so I was glad he was being so open about it now. Any information he could give me could only help.

"Right, so when Frankie and a couple of his pals were in their twenties, they were already up to no good. Their preferred method of villainy in those days was running a protection racket, you know the sort of thing. Go to a business, offer to 'look after them' for a few quid a week, and if they don't cooperate, start smashing the place up. Anyway, they tried it with my old man when he was still running the florists. To cut a long story short, when I found out he was giving them money, I got together with Reg and a few of the other boys, and we put a stop to it."

"How?"

"Let's just say we gave Frankie and his pals a lesson they never forgot. Which seemed like a good idea at the time. He disappeared for a few years to lick his wounds, but then he came back, tougher and more menacing than ever. By now, he was working for Vincent 'Boots' Maddox. You heard of him?"

"I've heard the name."

"Well, they nicknamed him Boots, because that's what his enemies end up wearing. Concrete ones. He's one of the biggest gangsters in London. Anyway, by now, Frankie wasn't interested in protection scams anymore. These guys were into the big stuff. Drugs, money laundering, casinos, and big crime heists; jewellers, wage van snatches, bank jobs, etc."

"Like the one you got lifted for."

"Exactly. And you know what Frankie said to me when he came back? He said he hadn't forgotten what happened all those years ago, when we gave him a good hiding, but it was all water under the bridge, and that it had taught him a valuable lesson, which he even thanked me for. I doubted his sincerity at the time, and I was right to do so. He was just biding his time, till he got an opportunity for revenge."

"Well, he did that alright."

"Didn't he just. The whole thing was planned down to the letter, right down to my fingerprints on that car radio cassette. I knew I should have known better than to touch anything Eddie was involved with. He tried to sell me one in the pub, even getting it out of the packaging and handing it to me to have a butchers at. They were top of the range with all the latest features, auto-reverse, graphic equaliser, the lot. But you know what Eddie's like, there's always something wrong with them, either they're defective or they've fallen off the back of a lorry."

"That's why you didn't buy one."

"Exactly. I was tempted, though. It would have gone very nicely in the van. But I passed him up on the offer. And then, somehow, that stereo, with my dabs all over it, ended up in the Capri they used for the robbery."

"Do you think Eddie was in on it?"

"I doubt it. He's a small-time dealer, verging on conman. Not always intentionally, but let's say, he doesn't ask too many questions about where his merchandise comes from. He wouldn't get mixed up with the likes of Frankie. He'd be too scared."

"So how did it end up in the car, then?"

"That, I'm not sure."

"I think I should find out. Perhaps Eddie knows."

"I told you before, you need to tread carefully. If Frankie thinks you're onto him, he'll be onto you."

"I know what I'm doing," I said, even though I didn't. My hopes of help lay with the bracelet, though it hadn't done a great deal to assist in the matter so far.

"Frankie leans on people. You know where I was the night of that robbery? Having a lock-in at The Salisbury, with Des and a couple of other fellas. Now that was highly unusual, because Des never does lock-ins. I suspect that was all arranged by Frankie, too, and when I tried to get Des to give me an alibi, he refused, claiming it was more than his licence was worth to admit to after-hours drinking. As for the other two, I hadn't seen them before and nor have I seen them since. I suspect they were on Frankie's payroll."

"And the eyewitness accounts?"

"More people paid off or threatened by Frankie, no doubt."

"And didn't Dicky Ritchie suspect any of this?"

"Bent stupid, remember? Even if he did, he wasn't going to let it get in the way of the kudos of being the officer to crack the case. No, I was diced, sliced, and served up every which way you care to mention. I'm just going to have to face it, son. I'm in here for the duration."

"There must be some way around this," I protested.

"None that I can see that doesn't invite more trouble," he replied. "I'm telling you, lad, leave it."

"Right, that's it, time's up," barked out a guard, as our brief time together was terminated.

I bade him farewell and walked back the mile and a half to home in the cold, mulling it all over in my mind. It seemed like an impossible task. How could I prove my father's innocence and incriminate Frankie instead, when, as far as the police and everybody else were concerned, it was an open-and-shut case?

Dad was dead right about one thing. I had to be cautious about what I said and who I said it to. So, I drew up a shortlist of people to approach and decided the best course of action was to try to get them on their own, bearing in mind what my father had said about Frankie having ears everywhere.

First on my list was disagreeable Des, landlord of The Salisbury, where I'd spent a few evenings since coming back to 1984. He truly was as horrible as I remembered, and it wasn't an encounter I was relishing at all. But I had come up with an idea, which I'd run by the bracelet, and it seemed to understand and approve.

I'd discovered that just by thinking something, I could elicit a red or green response, and had learned how to react accordingly. This had come in very useful at the flower market, where I lacked the experience my parents had when it came to buying and selling. While the flowers all looked very nice, their shelf life could vary considerably. Some would last in the shop for days, whereas others would wilt in no time. It wasn't always obvious at the point of haggling with dealers, so I asked the bracelet if it could lend me a helping hand.

When I say ask, I didn't speak aloud; it was all said in my head. So in the case of the flowers, I simply willed it to flash red or green each day to tell me what was worth buying and at what price. And to my delight, it worked. From then on, every time I went to the market, I came away with the best deals and the best stock, meaning less wastage in the shop and a significant upturn in our profit margins.

What also helped was that the shop did brisk trade in January, fuelled by a flu epidemic that saw the funeral parlours doing a roaring trade as a few old-timers succumbed. I know it sounds a little morbid or even mercenary to talk about profiting from these sad moments, but when the undertakers did well, so did we, with January and February bringing a steady stream of business from mourners of the recently dearly departed.

I decided to further explore the bracelet's capabilities by asking if it could tell me when people were lying to me, which again, to my delight, I discovered it could. That was a very useful addition to my arsenal when it came to helping Dad, though I was more than aware it was one thing discovering the truth, and quite another being in a position to take advantage of the information.

Des opened the pub at 11 o'clock sharp every morning, so I left Mum holding the fort at the shop, telling her I needed to nip out. She was used to this, assuming I was off to the bookies, which I still did, though I hadn't tried using the bracelet there since that first bet to help her at New Year. My visits had been mostly social, with only minimal bets, during a period of mostly low-class racing, none of which I had any real memory of. It was just a way of keeping my hobby ticking over and building rapport with the other betting shop regulars, because I might need their help sometime in the future.

At eleven on the dot, Des drew back the bolts and flung the door open to find me, his first customer of the day, waiting on the pavement outside.

"What are you doing here so bloody early?" he demanded. "Isn't it old Ma Jessop's funeral this afternoon? They're having the wake here afterwards, which is a bloody inconvenience."

"It's more business for you, though, isn't it?"

"What, a load of miserable old biddies drinking sherry and going on about the war? I can do without that sort of business, thank you very much. You do alright every time someone snuffs it, though, don't you? I'm surprised you're not rushed off your feet in the shop, given the number of grannies who've carked it lately."

"All the flowers for the funeral car were sorted this morning," I explained, as we walked across to the bar. "Can I have an orange juice and lemonade?"

"Is that all?" he scoffed. "What was the point of even coming in here? Why didn't you just get a can of Fanta from Patel's? This is a pub, not a youth club."

"I'm here because I want a word. It's about my old man."

"Enjoying his time at Her Majesty's pleasure, is he? Bloody fool, getting himself banged up like that, not to mention bad for my pocket. He was a good customer."

"So good, you let him have a lock-in with you the night he got framed for that bank job? You'd never done that before, so why that specific night?"

"That's bollocks!" exclaimed Des, though as I glanced at the bracelet, testing out its ability to tell me if someone was lying or not, I could see it glowing red.

"I don't do lock-ins," he added.

"No, you don't, do you, Des?" said a new voice from someone who had crept in behind me. "Because if you did, then let's say, your licence might be up for review, and not in a good way."

I turned to see DS Ritchie standing behind me, with his familiar sidekick, DC Ashe, just over his right shoulder. Ritchie was about forty, with a long chin, not dissimilar to Jimmy Hill off the telly, and a prominent nose, with thinning dark hair which was all over the place where it had been blown about by the wind. Like many plainclothes officers, his choice of attire instantly marked him out as a policeman, with his crumpled beige anorak over an off-the-peg suit, probably from Burton's.

Ashe was younger, around thirty, with neatly parted blond hair and a fresh complexion. He still had an air of enthusiasm about him, not having been in the force long enough to become jaded. His plainclothes, consisting of a navy jacket, jeans, and trainers, were far more casual, and he didn't tend to say a lot, simply radiating a quiet attentiveness that suggested he was more than aware of everything going on around him.

"What do you want, Dicky?" asked Des. "Haven't you got anything better to do than harass honest publicans, while all sorts are roaming the streets?"

"Most of whom drink in here," replied Ritchie.

"Their money's as good as anyone else's. Provided they behave themselves while they are in here, what's it got to do with me what they get up to elsewhere?"

"It's interesting you should put it like that, because what if their money isn't as good as everyone else's?"

"What do you mean?"

"I mean bent twenty-pound notes, turning up all over the manor. And I can't think of any more likely source than this place."

"That's nothing to do with me," said Des. "I check all my banknotes carefully before I put them in the till."

"I'm not surprised, given that Fingers McFee is a regular in here."

"Never heard of him."

"Don't give me that, Gittins. Angus McFee, three convictions for forgery, amongst other things."

"Oh, old Angus. I haven't seen him for months. I didn't know his nickname was Fingers."

That was two more blatant lies because I had seen McFee in here the previous night, and he was known as Fingers to all and sundry. I hadn't even known his real name was Angus until now.

"Really, that does surprise me, since the little gang of petty thieves and criminals you harbour in here all like to be known by their sordid little nicknames, don't they? Still, if you haven't seen Mr McFee recently, then you won't mind if I take a look in the till, will you?"

"Be my guest," said Des, lifting the hatch so Ritchie and Ashe could gain access to the bar. He pressed the button to open the mechanical till, which sprang open with a ding, so the officers could look inside.

"There's hardly any money in here at all, guv," said Ashe, pulling out the paltry four notes from within – one tenner, two fivers, and two one-pound notes, which were still around, but rapidly being replaced by the new coins.

"That's because it's opening time, and all that's in there is my float," explained Des.

"I told you it would be better if we came at closing time, sir," said Ashe.

"Don't tell me how to do my job, Ashe. I've been working for the Met since you were in short trousers."

"I know, sir, but…"

"No buts, constable. I'm the senior officer here, and I make the decisions. What about the safe, Gittins?"

"Empty, I'm afraid. I did the banking this morning."

"Most publicans normally go to the bank in the morning before opening time, guv," said Ashe, infuriating Ritchie even further, causing him to snap back at the junior officer.

"I won't tell you again, Ashe, now button it. Right then, Gittins, we'll be back later to check again. If there's anything dodgy going on here, I'll get to the bottom of it, mark my words."

"Like you did when you put my dad inside for something he didn't do?" I asked, piping up for the first time.

"Now listen here, sonny," said Ritchie, coming right up to me and wagging a finger in my face. "The evidence against your father was clear-cut. He had no alibi, for a start."

"Yes, he did. He was in here drinking late with Des."

"Mr Gittins here says otherwise."

"What about the other two blokes who were with them?"

"We looked into that in detail, and other than your dad's say-so, there is no evidence they even exist."

"Did we, sir?" said Ashe. "I don't remember us doing that."

"Yes, Ashe, we did. You were probably on leave that day, you have had enough of it lately. Now, if Des here says it never happened, it never happened. He's a man in a responsible position, and I trust his word."

"When it suits!" I exclaimed. "It didn't sound like that five minutes ago, when you were accusing him of handling forged notes!"

"I was just following procedure, young man. Now, if I were you, I would get back to your shop and tell Mrs Clarke to keep her eye out for these dodgy notes. Because we'll be checking all the businesses around here today, and anyone caught with them will be for the high jump. Come along, Ashe."

He turned on his heel and left, with his assistant trailing in his wake, but as he passed me, the younger man flashed me a look that hinted at doubt over what had been said. As coppers went, Ashe was a decent sort, and I got the impression that he was no more convinced my dad was guilty than I was.

As soon as they were out the door, Des started haranguing me.

"What the fuck do you think you're doing, you little shit, trying to drop me in it with Ritchie?"

"That's rich!" I replied. "Fingers McFee was in here last night, but you seem to have conveniently forgotten that, along with his name. Just like you forgot your lock-in, which could have cleared my dad's name."

"Let me give you a piece of advice, Nobby. You are way out of your depth. If you go around shooting your mouth off like this, especially in front of the filth, you're going to attract some extremely unwelcome attention. How old are you?"

"Twenty."

"Well, if you want to live to see twenty-one, you'll zip it, sharpish."

"So Frankie got to you, did he?"

"Seriously, kid, just saying things like that can get you killed. Now get out of my pub. Just by having this conversation, I'm putting myself on the line."

It wasn't worth arguing any longer, so I left. He'd never got round to pouring my orange juice and lemonade, but I hadn't wanted it anyway.

On the way back to the shop, I reflected on the encounter. Des and Ritchie had acted entirely true to form, but Ashe's reaction had given me a glimmer of hope, even if he wasn't necessarily in a position where he was able, or even willing, to help me.

We had an even busier spell coming up in the shop, as Valentine's Day was fast approaching, our busiest day of the year. With early-morning trips to the flower market in the dark, followed by full days in the shop, I often found myself putting in twelve-hour shifts. Come the evening, I was usually good for little more than collapsing in front of the telly, not that I minded, as the schedule on the main channels back then was vastly superior to the tripe served up in the twenty-first century.

I particularly looked forward to *Top of the Pops*, which I watched religiously every Thursday. Interestingly, for several weeks in early 1984, the song at number one wasn't played. The BBC, being rather stuffy in those days, had banned 'Relax' by Frankie Goes to Hollywood for obscene content, most notably after Mike Read took it off the air during his *Radio One Breakfast Show*.

It seems laughable now, given the graphic lyrics in rap and pop songs that would come along in the following decades, but back then, parts of British society were still desperately clinging to Victorian values. Ironically, the ban had the opposite of its intended effect as the controversy brought the song massive publicity. People were desperate to hear what all the fuss was about, and since they couldn't hear it on the radio, they went out and bought it instead. Within a fortnight, it shot to number one, stayed there for five weeks, and went on to sell over a million copies.

Despite the ban, *Top of the Pops* still delivered a cracking line-up in early '84, with appearances from the likes of The Smiths, Echo and the Bunnymen, Marillion, and Madness, amongst others. Another television highlight came that February, with the Winter Olympics in Sarajevo.

After a punishingly busy Valentine's Day in the shop, during which we racked up our all-time highest daily takings, Mum and I were fit for nothing more than ordering a takeaway from The Golden Dragon and flopping in front of the box. We watched, captivated, as Torvill and Dean took gold in the ice dancing, delivering a truly unforgettable performance set to Ravel's Boléro. I, of course, already knew the outcome, but I kept quiet, letting Mum enjoy the suspense of wondering whether they'd pull off the victory.

She was gutted not to be spending the day with Dad, but thrilled to receive a Valentine's card from him, one he'd somehow managed to obtain and post from inside. I assured her that this would be the last Valentine's Day they'd spend apart, but she remained sceptical, once again warning me to watch my step.

I did take the various warnings I'd had seriously, because intentionally charging into trouble would be foolhardy. I had to keep going, albeit carefully. So far, I'd managed to stay under the radar, and I'd figured the bracelet would give me fair warning if I was straying into dangerous waters.

The next person I was keen to speak to was Eddie, but not in the pub, surrounded by people. He had a warehouse where he stored and shifted his assorted gear, so I headed there one morning before the pubs opened, figuring it was the best time to catch him alone.

Eddie's Emporium was tucked down a scruffy side street, behind a set of rusted corrugated doors that screeched in protest when pulled open. Inside, it was a positive Aladdin's cave of mixed goods, from modern video recorders to ageing Teasmades, fondue sets, and other items that looked to have been gathering dust for years. There was even a rack with a collection of the kipper ties once favoured by Open University presenters in the early 1970s. *Good luck shifting them*, I thought.

I knew Eddie was in, as the unmistakable smell and drifting haze of his Park Drive cigarettes gave him away. Sure enough, there he was in his office at the back, on the phone in the middle of a deal, in his usual summery cream suit that gave him the look of someone heading off to Henley Regatta.

"I'm not a charity, Derek. You can have all twenty for a score apiece, and I'm practically giving them away at that."

There was a pause as he spotted me and waved me to take a seat, still listening to Derek, whoever he might be, on the other end. The negotiations went back and forth until they finally agreed on a price.

"Alright, twelve quid it is. We have a deal. Cash on collection. You'll send your brother over with the van, will you? Lovely job."

He put the phone down and turned to me.

"Well, that was a nice bit of business. I've finally got rid of those SodaStreams that have been gathering dust since the late seventies, to some dealer out Peckham way. Now, what can I do for you? I'm not in the flora business, as a rule, but I'll knock out anything if the price is right."

"It's nothing to do with the flower trade," I replied. "It's car stereos I'm interested in. I was thinking of getting one for the van."

"I do a very nice line in stereos, as it happens. My nephew, Kevin, supplies me. You name the model, he can get it for you."

"I'm sure he can. Minus the packaging, presumably."

"Yeah, well, that's a lot of faffing about, isn't it? You don't want to be wasting time unpacking it and reading all those instructions. He'll even install it for you. All part of the service."

"No, what I'm interested in is the models you had a few months ago. Remember? Specifically, the one you showed my dad in The Salisbury."

The salesman's smile faded from Eddie's face as he began to suspect what I was driving at.

"You're out of luck there, I'm afraid. That was a very popular model. They've long sold out."

"Ah, that's a pity. And the one you let my dad handle – can you remember who you sold it to?"

"I'm afraid I don't recall. And even if I could, I wouldn't be able to tell you. That would be breaking client confidentiality. Completely against the dealer's code of conduct!"

He was shifting about in his chair, giving off the uncomfortable air of a man who knew exactly what I was asking, and why. A quick check of the bracelet confirmed that he too was lying.

"That's a pity," I said. "Because I think we both know where that stereo ended up. What I want to know is just one thing. Were you in on it all along, or was it just a case of getting caught up in events without knowing what was going down?"

I eyed him carefully as he weighed up what he was going to say. Then he gave me an intense look and delivered his response.

"Fine, I'll tell you the truth, but it's strictly between me and you. You need to give me your word on that. If Frankie found out I'd told you, he'd kill me. And you as well, probably."

"It'll go no further," I promised.

"Good. So, first let me assure you, I was not in on it. Of course I wasn't. I like your dad, always have. That night when I showed him the stereo, I was just trying to sell it to him, I swear, that's the truth. He had a play with it, but declined, then put it back in the box, finished his drink and left. Trouble was, unseen by him, Frankie had just come in and clocked the whole exchange. He came straight over to me and offered me a hundred quid cash for it, there and then."

"That's way over the odds."

"Exactly. I was trying to knock them out for fifty. Unlike the ones Kev gets, these weren't ripped out of other people's cars. They fell off the back of a lorry outside the back of Dixons. So I was hardly going to refuse, was I? No one says no to Frankie. I'd have probably given it to him for nothing if he'd asked."

"And that's how it ended up in the getaway car, with Dad's fingerprints on it."

"Exactly. I'm not happy about seeing your dad go down for this any more than you are, but there was nothing I could say once I realised what had occurred.

At best, I'd have been nicked for handling stolen goods, at worst, filleted by Frankie."

"Thanks, Eddie, you've been very helpful," I replied. "Your part in all this is safe with me. All I'm trying to do is build up a picture of what happened."

That led to him giving me the usual speech about watching my back, the same one I'd heard from several other people, but at least I was reassured that he hadn't played an active part in Dad's conviction. He had been used by Frankie, who had seen an opportunity and taken it.

I left, confident that Eddie wouldn't say anything to Frankie about my enquiries. Why would he? There was no upside in it for him; he'd only be inviting trouble upon himself. But someone else had dropped me in it, as I found out during the last week of the month.

It was Tuesday, my mum's day off, and our quietest day of the week when I manned the shop alone. Not long after opening time, the bell above the door chimed, and in stepped the feared Frankie with two associates.

Incredibly, I had managed to avoid him up to this point in 1984, but he was exactly as I remembered him, slim and sharp-featured, with slicked-back black hair and a snazzy blue suit that reeked of Savile Row, with the gold sovereign rings on his fingers adding to the air of wealth, all ill-gotten, of course.

The two blokes with him were bulkier, with the classic build of hired goons. They wore cheaper suits that, like DS Ritchie's, had more likely come from Burton or Top Man. Doubtless they had no qualms about hurting people for a living, and probably enjoyed it.

Neither looked particularly bright, but these men were hired for their muscle, not their minds.

One of the heavies turned the sign to CLOSED and locked the door, which was never a good sign, but I wasn't about to be intimidated. I glanced at the bracelet. It was dormant, which offered some small reassurance. If I were in immediate danger, it surely would have let me know.

"Bud and Bloom," said Frankie slowly, in that way gangsters liked to speak, letting each word linger long enough to drip menace. "You know, I don't think we've been in here since Bert Gilroy's funeral, have we, Lenny?"

"That's right, boss," grunted one of his associates, in tones barely evolved from the Neanderthal era.

"Yes, shame what happened to old Bert. Fancy stumbling in front of that bus like that. Still, that's what happens when you don't look where you're going."

Then suddenly, his tone shifted as the small talk came to an end. He thrust his face close to mine, invading my personal space, and snapped, "Do you know where you're going, lad?"

"Of course, Mr Fowler."

"So, you know who I am. How do you know my name? Been making enquiries about me, have you?"

"You're a past customer, Mr Fowler. We pride ourselves on greeting all our customers by name."

"Then you'll know the other name I'm often known by. Do you like fish?"

"I'm quite partial to a portion of cod and chips on a Friday."

"And what do fishermen do to their catch when they get them back to shore?"

"Eat them?"

"Before that, they fillet them, don't they?"

He opened his suit slightly, revealing a brief flash of steel, a long, thin chef's knife strapped to his side in a holster, like a cowboy carrying a gun.

"You don't want to end up like one of those fishes, do you, son? Or swimming with their friends in the Thames?"

"Of course not."

"Good. Then we understand each other. I don't want to hear from anyone else on this manor that you've been asking questions about me."

He turned, picked up an elaborate funeral wreath I'd been preparing, and added, "Or the next one of these your mother makes will be for you. Do I make myself clear?"

"Perfectly," I replied, trying not to sound rattled, even though I was like jelly inside. I had been half-expecting this encounter and had mentally prepared myself, but it was still terrifying.

"Good," he said. "Mind how you go, won't you?"

And with that, they left.

It hadn't been as bad as I'd feared, but it had still rendered me severely shaken. On the plus side, they hadn't hurt me or done any damage to the shop. When they'd locked the door, I'd half been expecting them to smash the place up and me along with it. But this time, it had been a warning, nothing more. A chilling warning, all the same.

I'd been here two months and was no closer to getting my dad out of prison than when I'd arrived. Now that Frankie had visited me, it was hard to see what move I could make next, but I knew one thing for certain. I wasn't going to let this drop.

March 1984

"Go and see Reg."

That was the message, clear and insistent, that came to me during a night of restless sleep a few days after Frankie's visit. Once again, the bracelet's influence was filtering into my mind, probing both my waking moments and the night-time world of my dreams. Most importantly, the vivid depictions I saw that night were nudging me in the direction I needed to go.

I saw Tommy and Reg as young men, facing down Frankie just as my dad had described during my first visit to Pentonville. This version of Reg was barely recognisable from the current incarnation; fit and muscular, built like a brick shithouse, as the saying goes. That was more than twenty years ago, before the lure of full English breakfasts and evenings on the beer had taken its toll. These days, his six-pack had long since disappeared, replaced by a bulging sack of spuds that drooped over the waistband of his jeans.

Looking at him now, it was hard to picture how he could ever have been a match for someone like Frankie, and he certainly wouldn't be now. But maybe it was merely advice the bracelet was encouraging me to seek out, based on the past loyalties between him and my father.

So, the next day, I left Mum minding the shop and made my way down to the isolated corner plot. The exterior looked tired, its red-and-white striped awning faded by years of sunshine, and covered in birds' mess, with the paint on the door flaking off.

A menu outside advertised various combinations of breakfasts, from the basic, which was one each of sausage, bacon, egg, beans and toast for a quid, right up to The Gutbuster, which was three of everything plus various add-ons such as mushrooms, black pudding and even kippers. This came with unlimited tea and coffee for a fiver and was the option favoured by Big Mick and Brenda, who feasted on this every morning before opening the betting shop at ten o'clock on the dot.

I arrived mid-afternoon, when things were starting to wind down for the day, as this was the time the bracelet had suggested. I had assumed it had chosen that time because Reg wouldn't be rushed off his feet, giving him time to talk, but when I arrived, I discovered the real reason.

As I walked into the cheap and cheerful establishment, with its rectangular red Formica tables and an air thick with the scent of cooking fat, I could see that the place was in its usual unkempt state, rather like its proprietor. The laminated menus were peeling at the corners, their surfaces smeared from infrequent, hasty wipe-downs with a cloth that was probably dirtier than they were. Each table housed a small plastic condiment holder, containing glass bottles of Heinz ketchup and HP Sauce. These were crusted with dried residue around the lids, and were flanked by cheap plastic salt and pepper pots that moisture had got into, rendering even the most vigorous attempts at dispensing any of the contents futile.

Reg had visitors, two suited and booted official-looking types who seemed thoroughly out of place in these less than salubrious surroundings. Even I, who prided myself on maintaining a smart appearance in most settings, felt the need to dress down when I came here, and had put on a woolly jumper and jeans for the occasion.

For a moment, I wondered if the two visitors had taken a wrong turn on the way to an upmarket eatery, somewhere on Camden High Street. The few remaining customers were finishing up their lunches, and all the cooking was over, enabling Reg to come out from the kitchen to the floor, where he was now deep in conversation with his two guests.

His only other member of staff, his niece Mandy who waited the tables, was now clearing up and preparing bills. There would be no more orders from the lunch menu which, comprehensive as it first appeared, largely consisted of combinations of various items with chips.

I recognised the councillor as Rory Pollock, middle-aged and dull, with a suit greyer than his hair and a predictable nickname, one letter altered from his surname. The other chap, younger and more vibrant, I had not seen before, but later learned his name was Morland.

"You're too late for food," said Mandy, as I took a seat within earshot of the visitors.

"Just a coffee will be fine," I replied, and she turned and headed for the kettle and jar of Nescafé behind the counter. There were no frills and fancy coffee machines here. Mention an espresso to Reg, and he would probably think you were talking about some sort of bus.

While her back was turned, I listened in to what the three men were talking about.

"I think our offer is extremely generous," said Morland. "A man with clear business acumen such as yourself would be foolish not to accept it."

The words were said with a smile, but was it the slick, insincere smile of a snake oil salesman? There was a hint in his tone at dark undercurrents about what might happen if Reg did not play ball.

"You can offer what you want," said Reg, taking a draw on his half-smoked cigarette. "I'm not selling."

"Mr Harvey, do you think you ought to be smoking in a foodservice setting?" asked Pollock. "I think our environmental health department might have something to say about that. It would be unfortunate, would it not, if you were to be closed down for contravention of food hygiene regulations."

"Nice try, but I'm not in the food preparation area, am I?" said Reg. "I'm out here in the café where both my customers and I can puff away to our hearts' content. There's no law against smoking in public places, never has been, and never will be."

"And if Mr Pollock here were to take a look out the back, might he not uncover evidence of smoking in the kitchen?" asked Morland.

"He's more than welcome. I've nothing to hide."

About that, I had my doubts, having had a part-time job in the café when I was sixteen. Reg must have been assuming they wouldn't call his bluff, but noticing the bracelet flashing a red warning, I got up from the table and called out, "Do you want a hand clearing up, Mandy?"

"Cheers, Nobby," she replied.

I grabbed a couple of dirty plates from the next table and headed for the kitchen. Sure enough, there on the side, next to the sink, was an overflowing ashtray. Reg was not doing himself any favours here. I grabbed it and headed for the back door, knowing that I had to get rid of it, and fast. When I got back inside after disposing of the offending item, I heard voices approaching the kitchen door.

"I'm sure Mr Harvey won't mind if we have a quick look, will you, Mr Harvey?" said Morland.

"Here, you can't go in there," said Reg, but Morland was strong and practically barged his way into the kitchen. But the evidence was gone, and any remnants of the smell of tobacco were masked by the all-pervading stench of cheap cooking oil and bacon fat.

"And who might you be?" asked Morland.

"Oh, I'm just helping out," I said, as he cast his eye around the grimy kitchen. The evidence of Reg's smoking had been removed, but there were plenty of other causes for concern in the greasy surroundings.

"Well, you may not have been smoking in here, Mr Harvey, but it looks to me like some questionable practices are going on. When did you last change the oil in that fryer?" His nose wrinkled as he spoke. Whether it was down to the assault on his eyes or his nostrils, I could not say.

"Are you a member of the health department, Mr Morland?" asked Reg.

"Well, no, but…"

"And are you, Mr Pollock?"

"No, but I am a representative of the council."

"Doesn't matter. You have no jurisdiction, and by coming back here, you are trespassing. Now kindly step back into the restaurant area."

"Restaurant?" asked Morland, with a look of disbelief. "Is that what you call this…establishment?"

The pause suggested there were plenty of other words he'd have preferred to have used and was having to force himself to remain polite.

"I do. Now come on, sling yer hook."

"Very well, but you can expect an official visit from us very soon," said Pollock.

"And that aside, we have plenty of other avenues we can pursue to persuade you to cooperate," said Morland, as they made their way back into the café. "The structural integrity of the property, for a start. Take that patch of wasteland next door."

"Which you've recently acquired, I believe," said Reg.

"Indeed we have," said Morland. "As you know, the property that previously occupied that space was demolished after being hit during the Blitz. When we took ownership, we had the land thoroughly surveyed, and we have evidence that the damage caused has rendered your building unsafe. In short, there is a risk of collapse, and you are endangering every member of the public who steps in here. It's a toss-up as to what's going to kill them first, the ceiling falling in on them, or a coronary from the artery-blocking delicacies you serve up."

"Oh, very good," said Reg. "Let me guess, you're going to produce a fake report saying my place has got to come down. Well, I'll have you know my family's been here since before the war, and my uncle ran the biggest building firm in the district. The exterior wall and foundations adjoining the plot next door were completely rebuilt and are as sound as a pound. I've got the paperwork to prove it, insurance certificates, surveys, you name it, going back forty years or more. You've not got a leg to stand on."

"Be that as it may, Mr Harvey, one way or another, we are going to have this land. Still, I am pleased to hear that your insurance is up to date. I would hate to think of you being plunged into poverty, in the event that anything ... unfortunate occurs."

"Is that a threat, Mr Morland?"

"Just friendly advice, that's all. Right, I think we're done here for today, don't you, Mr Pollock?"

"I do. But we'll be back," replied Pollock. "In the meantime, I suggest you think very carefully about what we've discussed."

And with that, they left, allowing me to quiz Reg as to what this was all about.

"They're trying to get me out," he said. "They want to demolish this place, and together with next door, build a supermarket on the land."

"We can't have a supermarket here," I said. "It would be a disaster for all the local shops and the market." I knew this to be true because I had already seen it happen. Reg had indeed sold up in the old timeline, but I couldn't remember why.

"Exactly. And I'm not selling. This is my family business. My grandad started it around the same time as yours."

"They sounded pretty determined," I said.

"Pillock doesn't bother me," he said. "He's just your average council gasbag."

"It's the other bloke I'd be wary of," I replied. "And I don't want to sound critical, but you don't want to be giving them any open goals they can use to close you down. That's why I nipped out the back just now, to get rid of the ashtray. You're going to have to stop smoking in the kitchen."

"Yes, I guess you're right," he replied. "I appreciate you looking out for me like this. It's just like your old man used to."

I'd come here to seek Reg's help, but so far, it had been the other way around. Now was my chance to ask his advice.

"Speaking of which, it was Dad I came to see you about. We've got to clear his name."

"Nobby, I'd like as much as anyone to get him out, but you know the score. I heard on the grapevine that Frankie's already given you a warning. And you only get one off him, you know."

"There must be something we can do."

"Short of Frankie turning up at the station, handing himself in, and confessing all to Ritchie, I can't see what."

"That's the answer, then," I said. "That's what we need to get him to do."

"And how exactly do you propose to do that? Go and see Frankie and appeal to his better nature? Don't bother, he hasn't got one."

"He's only going to go and turn himself in if the alternative is something worse," I said, just as the bracelet began to glow green. I was on the right lines.

"And what's that exactly?"

"I haven't worked that bit out yet," I confessed. "But I am going to. When I do, will you help?"

"Without question," said Reg. "Your dad and I are as good as blood brothers."

"I'll hold you to that," I said. "And in return, I'm going to help you. Pillock and Morland are sure to try every trick in the book to hound you out of this place, and I want you to know I've got your back."

"What can you do?" asked Reg, a look of doubt in his eyes. To him, I was just a twenty-year-old kid, lacking life experience. He wasn't to know I'd lived a full adult life already.

"Whatever I can," I said. "If you and my dad are blood brothers, that makes me what, a blood son? Whatever loyalty you two have to each other, it extends to the next generation. You can count on my support."

"Thanks, Nobby," he replied. "That means a lot." Reg didn't have a son of his own, or any other family to fall back on, and I was glad to plug that gap.

Quite how, I wasn't sure, but I was confident the bracelet would let me know when the time came.

That moment arrived in mid-March, while I was testing out my Robin Hood strategy. I had done surprisingly little on the betting front since arriving in 1984, and had avoided poker altogether after getting my fingers burnt so badly on arrival. But the Cheltenham Festival gave me the opportunity to see if I could truly become a force for good.

Although I was no regular churchgoer, I had become aware of the difficulties facing our local parish church. St Mark's had fallen into a sorry state, with years of neglect taking their toll. The story had made the *Camden New Journal* a few weeks back, when it was reported that the roof was now in such poor condition that rainwater was pouring through, soaking not just the pews, but the organist and the organ as well. If the church could not raise £10,000 for urgent repairs, it would be forced to close its doors, possibly for good.

The local flock had done their utmost to rally around and, thanks to a relentless campaign of jumble sales, raffles, and collection plate appeals, had scraped together about a quarter of the total needed. But that had taken six months, and there was only so much the regular congregation, mostly elderly, retired folk, could manage. Without a major donation, it seemed inevitable that the old place would be lost, even, heaven forbid, falling into the hands of developers like those trying to force Reg out.

This, I decided, was as good a cause as any to make use of my knowledge, and when I floated the idea, the bracelet was amenable. I had been looking forward to Cheltenham coming around, as it had been a vintage year, and I clearly remembered some of the history-making performances, called home on BBC television by the legendary Peter O'Sullevan.

I knew the winners of the four biggest races across the decades off by heart, with this being a particularly notable year. Firstly, Dawn Run had claimed the Champion Hurdle, before going on to become the only horse ever to win both that and the Cheltenham Gold Cup a couple of years later. This year's Gold Cup was memorable for Burrough Hill Lad's victory, giving Jenny Pitman the honour of being the first lady trainer to win the race. Throw in Badsworth Boy, in the Champion Chase, and Gaye Chance in the Stayers' Hurdle, and I had the makings of a very tidy four-horse accumulator. With my clear intention to donate the winnings to the church appeal, I had the bracelet's full blessing.

Although I did most of my betting at Big Mick's, I had no intention of placing the bet there. Mick, despite the tarnished image of his profession, was an old-school independent bookie who conducted his business with integrity, always with a smile, whether you were winning or losing. I saw no reason to fleece him, even though, as a diligent and disciplined bookmaker, he would almost certainly lay off the liability if I did.

Instead, I set my sights on the Mecca shop on Kentish Town High Street. Mecca was one of the biggest bookmaking chains in the country at the time, though the name would disappear from Britain's streets in the late 1980s when it merged with William Hill. I would be quite happy to relieve this large corporation of a few quid, especially in this shop, where the sour-faced manager, Ted Mills, was notorious for knocking back punters. He had once refused me a tricast at Thirsk after

I had spotted that one side of the track had a hugely favourable bias in sprints when the going was firm. He said by combining all the high-drawn horses in a bet, I was cheating, but I saw it as being shrewd.

None of my four horses were big prices, but accumulators multiply up nicely, which was just as well given my parlous financial state. I had managed to squirrel away a bit of money, thanks to Bud & Bloom doing well, but I still needed about a hundred quid to place the bet I wanted to get enough money for the church, and that was a lot to risk.

The bracelet assured me I was doing the right thing, but I still felt a twinge of anxiety. It was all very well knowing the results in advance, but there was still this nagging worry that somehow, just by being here in the past, I might have altered things without realising it. Could it be that events might not unfold exactly as they had the first time around, even though I hadn't been anywhere near Cheltenham or any of the participants?

My fears had eased by the final day of the meeting, which in those days fell on a Thursday, by which time my first three selections had all won, leaving just Burrough Hill Lad to come. Rather than watch the race on television, I decided on a whim to go down to Mick's, even though I would not be able to see the race there. Television screens were banned in betting shops until the mid-1980s.

I loved Mick's place. With no TV, the only way to follow the races was through a tinny, crackly speaker mounted in one corner, where the motley crew of regulars would huddle round, listening to commentaries of dubious quality. With no pictures to rely on, there was often a suspicion that the commentators were making some races seem far more exciting than they truly were, with the favourite always 'still in with a chance' at the furlong pole. Later study of the form book would reveal it had, in reality, been tailed off and beaten by a distance. But that was all part of the charm, and infinitely preferable to the depressing, dismal places that betting shops would ultimately become.

Many of the punters in Mick's shop were pensioners, betting in tiny amounts, there more for the companionship and the free heating than for any serious gambling. The place was packed on this busiest of racing days, and both Mick and Brenda were behind the counter. When I showed Mick my betting slip and pointed out where I had placed it, his face lit up, not so much because he hadn't taken the bet, but because he disliked Ted Mills every bit as much as I did.

They were all there that afternoon, the old faces. There was Stan the boardman, whose name caused mild amusement due to comparison with Stan Boardman, the television comic. His job was to write the betting shows and results up on a massive whiteboard in marker pen, a job soon to be rendered redundant by the arrival of electronic screens.

Among the punters was Jinxy Jack, a milkman who had chosen his profession for its early hours, allowing him to spend the rest of the day in the bookies after finishing his round. He had acquired his nickname due to his uncanny ability to put the mockers on any horse. If you discovered you'd backed the same horse as him, you would almost certainly have done your dough. He was also forever coming up with miracle systems, none of which ever worked.

He was perched on a stool next to Sid the Snuff, an ancient and almost incomprehensible pensioner who spent the entire day in the shop, stuffing pinches of powdered tobacco up his nose. Sid was an anachronism from another era, his habit long out of fashion even then. He carried a small, battered tin of snuff, from which he would take frequent pinches, rubbing the fine, brown powder between his fingers before inhaling sharply. The residue clung to his heavily stained shirt, leaving dark smudges across the fabric. He is the last person I can ever recall taking snuff, a practice that seems to have died out.

Another regular, a morose-looking chap universally known as Doctor Death, stood by himself, scanning the race cards pinned to the wall. People tended to keep their distance from him because, for some unnerving reason, his close acquaintances had an unfortunate tendency to meet untimely ends, whether by heart attack, traffic accident, or some other misfortune. Too much association with Death, as he was known for short, was considered very bad for one's health.

Some of the other regulars were rather more amenable. I was pleased to see my best friend from school, Billy, who worked as a delivery driver and often ran errands for Eddie, along with a couple of poker players, Danny and Chris, whom I remembered from the circuit. They were decent fellows, fair players, and tough men who could handle themselves if the need ever arose. And as it turned out, that need was about to arise, right now.

Sometimes the bracelet gave me hints as to what I should be doing with just a green or red flash, and other times, it furnished me with more details. Today, it was a case of the latter. Not long after cheering Burrough Hill Lad home, I got a strong inkling that I was needed at the café. I stepped outside to be greeted by the sound of breaking glass coming from down the street. I turned and went back into Mick's, instinctively sensing I needed backup.

"Mick, Billy, the rest of you. There's trouble at the café. Reg needs our help."

Despite the shop being busy, Mick left Brenda to hold the fort while he, Billy, the poker players, and I rushed the short distance down the street to Reg's, where trouble was seriously kicking off.

A group of yobs, bovver boys, call them what you will, were inside, wrecking the place, throwing chairs around and smashing plates, clearly intent on causing as much damage as possible. It was late afternoon, just as the place was winding down, and I could see a terrified Mandy through the window, cowering behind the counter, as Reg brandished a frying pan at one of the youths. Before he could make use of it, one of the others knocked it out of his hand and shoved him to the floor. As handy as he might have been in the past, Reg was no longer up to dealing with this sort of aggravation.

The gang were the sort you would not want to meet down a back alley. Shaved heads, bomber jackets stretched tight over wiry frames, and faded jeans tucked into heavy boots with steel caps that could dish out plenty of damage to any body part unfortunate enough to come into contact with them.

None of that was going to intimidate us, since we outnumbered them five to three, or would do when Mick caught up. He was lagging a little on account of a few too many Gutbuster breakfasts, but we did not hang about and charged through the door, like the cavalry coming over the hill to Reg's aid.

The yobs were taken by surprise, and Danny managed to land a punch on the first one before he even saw him coming, catching the side of his head and sending him reeling right into a wall, where he sank, winded, to the floor. Billy, meanwhile, ducked a clumsy swing from another before delivering a punch straight into the lad's stomach, leading to him staggering backwards into a table, sending crockery and cutlery flying everywhere.

Reg, for his part, was not standing idly by either. Rejuvenated by the reinforcements, he got back to his feet and planted a solid right hook on the third lad's jaw, who didn't know where to look with opposition bearing down on him from all directions. It looked like Reg still did have a bit of his old gusto after all.

In less than a minute, it was all over. The yobs, thoroughly battered and recognising that they were beaten, were practically falling over each other in their eagerness to escape, shoving past us and stumbling into the street, where they broke into a panicked run, one of them limping from where Chris had put the boot into his shin..

We stood there catching our breath, surveying the scene of overturned tables, smashed crockery, and broken glass. Mandy peered up from where she had ducked down behind the counter, shaken but unharmed, as Reg offered his thanks to all of us.

"What was that all about?" asked Billy.

"Oh, just random yobs, looking to cause trouble," said Reg. "Thanks again, and if you are in The Salisbury later, the drinks will be on me."

I hung about a bit after Billy and the others had gone, eager to get Reg on his own.

"I do not think those were random yobs any more than you do," I said. "It is too much of a coincidence, after what Morland said last week. Has anything like this happened before?"

"We have had the odd troublemaker from time to time, but nothing like this. I didn't want to say anything in front of the others, but the more I think about it, the more likely it seems. He said something about finding other ways to get me out."

"And it is not likely to stop there," I added.

"I doubt those skinheads will be back in a hurry, not after the pasting they've just had."

The bracelet was flashing red at me. This was certainly not over yet.

"Maybe not them, but Morland does not strike me as the type to give up easily. You're going to have to be extra vigilant from now on. Have you thought about getting a minder? I am pretty sure that Danny, who was here earlier, is in that game. Perhaps you could hire him."

"I will think about it," said Reg. "Let's see what they try next."

"I'll come in each day as well as keeping my ear to the ground," I promised. By that, I meant that I hoped the bracelet would continue to tip me off, because I was sure it wouldn't be long until Pollock and Morland pulled their next trick.

The next day, I had the great satisfaction of going down to the Mecca to collect the winnings from my Cheltenham bet, which amounted to £7,850.77. The pleasure was heightened when miserable Mills himself was called out from the office to authorise the payout. I asked him for a hundred pounds in cash, and the rest in a cheque made out to the church restoration fund's account. He was clearly not a charitable man, as I could see him wince with almost every stroke of the pen as he wrote it out. Then I headed for St Mark's.

The bracelet seemed happy for me to retain my initial stake, which was only fair, and now that the rules of the operation were clearly defined, I was already thinking ahead towards future projects. There were plenty of good causes around our way, and indeed further afield. But for the moment, I was about to make the local vicar's day.

He was thrilled when I handed him the cheque, though I noticed a frown cross his brow when he saw the source of the funds. He wasn't going to go all pious on me, was he? Perhaps if it had been a Mormon church there might have been a problem, but in this case, the bountiful windfall I had come bearing was more than enough to offset any reservations he might have had about gambling as a source of funds for the restoration.

I asked only one thing: that my part in all this remain anonymous. Whether that would be possible, I didn't know, as I couldn't guarantee word of my win wouldn't get around. I knew I could rely on Mick's discretion, but what about the punters who'd witnessed me collecting at the Mecca? Thankfully, it seemed they soon returned to their preoccupation with their Union Jack bets and reverse forecast doubles, and quickly forgot about me.

Reg reluctantly employed Danny as a minder at the café, but he didn't come cheap, and when nothing happened for a week or two, he promptly dispensed with his services, as he was basically paying him to sit around drinking tea all day. Those looking to drive Reg out weren't stupid and weren't in any hurry, so they were quite happy to wait it out for another opportunity to strike. Sending the heavy mob in hadn't worked the first time, so now they turned to more devious tactics.

If it hadn't been for the bracelet helping me to foil these schemes, Reg's hopes of hanging on to the café would surely have been scuppered. Thankfully, I was once again tipped off, this time that a health inspector would soon be visiting. Reg had no forewarning of this because he didn't receive prior notification. That would have given him time to clean up his act, and why would those trying to close him down want to do that?

I turned up late afternoon to warn him they were coming the next day. When he asked how I knew, I gave him some fluff about getting a tip from someone working at the council, which he accepted, so the three of us, him, me, and Mandy, spent the entire evening scrubbing the place from top to toe.

To be fair to Reg, he had already cleaned up a lot since the previous visit and assured me there had been no more smoking in the kitchen. I could see the walls had been washed, and you could now see the actual paintwork beneath the layers of fat that had built up over the years.

It was good, but not quite there, and during that evening we disposed of various chipped and damaged bits of crockery, pulled out all the appliances and cleaned behind them, as well as checking the dates on all the goods, particularly in the fridge, where I discovered some sausages three days past their sell-by date.

I enjoyed working with Reg, and the feeling was mutual, as he expressed his gratitude.

"Nobby, I can't thank you enough for all you've done to help out these past couple of weeks," he began. "But how do you find the time? Don't you have your work cut out at the florists?"

"Most of the hard work is in the morning, and Mum's quite happy holding the fort the rest of the time," I explained. "Besides, I want to help. My dad can't look out for you anymore, so it's down to me to take his place."

"Your old man would be proud of you," said Reg. "A real chip off the old block."

His words filled me with a warm glow and the reassurance that I was making far better use of my time this second time in 1984 than the first, when I'd probably have spent most of it in the bookies or holed up in a poker game somewhere. My number one mission was still to get my dad out, but saving Reg's business was now a clear second.

By the time we went home that night, the place was spotless. It looked like a brand-new business opening up for the first time. There was no way the health inspector could find anything wrong with it ... could he?

Not with what we'd done, no. But Reg's enemies weren't leaving anything to chance.

The bracelet had suggested that the visit would take place at 9.30 in the morning. This was a most inconvenient time, as it was when Reg was still in the middle of the morning rush. But health inspectors didn't take other people's schedules into account when planning theirs, and sure enough the visitor, a Mr Braithwaite, arrived right on cue.

It was busy in the café, with Brenda and Mick busy demolishing their bacon and sausages and already onto their second cups of tea. It wasn't an ideal time for me either, as Mother's Day was coming up at the weekend, and we had a lot of orders to prepare but I had to go because I'd been getting red warnings from the bracelet suggesting that, despite all our efforts to clean up, further help was needed.

Reg was dealing with Mr Braithwaite in the main café area when I arrived, which was causing unrest among the punters, because while he was out there, he wasn't cooking orders. Mandy was doing her best to quell the growing tide of discontent, but builders waiting too long for their bacon and eggs tend to get irate. I thought about offering to help, but cooking was out of the question. I was no trained chef, and if the inspector caught me in the kitchen, contravening regulations because I didn't know what I was doing, I could easily mess this up all by myself.

However, I still felt drawn to the kitchen, where I knew something was wrong, so like before, I offered to clear a few tables, scooping up a stack of dirty plates and cutlery from a group of road workers who had just left. That was when the next dastardly scheme was revealed.

The back door was usually left unlocked, as Reg had taken to smoking out in the yard instead of in the kitchen, and as I entered, laden with crockery, I saw the handle turn and the door begin to open, slowly, as if the person behind it was worried about being seen by someone on the other side.

I knew that whoever this was, they had to be up to no good, so I offloaded my pile of plates and rushed towards the door, just as it was opened wide enough for me to see who was there. It was one of the yobs from the other night, and he was in the process of unzipping a large plastic holdall, emblazoned with the colours and crest of Tottenham Hotspur. It was the type of bag favoured by kids for their school sports kits in the 1980s.

I charged into him, knocking him backwards, and in his surprise he dropped the holdall just outside the back door, causing it to burst open as it hit the ground with a thud and rolled over. What happened next turned my stomach. Dozens, perhaps even hundreds, of cockroaches erupted from within, swarming across the concrete like something out of a horror film.

They scattered in every direction, some skittering down a drain, others disappearing behind the bins, and a few squeezing through cracks in the wall. Others followed the yob's example and headed for the back gate, through which he was now sprinting. He didn't look keen on hanging around these creatures any more than I did.

I've seen cockroaches before. An apartment block in Tenerife I once stayed in was riddled with them. But never in Britain, not even in the roughest takeaway.

Pursuit of the yob was out of the question. He was already legging it down the alley, and I had more important things to worry about. Because when I said the little blighters had scattered in all directions, I meant it, and I was sure I'd seen at least one make a dive for the open kitchen door behind me.

I darted back inside, slamming the back door shut behind me to stop any more from coming in. The kitchen looked calm and still spotless, apart from the piles of washing up, but I wasn't about to get complacent. There was one in here somewhere, and if the inspector found it, then the game would be up. Thank goodness the bag hadn't been opened in the kitchen itself, which had obviously been the intention. I would never have been able to deal with them all.

I dropped to my knees and examined every hiding place I could think of, down the side of the fridge and cooker, in the food cupboards, behind the broom and the bins. Then I opened the cleaning cupboard beneath the sink and saw it, big and bold, feelers twitching next to a packet of Vim. How it had got in there, I couldn't see, perhaps through the gap beneath the cupboard that housed the waste pipe.

I could hear the voices of Reg and Mr Braithwaite just outside the door, so I did the only thing I could think of. I grabbed a mug from the counter above and slammed it down, trapping the insect. I then shut the cupboard door and leapt to my feet, moving away and trying to compose myself, just as the door swung open.

Mr Braithwaite was one of those officious types, tall and thin, with a neat moustache, in a pinstriped suit and carrying a clipboard. He entered with a brisk stride, pausing briefly to sniff the air, as if in disapproval at the reek of bacon fat, though that was not an offence, or at least I didn't think it was, because Reg did have a working extractor fan. We'd had mended it the day before. Nonetheless, he gave the impression of someone who was a stickler for seeking out infractions, perhaps even taking pleasure in it.

"I'll begin with a general inspection of the food preparation area, then take a look at your refrigeration and storage facilities."

He was bound to look in the cupboard, and was likely to wonder what an upside-down mug was doing among the cleaning products. These people were trained to poke their noses in and sniff out things that were out of place. I had to get it out.

I waited while he poked about, examining the surfaces and the cooker, hoping he wouldn't ask me any questions, though it was Reg who was getting the grilling. My presence was ignored completely. Perhaps, given my youth, he just assumed I was some lackey and of no consequence.

My opportunity came as Braithwaite moved towards the fridge, which was opposite the sink, so he would have his back turned for a few moments. I sidled back towards the offending cupboard as casually as I could and opened it an inch, focusing on the upturned mug. It was shifting ever so slightly, and my stomach turned again in disgust at the thought of what I was going to have to do.

I reached in and slid the mug towards the edge of the shelf, placing my hand so that I could slide it right onto it. I could hear that Braithwaite was preoccupied, going on about what should be stored on which shelf, but it sounded as if all was in order. I took a deep breath and brought the cup over the edge, instantly feeling the thing within, alive and wriggling on my hand. I wasn't sure if it could bite or sting and didn't fancy finding out, so as fast as I could without attracting attention, I made my way to the door, inverting the mug to the upright position as I went, keeping my hand clamped tightly over the top.

When I got to the door, I realised there was a problem. How did I open it without taking my hand off the mug? I couldn't, so I would just have to be quick and snatch my hand away, turn the handle, and clamp it back on top before the insect could escape.

I almost made it to safety, and the cockroach didn't leap out or bite me, much to my relief, but as I made my way through the door, I caught Braithwaite's eye as he closed the fridge door.

"Wait," he said. "Where do you think you're going?"

"Just nipping out for a bit of fresh air and a cuppa," I called, hoping he wouldn't call me back.

"Well, don't be long," he said. "I want to speak to all the staff before I go. And when you come back, you can make me a cup of tea. Milk and two sugars."

Free at last, I went to the far end of the yard, flung the cockroach over the wall, then checked the inside of the mug. It looked clean, as if it had been just washed up, with no evidence that anything had ever been inside.

Then I went back in to make Braithwaite's tea, deciding, much to my amusement, to use this very mug. It was the least I could do under the circumstances.

By the time I handed it to him, he was wrapping up and giving Reg his summary. I didn't face any further interrogation, because Reg had explained I wasn't on the payroll and just helped with collecting a few plates and glasses, rather like a potman in a pub.

"Well, this all appears in order, Mr Harvey. You'll receive a written report within fourteen days. Nothing to worry about here. Keep up the good work."

And then he left, to a huge sigh of relief all round.

This had been far too close for comfort, but thankfully, I didn't think Braithwaite had been in on the scheme. He hadn't given any indication that he was specifically looking for cockroaches. But there was no doubt it was Pollock and Morland who had sent the yob, knowing what time the inspector was coming.

When I told Reg the full story, he was extremely relieved at my intervention, particularly given that Braithwaite had looked in the sink cupboard after I'd gone outside. He was going to have to keep a close eye out for cockroaches for a few days, but the immediate danger was past.

So Reg's café lived on to fight another day. But I was pretty sure it wasn't over yet.

April 1984

"Know anything about salmon, Carter?"

"Indeed, I do, Mr Ritchie. Did you know they swim upstream to mate? Even up waterfalls if necessary. Me and the missus were watching a documentary on BBC2 about it only the other night. Sounds like a lot of hard work, if you ask me."

It was Sunday lunchtime, the start of a new month, and I had gone for a drink with Billy at The Salisbury. Shortly after our arrival, Ritchie, accompanied by Ashe, had arrived on one of their regular investigations into whatever had been half-inched in the neighbourhood this week. It was a routine I had seen played out many times, and, as was often the case, the first person they made a beeline for was Eddie. A hush had come over the pub, with everyone keen to eavesdrop as Ritchie continued his interrogation.

"I'm talking about smoked salmon. Cases of smoked salmon. They're nicked."

"Well, I can't help you there, I'm afraid. The missus won't have it in the house, not after that food poisoning scandal a couple of years ago. We aren't fans of botulism around our way."

"That was canned salmon, Carter. I'm talking about the high-end stuff here. Scottish smoked salmon, from the most prestigious farms, bound for some of the finest restaurants in the West End. Twelve cases of it disappeared off the back of a truck when it stopped for petrol, not half a mile from here, on Friday afternoon. And practically on the doorstep of your Emporium, or whatever other glorified title you're giving that warehouse full of tat this week."

"Are you sure you aren't winding me up, Mr Ritchie? It is April Fools' Day after all. I didn't think the CID worked Sundays. I thought you were all Monday to Friday men."

"A good policeman is never off duty," volunteered Ashe.

"We know that, but what about the bad ones?" asked Des from behind the bar, prompting laughter from the half a dozen or so regulars gathered around.

"This is not a joke," insisted Ritchie. "Because if I recall correctly, April Fool pranks have to be carried out before noon, and if it was prior to midday, Mr Gittins, I would be nicking you for operating outside of legal licensing hours. Now, what about you? Do you know anything about this salmon?"

"No. We don't do food in here. That's for poncey tourist pubs. But I've got some prawn cocktail crisps if they're any good to you?"

"I don't think we're going to have much luck here, sir," said Ashe, as more laughter reverberated around the bar. "Maybe we should try that new bistro on Camden High Street."

"Very well," said Ritchie, whose face had gone a noticeably darker shade of red. The regulars had run rings around him as they always did, and he knew it. "But I'm sure you know something about that salmon, Carter. If I find your mucky paws have been anywhere near it, I'll have you, make no mistake."

As soon as they went, a couple of the regulars began badgering Eddie in the hope that he did have the salmon and would sell some of it to them. As Ritchie well knew but could never prove, half the dodgy deals in the area took place in The Salisbury, but the patrons were out of luck, because for once Eddie genuinely didn't know anything about the stolen fish. So Billy and I enjoyed our pints and had a game of pool, while I reflected on my latest successful Robin Hood mission.

The previous day had been the Grand National, and I had once again gone down to the Mecca to fleece them. Perhaps I was pushing my luck because I doubted Ted Mills was going to tolerate another caning from me, but what the hell, I decided to do it anyway.

My charitable cause this time was a new minibus for the old folks' home. Their previous one had conked out for good, and they'd been trying to raise the funds for a replacement. Without it, their regular day trips to the countryside, the seaside at Southend, and even just the local garden centre, had been put on hold. For many of them, it was these little outings that kept them going.

Just backing the winner of the Grand National with the stake money I could muster wouldn't raise enough, with the winner returned at the rather unusual starting price of 13/1. But I knew the history of the race well, which meant I also knew who had come second. That allowed me to place a bet known as the Computer Straight Forecast, which involved picking the first and second in the correct order. With Hallo Dandy winning at 13/1 and Greasepaint coming second at 9/1, I knew I'd be looking at a payout of over 100/1.

These forecast bets were a mug's game most of the time, with the dividends they paid out woefully short of the true mathematical odds. However, with most punters unable to figure out the extent to which they were being ripped off, it remained a popular bet. That was particularly the case on the dogs, where the clientele at Big Mick's shop loved to fritter away their pension money in combination bets on their favourite trap numbers, without any form study whatsoever.

The bet served my purposes very well, though, and I was able to slip it in under the radar on Saturday morning, the shop's busiest time of the whole year, when hundreds of once-a-year punters were queuing up to place their bets. I decided that I would risk no more than fifty quid this time, fearful that any more might set off alarm bells, but the shop was so busy processing bets, there was no time to scrutinise them. No one was expecting clever money on the Grand National, generally regarded as a lottery, so this was the perfect day to pull a stroke.

I had kept quiet about it afterwards, and when Billy asked me how I'd got on when I met him in the pub, I just said something about having a couple of quid each way on the winner and left it at that. I wanted my betting coup to stay under the radar. It didn't stop him scrounging a couple of pints off me, though. But at 75p for a Löwenbräu, I could afford it.

I waited until Monday morning to go and collect my winnings, where this time I had no choice but to take the money in cash, as I did not know to whom a cheque should be made payable. I did know, though, that the fund-raising committee for the minibus was having a meeting at St Mark's church hall that evening to discuss plans for a proposed Easter fête. This had been reported in the previous week's *Journal*, in an article in which they were asking for volunteers.

I planned to turn up at the meeting, like the fictional Robin on his trusty steed, riding to the rescue with all the money they needed. But as things turned out, between collecting the money and handing it over, I was to be called on again to bail Reg out of trouble.

I was most uncomfortable about walking round London with over five thousand pounds burning a hole in my pocket, especially since, having stuffed my jacket with the twenty-pound notes that Ted had reluctantly handed over, I was distinctly bulging at the seams. I intended to go home, stash the cash, and then take it out again in the evening.

I was informed while being paid out that my custom was no longer welcome at this branch of the Mecca, though he stopped short of saying I was banned from any of the others. Even so, I knew I'd have to tread carefully from now on, as I'd learnt over the years that the different branches shared information about certain clients. Thankfully, there were dozens of betting shops within a mile or two in this part of London, and it was a lot easier to maintain anonymity in this pre-internet era where cash was king. I'd just have to spread my bets around a bit in future.

My plan to go straight home evaporated when, just as I was leaving the shop and looking around carefully, given that this would be a very bad day to get mugged, the bracelet started flashing red. I didn't know why, yet, but I sensed I needed to get to Reg's fast. When I arrived, I saw him deep in conversation with Ritchie and Ashe.

"Are you serious?" asked Reg. "Does this look like the sort of establishment that serves smoked salmon? As far as the punters in here are concerned, the height of sophistication is a slice of toast cut into triangles. What on earth would I want with smoked salmon?"

"Acting on information received, we have reason to believe that you've taken delivery of a consignment of this stolen salmon," said Ritchie.

"And I told you I don't sell salmon. The only fish I do in here is kippers for breakfast and fish fingers for the kids at lunchtime."

The bracelet flashed red like crazy at the mention of kippers. That was the hint I needed. Unfortunately, Reg, Ritchie and Ashe were standing between me and the kitchen. There was no way I could get past them without attracting attention.

Instead, I turned and went back outside, walking to the edge of the property and sprinting round to the back, hoping Reg would have left the door unlocked again for his smoking breaks. Judging by the number of cigarette butts outside, he had, and I was relieved, on entry, to discover they hadn't come into the kitchen yet. It wouldn't be long, though, because I knew Ritchie wouldn't have come without a warrant, and they would be through in any moment. For the third time in as many weeks, I found myself in a race against time to remove something incriminating from the kitchen.

I flung open the large refrigerator Reg used for storage, and sure enough, right on the middle shelf was a large case marked kippers. I grabbed it and backed away, turning and making for the rear door.

I closed it behind me just as I heard the police enter. "Acting on information received," they had said. I imagined they knew exactly what they were looking for, and that was the large case I was currently holding. I was painfully aware that I was also carrying over five thousand pounds on my person. If I were caught with that and what was almost certainly inside this box, even a copper of Ritchie's limited deductive powers wouldn't have too much difficulty putting two and two together. I'd be rubbing shoulders with my dad in Pentonville before I knew it.

I didn't hang about, racing across the yard and around the corner, only slowing down once I was out of sight of the back door. I should have dumped the box there and then, but curiosity got the better of me. Pausing in the alley, temporarily out of view of prying eyes, I tore it open to look inside.

Sure enough, there it was, the missing salmon, labelled with the name of the farm in the Scottish Highlands it had come from. Tempted as I was to take some home as a treat for Mum, I couldn't afford to take such a risk. This lot had to be disposed of fast.

The bracelet glowed green, prompting me to move on, directing me back towards the main road, which seemed an odd choice. What if Ritchie and Ashe caught me on their way out of the café? The box might be labelled kippers, but they knew what they were looking for, alright.

Then, the logic of the bracelet became clear. There was a builder's skip just where the alley emerged onto the road, so without a thought, I tossed it in, prompting a cry of "Oi!" from someone on the scaffolding behind me. I didn't turn around, but just legged it, getting back to the front of the café just as a glum-faced Ritchie was leaving empty-handed.

When I told Reg about this latest scrape, he was extremely relieved, but also curious as to how I seemed to be so well-informed about everything that was going on.

"Obviously, I'm grateful. If it wasn't for you, I'd have been finished by now. But how did you know?"

"Just a stroke of luck, really," I said, making up something on the spot. "I overheard Morland tipping Ritchie off in the pub toilets last night. They didn't know I was in the cubicle. The whole thing was a set-up. When were those kippers delivered?"

"Only this morning."

"That'll be it then. They must have switched the boxes in the delivery, then got Ritchie to come the same day, knowing you probably wouldn't have had time to check them. It would have been an open-and-shut case. Except, I got there first. Disaster averted."

"This time, maybe," said Reg. "But how much longer are we going to be able to withstand this? We've managed to deal with everything they've thrown at us so far, but we can't ride our luck forever."

He had a good point. We knew they weren't going to give up, and they hadn't left any sort of trail that would allow us to turn the law back onto them. On my way home, I mulled it over, wondering what we could do to bring this to a close. In the meantime, I had a donation to make.

The bracelet didn't tell me everything that was going to happen, so when I met the committee at the church hall, I was in for a surprise. There were just four of them, and as I entered the room, turning up early before any other attendees, I saw that one of the women was much younger than the others, who were mostly middle-aged. My heart leapt when I saw it was Molly.

I hadn't seen her for weeks. She had been seeing that mechanic for a while, and I'd spotted them in the pub together a couple of times back in the winter, but not since. And we hadn't spoken since New Year's Day.

If anything, it was more of a surprise to her that I'd turned up, as in my old life I hadn't exactly been known for supporting charitable ventures. Would she still be so hostile towards me now that I'd come in aid of a good cause?

"Nobby!" she exclaimed, without the animosity of before, but not with any hint that she was pleased to see me either. "What are you doing here?"

"I heard about your minibus campaign, and I've come to make a contribution," I said. "How about you?"

"My gran's in the home. She's got dementia, bless her, and I can't bear to think of her cooped up. The outings they used to take her on before always brought her out of herself."

"Well, now you can," I said, opening my jacket and pulling out five wedges of a thousand pounds each in twenty-pound notes, plus the odd few extra notes that made up the total of my winnings.

The other ladies were thrilled, but I could see that Molly wasn't impressed. I wasn't going to win her over that easily.

"Where did this come from?" she asked. "More dubiously acquired gains? If this has come from gambling, we can't touch it."

But Molly was outnumbered. The howls of derision from the other ladies at the suggestion of looking this gift horse in the mouth soon drowned out any argument she had. The money they needed for the bus was sitting there, on the table. Whatever beef Molly had with me, there was no way they were turning this donation down.

As before, I urged all of them not to reveal the source of the money, just as other eager volunteers began shuffling into the hall. Whether they wanted to continue with the rest of their activities now was up to them. Five grand would be enough to pick up a decent second-hand bus in 1984 that would keep going for years. Provided they didn't buy it off Eddie.

Molly still didn't look happy, though. I stayed for the rest of the meeting, during which there were huge cheers when it was announced that an anonymous donor had put up the money they needed, without the people around having any idea it was me. Afterwards, I approached her to ask if she'd meet me for a drink. What I was going to say, I wasn't sure, but I couldn't pass up the opportunity.

"What? You must be joking. You think just by coming here and dropping five thousand pounds into my lap, you're going to impress me?"

"Well, I thought it was pretty impressive," I said. "And so did all the others."

"Yes, but they haven't been in a relationship with you and had to play second fiddle to your gambling addiction. Which I assume is where that money came from."

"Yes, but it's not an addiction. And you know the mysterious benefactor who paid for the church roof to be fixed up? That was me as well."

I looked as she mulled it over, wondering if her stance was softening at all, but she still looked doubtful, as if all this were too good to be true.

"But the money still came from gambling, right?" she asked.

"If it's for a good cause, does it really matter? It's all legal. It's not like I robbed a bank or anything. Come on, just one drink, then I'll explain all about it."

I wasn't sure how I was going to do that, but she did agree to have one drink with me, so we went to The Grafton, where we'd hopefully be able to talk undisturbed. There was no way I was taking her to The Salisbury.

I couldn't tell her about the bracelet, so I just went with the angle that I had a talent for poker and betting on the horses, and I wanted to use those skills for something worthwhile. The point I was trying to get across was that it had all been done with good intentions and not for any personal gain. She seemed to understand what I was saying, but it didn't appear to be getting me anywhere.

"I'm not going back out with you, Nobby. You let me down badly, and despite your current knight in shining armour act, I can't forgive that."

"But you don't hate me anymore? We can be friends?"

"Friends is pushing it. But no, I don't hate you, and I won't cross the street to avoid you if I see you in the future."

That was something, I supposed. Progress, of a sort. Despite my focus on helping Reg and trying to free my dad, winning back Molly had also been on my mind.

"What have you been up to these last few months?" I asked. "You haven't been in the pub for ages. I saw you with Martin a couple of times, but not lately."

"I'm not with Martin anymore," she said. "He's too obsessed with his cars. It's all he cares about. At times it felt like, given the choice, he'd rather stick it up the exhaust pipe of his latest motor than me."

That wasn't what I wanted to hear. I mean, I was glad that she wasn't with him anymore, but the way she described it suggested that they had been having sex at some point. And that cut like a knife, even more so because it would never have happened if I had treated her better in the first place. Sometimes, the wounds that hurt the most are the ones we inflict upon ourselves.

"Oh, well, I'm sorry to hear that," I lied, relieved that at least it was now over.

"I've got a new job, too," she said. "At that new club, Nirvana."

"You're joking," I said, aghast at the revelation. "That's Frankie's new venture. You know he's a gangster, right?"

"So what? He pays well."

"So what? I'll tell you so what. It's down to him that my dad's in prison. He carried out that robbery and framed Dad for it."

"You never mentioned that before. You were convinced Tommy was innocent, but you never said anything about Frankie being involved."

"Because we haven't spoken in months. I know a lot more now than I did then."

"Right, well, I am sorry I didn't know. If I had, I might have thought twice. But at the end of the day, it's a job. I can't live on fresh air. And I'm good at it. My boss at the last casino gave me a glowing reference."

She did seem genuinely contrite, and I could hardly expect her to quit just to spare my feelings. Then a thought struck me. A glance at the bracelet confirmed it was a good one. Perhaps she was in exactly the right place.

"Look," I said. "It's fine. You were not to know. But I need to warn you; Frankie is a very bad man."

"You don't need to tell me that. I know all about how he got his nickname. But I've nothing to be afraid of. I'm just an employee."

"Exactly, just an employee. To him, you're probably no more than a pretty face, a bit of decoration around the place. However sexist that might sound, that's how these people think. But perhaps we can turn that to our advantage."

"Our advantage? I'm hearing a 'we' in this, and I thought I made it clear there is no 'we' about us, anymore."

"Even if it means working together to clear my father's name? Surely you can't be opposed to that. You used to get on great with him before."

"I don't know what you think I can do. I'm only a waitress."

"There's no 'only' about it. You're in a prime place to keep your ears to the ground and your eyes peeled. See what he does, who he talks to, what makes him tick. If there's a chink in his armour, I want to know what it is. You don't have to do anything dangerous."

"Fine, but I don't know what you think I'm going to be privy to."

The bracelet, still glowing green, seemed to think otherwise.

"I don't know," I said. "Perhaps nothing. But will you keep an eye out? If not for me, then for Tommy?"

"Alright," she agreed, downing the rest of her drink and getting up. "But this changes nothing between me and you, understand?"

"Yes," I said. "So, if you find anything out, you'll be in touch? Promise?"

"I promise," she replied.

I felt curiously optimistic in the days after this reconciliation of sorts. I had a strong sense that Molly working at Nirvana was the route into Frankie's life I had been looking for.

April seemed to rush by, with the weather improving and Easter on the way. I worked hard in the shop and tried to spend as much time with Mum as I could, particularly on Sundays when we had our roast dinners and then watched television together in the evening. The first series of *Spitting Image* had just begun and was rapidly becoming a staple of Sunday evening viewing, with its send-ups of everyone from the Royal Family to Arthur Scargill. He was a familiar figure on TV due to the miners' strike, which had come to dominate the news schedules since it had begun a few weeks ago.

On the Sunday before Easter, I witnessed a tragic event when the legendary comedian Tommy Cooper collapsed and died live on stage while we were watching *Live from Her Majesty's* on ITV.

I had remembered hearing about this on the news first time around, but hadn't witnessed it at the time, and didn't recall the date, so it still came as a shock. I recalled that there had been a spate of celebrity deaths in the light entertainment world around this time, with Diana Dors and Eric Morecambe also passing away within weeks of Tommy Cooper.

I wondered if there was anything I could do to help the others, but the bracelet didn't seem to think so. Perhaps it was just their time to go. But there was plenty to do closer to home, because the ongoing situation at the café was about to come to a head.

Things had been quiet for a couple of weeks, but I knew Pollock and Morland weren't done yet. Quite the lengths they would be prepared to go to, though, I hadn't anticipated.

Of all the visions the bracelet had shown me, none had been as unsettling as the one that came after I went to sleep on Maundy Thursday. Forget the Last Supper, if this was anything to go by, Reg's was heading for its final fry-up.

In my dream, I saw the yobs, led by the ringleader I had since learned from my local enquiries was named Warren, pouring petrol through the rear of the building at the dead of night before setting it alight. Within minutes, the café was an inferno, and by morning, it was nothing but a blackened shell. That would have finished Reg, and possibly in more ways than one. He lived alone in the flat above the shop, and with the speed the fire took hold, I didn't fancy his chances of getting out alive.

I knew what was going to happen, just not when, but further dreams the following night filled in the missing details. This time, I saw Pollock and Morland meeting with Warren in a disused railway siding a mile or so away, a place I knew, as Billy and I used to play there as kids. Most of the time it was deserted, being derelict, overgrown, and forgotten, a stretch of rusting track half-swallowed by weeds, surrounded by crumbling brickwork and filled with junk. Hardly anyone ever went there, so it was the perfect location for local ne'er-do-wells to get up to no good.

The bracelet had come up trumps this time, giving me a detailed plan of action. I just had to play my part. It was Saturday, a busy day for Bud & Bloom before we closed for the Easter break, and my mother needed me in the shop, but I was going to have to let her down, not for the first time. She was not best pleased, but this had to take priority, being likely to take up a sizeable chunk of the day.

The first thing I did was get hold of my father's camera, his beloved Olympus Trip 35, which had accompanied us on family holidays throughout my youth. He was well into his photography, though not to the extent that he'd invested in a lot of expensive equipment. He swore by this camera and was adamant it was the only one he'd ever need.

I'd rarely used it myself, as he only trusted me with it when he handed it over to take a snap of him and Mum, and always took it right back afterwards. I knew it was easy enough to use, though, being pretty much point and shoot, as promoted by David Bailey in a long-running TV advertising campaign.

Point and shoot was all I needed, and thanks to the bracelet, I knew where and when. So after breakfast, with Mum busy in the shop, I headed for the disused siding, a place I hadn't been for years. Other than the addition of copious amounts of graffiti and a lot more weeds, it had barely changed at all.

Thanks to my dream, I knew exactly where I needed to be to get the shots I wanted, and concealed myself in an old railway carriage, in which Billy and I had once delighted in recreating scenes from the Bond movie *From Russia with Love*.

The carriage was as horrible as you might expect inside, given that it had been abandoned for at least a decade. The roof leaked, leaving the place reeking of damp, with torn seat cushions spilling yellowing foam and rust-streaked window frames holding in the few panes of glass still intact. But it was the ideal cover, and from inside I had a clear view through one of the broken windows, from which I could take my snaps.

This was fraught with risk. Pop my head up at the wrong time, and I risked being spotted. Then there was the tell-tale click and whirr of the shutter. I knew how loud it was, because I'd already had a couple of practice goes with the new roll of film I'd installed. I just hoped I was near enough to get a clear view of their faces, but not so close that they heard the camera.

Warren arrived first, looking furtive and casting glances around to reassure himself that no one was present. He was soon joined by Morland and Pollock, who arrived together. They were barely ten yards away from me, but it was a clear day, and the sun was behind me. So if they looked this way, they'd be less likely to see me with the sun in their eyes. The angle of the rays lit up their faces, and even before any money changed hands, I managed to get a couple of decent shots of the three of them. A main road ran behind the siding, and the steady flow of traffic drowned out the click of the shutter if I timed it right.

Then came the payoff, the real money shot, as Morland opened a briefcase and began handing Warren bundles of banknotes, rather like the ones I'd been given for my Grand National winnings. I couldn't see the exact amount, but it was a lot, maybe a couple of thousand or more. Given the seriousness of what Warren was being asked to do, it seemed a fair price, and probably a fortune to an unemployed yob, even if it was pocket change to a businessman like Morland.

My next task was simple: take the film to a same-day developing service on Kentish Town High Street, which promised to have it ready by the afternoon. Then it was off to the café, where I fully expected to see our enemies again, because the bracelet had told me that's where they would be.

Sure enough, there they were, being all sweetness and light this time, pretending to offer Reg an olive branch. But Reg, being Reg, was naturally suspicious and not playing ball.

"Come on, Mr Harvey, all we want to do is talk," said Morland. "Let's have dinner this evening, and see if we can't come to some sort of arrangement."

"The only arrangement I'm interested in is one that involves you leaving here, right now. Don't think I'm not aware who was behind that cockroach wheeze. Or the salmon."

"We just want to let bygones be bygones," said Pollock, at which point I intervened.

"It wouldn't do any harm to have dinner with them, would it?" I suggested.

"All at our expense," added Pollock. "It's the least we can do."

"Tried the stick, and now it's the carrot, eh?" said Reg. "It won't make a blind bit of difference. I'm still not selling."

"You may as well go along and see what they've got to say," I said. "Eat, drink and be merry on their money."

"Fine, if you insist," said Reg. "Waste your money. But don't think that by getting me drunk, you'll get me to sign anything."

"Eight o'clock at Andy's Greek Taverna," said Pollock. "Don't be late."

Reg remained suspicious, but I was hugely relieved he'd agreed to go. I knew what Morland and Pollock were up to. They needed to get Reg out of the café. It seemed that while they were happy to commit arson, they weren't prepared to go as far as murder, which was a relief. It also gave them an alibi, because if they were with Reg on the night his café went up in flames, they could hardly be accused of starting it.

By getting Reg out of the way, I was helping enable their plan, but if I had prevented it from happening tonight, there was nothing to stop them from trying another time. At least this way, I knew exactly when Warren and his mates would strike, and I could prepare accordingly.

I went back to the camera place and picked up the developed film. I was slightly concerned the proprietor might question the content of my snaps, but nothing was said, so armed with my evidence, I was ready for the next step.

I phoned the local nick and asked to speak to Ashe. I'd found he could be quite reasonable when Ritchie wasn't around, and I arranged to meet him in a different café, a couple of miles away, telling him it would be worth his while.

I did have a few reservations about doing this. It was an unwritten rule in our community that nobody ever grassed. Even those who got caught in possession of something dodgy bought off Eddie generally took the fine, rather than land him in it. But this was different. I wasn't grassing on one of our own for knocking out bent video recorders. Pollock wasn't one of us, and neither was Morland. As for the yobs, anyone willing to set fire to someone's home deserved everything they got.

I told Ashe the full story, even risking landing myself in it by telling him the truth about the salmon, figuring, if you'll pardon the pun, that there were bigger fish to fry. I showed him the photographs I'd taken at the railway siding, and then embellished things slightly, claiming I'd overheard them confirming the time and place of the planned arson attack. That information had come from the bracelet, but the outcome was the same, and he agreed to post some officers in the yard to catch them in the act.

It was all highly irregular and outside of official procedure, but Ashe was smart and saw the logic. He was confident he could swing it at the station if he claimed the information had come from a reliable source.

"Ritchie's going to hate this," he said. "He's gone away for the weekend."

"Good," I said. "He's been taking the credit for your work for years. It's about time you got a bit of glory."

And that was exactly what he got. It all went like clockwork. Warren and his two mates arrived right on cue, about half an hour after dark, one of them posted at the back gate as a lookout. That was of little use, given that the police were already inside. The officers waited, out of sight, until Warren started splashing petrol from a jerry can on the back door, and then pounced. Within minutes, they were all being bundled into the back of a police van.

From there, everything fell into place. The yobs turned out to be far less tough than they made out, and folded quickly under questioning, especially once it was suggested they might get lighter sentences if they dropped Morland and Pollock in it. Which they did, quite happily. Within a couple of days, both were helping the police with their enquiries, and with more revelations surfacing, some even I hadn't known about, the pair ended up being charged with multiple offences. A stretch behind bars seemed inevitable.

The café was safe, resulting in a very grateful Reg who couldn't thank me enough, while we were hosing down the back door to get rid of any trace of the petrol, given that this was now his preferred smoking place. Ashe, meanwhile, had earned some long-overdue credit for his work, much to Ritchie's disgruntlement. Then there was Molly, back on speaking terms with me, and now my eyes and ears at Frankie's club. My dad might still have been inside, but at last it was beginning to feel like the tide was turning my way.

May 1984

I'd forgotten just how ever-present the fear of nuclear war had been in the 1980s. It was a constant, looming threat. The Soviet leadership changed hands three times in as many years, and with Chernenko taking the reins in 1984, there was still no sign of the thaw his successor would eventually bring. The Cold War was still very much alive.

This undercurrent of anxiety seeped into popular culture. The previous autumn had seen the hard-hitting American TV film *The Day After* portraying the reality of a nuclear conflict, while in music, '99 Red Balloons' explored the theme, hitting the top spot in the spring of 1984. Frankie Goes to Hollywood's follow-up to 'Relax', the apocalyptic anthem 'Two Tribes', would soon do the same, holding on to the top spot for an impressive nine weeks during the summer, the longest any record topped the charts in the 1980s. Meanwhile, the women's peace camp outside RAF Greenham Common kept the issue firmly in the headlines.

I also remember another drama called *Threads* being broadcast around this time, but I don't think it had been shown yet.

Everyone was living with the realistic possibility that we might all be annihilated at any minute, and it was a topic frequently discussed by those around me. Possibly the most bizarre such conversation took place one lunchtime when I was in the bookies.

It's almost a forgotten custom now, but back in 1984, we still used to close our shop for lunch between half past twelve and half past one every day. It sounds bizarre when you think about it from a business perspective. Why close for an hour at the very time of day that working people are also on their lunch breaks? It's probably the only time during the day they might be free to do any shopping.

On top of that, we, and several of the other establishments on our road, used to close for a whole afternoon on Wednesday. We called this half-day closing, another common practice that has long since disappeared, as far as I know. Perhaps they still do it in some rural areas.

I often used this spare time to pop into Big Mick's. Not necessarily to have a bet, as I wasn't doing much on that front, but more for the social side of things. I found the hapless betting antics of the patrons amusing, as they formulated their bets each lunchtime for the afternoon's racing, which usually started around two o'clock. It was on one of my lunch breaks that I overheard Doctor Death and Jinxy Jack discussing the topic of nuclear war.

"I'm telling you, the balloon's going to go up soon," said Death, putting his usual bright and breezy perspective on things. "It's just a matter of time. Mutually assured destruction."

Not only did Death seem to have a negative impact on the health of those around him, but he also seemed to relish the possibility of everyone on the planet perishing in a nuclear holocaust, or whatever other possible calamity might befall humanity. Thankfully, I knew this would not be the case, at least not for another forty years, and said as much, but he was adamant.

"You don't know what you're talking about, Nobby. In fact, I'm so confident, I'm going to ask Big Mick to lay me odds on it."

Which is exactly what he did, marching up to the counter and asking Brenda to get Mick out of the back office so they could negotiate a price.

"Oh, I don't think it's that likely," said Mick.

"What odds will you give me, then? I want to put a tenner on that we're all wiped out in a nuclear war by the end of 1984."

"Alright, Doctor, it's rather unorthodox, but I will indulge you. No credit, though. If you bet cash up front, I'll lay you odds of 100/1."

"Blimey, that's generous!" exclaimed Death.

"You wouldn't get that price down the Mecca," said Mick. "You see, I look after my regulars."

Business concluded, he returned to the back office, as Death came back over to me and Jack, excitedly clutching his slip.

"Look at that, 100/1. When the bomb drops, I'll cop for a grand!"

"I wonder if he'll let me have the same odds," said Jack. "Not that I've got a tenner spare. I might be able to scrape together a few quid, though, if I get a couple of winners up on my Yankee at Newmarket."

"Mick has had you right over, you bloody idiot," I said, unable to believe how gullible these two were.

"How? Surely the odds of nuclear war are less than 100/1," said Death. "It's a value bet."

"And how are you going to collect your winnings when the betting shop, and all of us in it, have been reduced to a pile of radioactive ash and rubble?"

"Oh," he replied, as the flaw in his plan sank in. "I hadn't thought of that."

Ridiculous conversations like this went on all the time, with the regulars always coming up with new ideas and systems to try to beat the bookies, none of which ever worked. Jack was particularly prone to this sort of thing, and was forever scouring the racecards and trying to make up systems from past results, or worse still, buying them from dubious 'experts' who advertised their wares in the classifieds in *The Sporting Life*.

"I've got a new system!" declared Jack, misplaced optimism all over his beaming face, while Death was up at the counter, trying to persuade Brenda to cancel his nuclear war bet. "It's called the Ted Rogers!"

"Ted Rogers?" I asked, fearing the worst.

"Yes. As in *3-2-1*. You must have seen it on the telly."

"Unfortunately, yes."

"OK, well, it's easy. All you have to do is find a horse that finished third two races ago, and then second last time out. So its last two form figures are 32. That means it's improving, right, and is due a win this time."

"With no other consideration as to the form whatsoever?" I asked.

"That's the beauty of it," he said. "The simplest ideas are often the best."

"So you don't think, for example, that coming a close second in the Gold Cup might be different from, say, finishing second in a two-horse race, beaten by twenty lengths?"

"Oh, you don't need to worry about any of that. It all evens out in the long run."

"So, did you come up with this system yourself, or is it one you got out of the paper?"

"It's one of Systematic Syd's," he said. "He's brilliant. You just send him a five-quid postal order every week and he sends you back a winning system in the post."

"Uh-huh. And is this the same Systematic Syd that sold you the infamous Romford Dog Dump method?"

"There was definitely something in that," insisted Jack. "It stands to reason, doesn't it? Any dog that takes a dump before the start is going to be lighter, so will run faster. We made quite a few quid on that the night we all went down to White City, don't you remember? It doesn't just work at Romford, any track will do. It's a shame we can't watch dog racing in the shop, or we could do it all the time."

This riveting conversation was interrupted by Danny, who came into the shop with a concerned look on his face. Something was up, and whatever it was, it was me he was looking for.

"It's Billy," he explained. "He's in hospital. He's been beaten up."

"When?" I asked, concerned not only that something had happened to my best mate, but also that the bracelet hadn't done anything to help me prevent it.

"Last night. He got into a poker school with the Georgiou brothers. It seems like there was some sort of kerfuffle, and the upshot of it was, he got a good kicking."

"Where is he now?"

"In the Royal. I thought you'd want to know."

I did want to know, and I also wanted to find out exactly what had gone on, so that evening, I took a walk in the pleasant evening sunshine to the Royal Free Hospital to see Billy during the strict visiting hours that had to be adhered to. He was on one of the older general wards, a long, high-ceilinged room where the only privacy afforded came from a flimsy curtain.

Billy was propped up in bed looking sorry for himself, with a face that bore the unsightly evidence of a sound beating, one eye purple and swollen almost shut, his bottom lip split and crusted. A dressing on his forehead hinted at a deeper cut beneath, and his right arm rested awkwardly across his chest, cradling what I assumed to be a cracked rib or two. Even so, he managed a weak smile, clearly pleased to see me.

"Alright, mate? How's it going?"

"A lot better than you by the look of it. What the hell happened?"

"I got suckered into playing poker with the Georgiou brothers, that's what happened. Above the launderette, after the pubs kicked out last night."

"Are you insane? You know they've got a reputation for cheating like crazy. Whatever were you thinking?"

"Let's say my judgement was impaired. It was payday, and I'd had a few. One thing led to another, and this game was suggested, and I thought, what the hell, why not?"

"How much did you lose?"

"My whole week's wages, minus what I drank in the pub. About a hundred quid."

It wasn't that much in the grand scheme of things, but I knew Billy couldn't afford it.

"That doesn't explain how you got beaten up."

"Yeah, well, I probably brought that on myself. The thing is, you're right, Andreas and Theo do cheat. I strongly suspect they were signalling to each other, and there were a couple of other blokes there who I didn't know. Perhaps they were in on it as well. I'm convinced they knew what cards I was holding, too. I was dealt three aces face down on one hand, and they all folded, even though Theo had a very tasty-looking hand. When I kicked off about it after they'd cleaned me out, things turned nasty. That's when they decided to give me a pasting and dump me out in the back alley."

"I see," I replied. "Well, perhaps it's time those two were given a taste of their own medicine."

"What can you do? If they're cheating, they'll just do the same to you."

In my original timeline, he would have been right, and that's why I had always steered clear of the two brothers. However, things were somewhat different now.

"Oh, I don't think they're quite as clever as they think they are. I've got a little something up my sleeve that they won't be expecting."

I meant that quite literally, glancing at the bracelet as I spoke, encouraged to get the green response I had been hoping for. If the brothers wanted to cheat, then I'd just have to out-cheat them, in a way that would be completely undetectable.

I wasn't stupid, and I knew if I didn't want to end up in the bed next to Billy, I'd need a bit of support, so when I got back, I sought out Danny and gave him the full story about what had happened to Billy. Few people messed with Danny, so he agreed to come along as backup, if we could get ourselves into one of the brothers' bent spielers.

Asking around, we found out that the games usually took place on Friday nights, and that Andreas and Theo usually tried to entice a couple of well-oiled individuals whom they picked up in pubs. They knew that most people still got paid in cash on a Friday and often went straight to the pub after work with their entire wages in their pockets. All we had to do was locate them, accidentally bump into them, and convince them we were the sort of mugs they were looking for.

They had found Billy in The Salisbury, so that was our first port of call, but they weren't in there. Des was pissed off when we left without buying a drink, telling us to 'fuck off then, you pair of wankers' for good measure. Fair enough, but we didn't have time to hang about. I theorised that they didn't like to hit the same pub two weeks running in case there was any comeback, and the bracelet agreed, kicking in and acting like a satnav.

It directed us to a pub called The Fox, over towards the eastern side of Kentish Town.

The Georgiou brothers must have known who I was, since we lived on the same street, but thankfully I'd had little interaction with them. They didn't tend to hang out in Reg's or Mick's, and we had a washing machine, so I didn't require their services. When we got into the pub, they were playing pool, with Theo, the more flamboyant of the two, leaning over the table, medallion dangling from his half-open floral shirt, as the more reserved Andreas watched on.

This was perfect. We had already worked out what roles we were going to play, the pissed-up lads splashing the cash, so we got a couple of pints of lager and headed over to the table.

"Fancy a game, lads?" I said, acting drunk even though it was my first pint, reaching into my pocket and slapping a ten-pence piece clumsily down on the table. That was all it cost to play in 1984.

"Sure," said Theo. "But why not make it interesting? How about we play for a fiver? My brother and I against you two."

"You're on," I said, pulling out a little brown envelope stuffed with cash, a familiar sight up and down the country on a Friday night. I did not get paid that way, nor did Danny, but this was all part of our act, and we saw their eyes widen at the sight of the cash. Our deliberately inept efforts at the pool table, playing badly, sloshing drink around, and generally acting like a couple of morons with more money than sense, was an excellent convincer, and by the time we finished the game and they collected the fiver, they had us down as the perfect targets.

"Pool is all very well," said Andreas, "but how do you boys feel about playing a man's game? Either of you enjoy a game of poker?"

Our responses were enough to convince them we knew how to play, but that we were probably mugs who didn't know what we were doing. Hence an hour or so later, we were entering the launderette via the back entrance and making our way up the stairs to where the game was to take place.

Danny was in the dark about how I was going to beat the brothers. I had just convinced him I knew what they were up to and was going to play them at their own game. He was there merely as my bodyguard, to protect me if things got rough, which they very well might, if my plan came to fruition. He hadn't even brought his own cash. I was staking him with the promise he'd get a cut of the winnings for his support. All he had to do was play cautiously, not get involved in big pots, and let me work my magic. With the aid of the bracelet, of course.

There were two other men in the room when we arrived, both Greek, one of whom looked like he could handle himself, and one who was much older, an uncle, perhaps. The younger one was very well-built and wearing a suit, and was almost certainly the brothers' muscle. It wouldn't have surprised me at all if he'd been the one who had beaten Billy up, and if it came to the crunch, I hoped Danny could take him, especially given that we were outnumbered.

I couldn't discuss tactics with Danny during the game, but he was no slouch at the poker table and would no doubt be focused on what was going on. As long as he left the big decisions to me, as instructed, I saw no reason why I couldn't take them apart.

Billy had briefed me on what to look out for, and I soon figured out what they were up to. It was a combination of two things, most notably some almost imperceptible markings on the cards. I'd never have noticed it with my sixty-year-old eyes, but at twenty, my vision was razor sharp. Billy reckoned they always seemed to know when he had an ace, so when I was dealt my cards, I paid particular attention to those, scrutinising the backs until I saw it: a tiny alteration in the design on the aces. It would have been hard to spot if I weren't looking for it.

When I told Danny beforehand that Billy suspected them of using marked cards, he had suggested we take our own decks, but the whole point was, I wanted them to use their cards. My entire scheme revolved around them believing they had the edge. Knowing where the aces were in a game of poker would be enough to tip the odds in their favour, but that was only half of their modus operandi. Seated opposite each other at the table, the two brothers had also developed an elaborate signalling system, which it took me a few hands to work out. During that time, I mostly kept my powder dry and let them win a few small pots.

It was all about building their confidence. That's where the 'con' in 'conman' comes from, which was effectively what we were tonight: scammers playing other scammers at their own game. Through little signals, like Andreas running his fingers through his hair, or Theo fingering the edge of his medallion, I soon had them both sussed. Now it was just a case of waiting for the right hand to strike.

They might have known whether I had an ace or not, but what they didn't know was that I could see every single card every player had in every hand, courtesy of the bracelet, which was relaying the information into my head every time a card was dealt. How it was doing it, I didn't know; all that mattered was that it was.

Danny and I had come in with about two hundred and fifty pounds each, and I had allowed myself to lose about fifty of mine over the first hour by deliberately playing badly, to lull them into thinking we were easy pickings. I needed to take my time to set up a major strike, and on about the tenth pot, I saw my chance, with the bracelet backing me all the way.

I had no aces in my hand, and I was confident they did not know what the other cards were, but what I did acquire as the hand progressed was a very handy three threes, two of which were face down. Both the brothers had good hands too, staying in through the opening rounds, until Theo signalled to Andreas to drop out and with good reason. With one card to be dealt, he was sitting on a full house, aces over kings: a stunning and almost unbeatable hand given what was on display. Of course, he did not know I knew this, given that not all his cards were visible, and that enabled me to spring the trap.

It was the perfect scenario. All I had face up was a three, seven and two kings, which looked pretty weedy by comparison, especially since he knew I couldn't have another king as he had the other two. From his perspective, no full house I could muster, even with my hole cards, could beat his, which meant there was only one card in the entire deck now that could win me this hand. The odds were stacked against me, you could say. In any normal game, this would be an obvious time to chuck in one's cards.

And that's when I began upping my bet, because I knew with unswerving certainty that the card I was going to be dealt was the one I needed. The bracelet was giving me the green light all the way, so I began raising big, with Theo matching me each time. My guess at this point was that he thought I also had the makings of a full house or was bluffing, but there was no way he was going to back down from what he was holding.

It was time for the river, the final card to be dealt in seven-card stud, which came face down. I didn't even need to look at it, a move which raised eyebrows when I confidently doubled the bet again, leaving me with only about fifty in front of me.

"What are you doing?" asked Danny, scarcely able to believe that I would make such a crazy move.

For a moment, I saw a flicker of doubt cross Theo's eyes. I knew what he was thinking. No one could be this stupid, could they?

A gentleman would have seen me at this point, knowing that I didn't have enough money to cover another bet, but he had to be an arsehole and raise again. I was at least a ton short of what I needed, so I turned to Danny, as prearranged, for a sub.

We might have agreed beforehand that that's what we would do in this scenario, but even he baulked at the suggestion.

"Are you insane? You haven't even looked at your last card? Is this how you ended up losing all your money at New Year?"

"You know about that?"

"We all know, Nobby," said Theo, smiling as his medallion glittered in front of his hairy chest. "Why did you think we were so keen to get you here tonight? We've had our eye on you for some time, ever since we saw you playing on the fruit machines in the chip shop as a kid."

"I don't care," I yelled, trying to act as if I was losing my rag. "Just give me the money, Danny. I can beat him, I know I can."

It was a masterclass in acting as I pleaded pathetically, with desperation in my eyes, like a drowning man about to sink below the waves for the final time. Danny paused for a moment, then shrugged and passed the money over. I had briefed him that I might behave like this as part of the con, but you couldn't blame him for having doubts. And when the cards were flipped over, I don't know who looked the most shocked, him or the brothers, particularly at that final card, the three of hearts, which they couldn't believe I hadn't looked at.

"Quads," I said, reaching into the middle of the table to claw in the loot. "I think you'll find that beats your full house."

"You cheating little shit!" exclaimed Theo, leaping to his feet.

"That's good coming from someone using marked cards," I said. "Did you think I wouldn't notice? The subtle difference in the design on the aces? Do you get them printed specially that way?"

"Bollocks," said Andreas. "You're the cheat. You knew that last card was a three. You didn't even look at it, for fuck's sake. So who's cheating now?"

He turned to the hired muscle, who had played very little part in the game, reinforcing my belief that poker wasn't what he was here for.

"Stavros. Do him," he ordered. I admired how concise and to the point his instruction was, but this was tempered somewhat by the prospect of being the one that was to be 'done'.

"I don't think so," said Danny, getting to his feet to show he meant business. I was seriously glad I'd brought him, because I'd have been mincemeat if I hadn't.

Danny's great advantage in these situations was his speed. He couldn't half shift when he needed to, and before Stavros could gather breath, Danny was across the room and swinging a right hook squarely on his chin. It was so well placed that it sent him straight into Theo, who had been seated next to him at the table, knocking the pair of them to the ground.

With the older player wisely vacating the room, it was game on, three against two, but Danny was so quick, he more than made up for our numerical disadvantage. He skilfully ducked every blow aimed in his direction while raining punches on the opposition from every angle. My only serious contribution was whacking Andreas over the head with a chair just as he was about to leap on Danny from behind.

When all three had had enough, I scooped up the remainder of the pot, along with our stake money, from the table, which remarkably had remained upright during the fracas.

"And I'm taking these," I said, picking up an unopened pack of cards from the side of the table. "If there's any comeback from tonight, or I hear you've cheated anyone else, I'll make sure there's not a poker player this side of the river who doesn't know you use marked cards."

And with that we left, though I couldn't resist giving Stavros a boot in the stomach on the way out, which was rather unlike me. But this was personal.

"That one was from Billy," I said, before we made our way down the steps at the back and then a couple of doors down to the safety of home, where I let Danny in and we drank coffee in the kitchen while we sorted out the money.

We had about eight hundred quid altogether, which wasn't hugely profitable, considering we'd gone in with five hundred. But it wasn't about the money; it was the principle of the thing. My best friend had been wronged, and now I had avenged him.

I gave Danny a hundred quid for his trouble, kept back my stake, and took the other two hundred round to a grateful Billy the next day. He was now out of hospital and on the mend. It was about double what the brothers had taken off him in the first place, so all in all, this had been a most satisfactory venture.

As for the Greek brothers? They'd been well and truly put in their place and kept a low profile from then on. Which, all things considered, suited me just fine. It was one less thing to worry about.

June 1984

Every year, since the end of the war, one of the social highlights in our community was the annual charabanc trip to the Epsom Derby.

After the race was moved to a Saturday in the 1990s, it lost its unique place in the calendar, now jostling for attention among the glut of weekend sporting fixtures. But back when it took place on the first Wednesday in June, it still commanded the nation's gaze. In Australia they still talk about the Melbourne Cup, held on a Tuesday, as the race that stops a nation. It used to be the same here for the Derby.

Charabanc trips, when a bus would be hired for the day so large groups could enjoy an outing, were immensely popular in the post-war years. I had many fond memories of our annual pilgrimage to Margate every August Bank Holiday, crammed onto the bus with multiple generations of the same families, laden with sandwiches, fizzy pop, and buckets and spades. The spades were often more in hope than expectation, as we peered out at grey skies and drizzle through misted-up windows on the A2.

The Derby trip, though, was strictly for adults, falling as it did on a school day. I didn't get to experience it until I'd left the education system, and even then, only for a few short years, with 1984 marking its final outing. It was mostly men who went, a proper boozy day trip, organised through the pub, where the regulars would give Des a quid a week which he would drop into an oversized whisky bottle behind the bar. This would pay for the bus and the copious crates of ale which I was helping to load aboard.

"What's this, a villains' day out?" remarked Ritchie, who, along with Ashe, had come nosing around the coach just as the regulars were clambering aboard.

"This is a perfectly legitimate outing," replied Des, who drove the bus each year, but you could see where Ritchie was coming from. The Salisbury was a haven for every suspect character in the area, and a good few of them were on this trip. One of these was Fingers McFee, who Ritchie had rightly pegged as the source of the dodgy twenty-pound notes doing the rounds earlier in the year. He hadn't managed to pin it on him, though. Bent stupid, my dad had called him, and that had stuck in my head ever since.

Sitting next to McFee was Slippy Sammy, a seasoned shoplifter who nicked to order, getting anyone in the pub anything they wanted at half of high street prices. He proudly claimed his grandfather had been the greatest three-card-trick merchant London had ever seen, and was another one who had been running rings around Ritchie for years.

Then there was Eddie, along with the various dealers who supplied him or bought from him, and a smattering of other shady sorts. Not hard-core villains, just the ducking and diving types who used to be everywhere when I was growing up.

Ritchie, convinced something was afoot with so many suspicious characters gathered in one place, was on the lookout for imported pornographic videos. He got Des to open the boot and instructed Ashe to search, but all they found were several crates of light ale and a stack of corned beef and Spam sandwiches.

"It's not exactly gourmet dining, is it?" remarked Ashe.

"What did you expect, smoked salmon?" asked Des. "Managed to find your missing cases yet, have you?"

"No," said Ritchie.

"Well, perhaps that's just as well. They're probably stinking worse than a tart's washing basket by now. You certainly won't find them here. These are working-class men, Mr Ritchie. And this is working-class grub."

"I would think the evidence has probably long been eaten, if you ask me, sir," said Ashe.

"I didn't," said Ritchie. "And as for working-class men, I doubt most of the dubious individuals on this bus have done an honest day's work in their lives."

"Be that as it may, Mr Ritchie, they've all paid good money for their Derby Day trip, so may we go?"

"Be my guest. With this lot off the manor for the day, we should have a nice quiet time. They'll be the Surrey Police's problem, not mine."

With Ritchie pacified, Des clambered into the driver's seat and fired up the engine, sending a thick plume of black smoke billowing over the two officers as the ageing bus rumbled into life. Des rarely laughed, but I saw him stifle a chuckle as Ritchie and Ashe coughed and spluttered in his mirrors.

Eddie had acquired the bus through one of his contacts, and it wasn't exactly in mint condition. Thankfully, Ritchie hadn't asked to see the MOT certificate, as I doubted it possessed one, certainly not one that was genuine. But it got us to Epsom all right, which was where the real fun began.

Big Mick and Brenda couldn't make it, what with it being a busy day in the shop, but plenty of my other friends were along for the ride, including Billy, Danny and Chris, plus Reg, who'd closed the café for the day, such was his fondness for this annual outing. So I had plenty of support with me, which was exactly what I needed. Because it was on this day, forty years ago, that some of us were well and truly fleeced, and I was going to make damned sure it didn't happen again.

Since the Derby began in the eighteenth century, hundreds of thousands of people had been flocking to see it each year. One of the reasons so many came was because the hill behind the racecourse, up on the Downs, was completely free to enter. Over the years it had built up a festival atmosphere, with a large funfair, coconut shies, Punch and Judy, and all manner of stalls, food and entertainment. It was a real carnival, and of huge appeal to the masses, especially after rail travel enabled easy access from London.

Inevitably it also attracted dozens of dodgy types, from dubious tipsters and pickpockets to bent bookies and assorted con artists, including, no doubt, Slippy Sammy's grandfather, who would have had a field day fleecing the unwary.

Skulduggery was rife around horse racing in the past, and not just at the smaller tracks. The big race itself had been rocked by scandals and cheating over the years, including one occasion in 1844 when the winner turned out to be a four-year-old imposter, passed off as a three-year-old.

By the late twentieth century the sport had cleaned up its act, and it was reasonably safe to attend the Derby without worrying about one's wallet being lifted. Even so, in 1984 we all became victims of a scammer, an experience that soured us so badly that we never went again.

The man in question went under the alias John Smith, which should have been a red flag in itself. Unfortunately for us, he was the man many of us placed our bets with for the race.

Bookmakers on British racecourses normally bet at fixed, allocated pitches, which are highly regulated, preventing any form of misdeed. But on the free hill at Epsom, it was somewhat different. In theory, any bookmaker could acquire a badge and set up there for the day, provided they had an official permit, which I remembered Fingers McFee telling us at the time was easily forged.

This character, Smith, really looked the part. He was dressed in all the classic bookie's garb: a loud, chequered suit, complete with a trilby. His mutton-chop sideburns looked like a deliberate throwback to an earlier era, rounding off an appearance designed to evoke nostalgia and authenticity. His pitch sported a sturdy betting board painted in bold lettering, boasting that his firm had been established in 1948. There was little to give rise to suspicion that he might be anything other than a bona fide bookmaker.

I had long fancied Secreto for the race, and backed it with Smith because he was offering 16/1 on the horse, while everyone else was top price 14/1. If I had been paying closer attention previously, I would also have noticed that he was laying over the odds on the hot favourite, El Gran Senor, who had recently won the 2000 Guineas. That would have been another warning sign. His seeming generosity meant that there was a lot of money pouring into his satchel.

Secreto did triumph, and Smith would probably have made a profit, given the amount wagered on the favourite, even if he had stayed put. But he hadn't hung around to wait for the result. While the crowd was engrossed in watching the race, which takes just over two and a half minutes to run, Smith packed up and absconded, taking all the stake money with him. When I returned to the pitch, expecting to collect the tidy sum of £340, he was nowhere to be seen. And nobody ever saw or heard of him again.

I was furious, as were a couple of the other punters on our trip who had also backed the winner, but there was nothing we could do. So this time around I was going to make sure I got paid out, and what's more, I was going to ensure we took all the money he'd laid on the favourite for good measure.

I didn't even need the bracelet's help on this one, because I already knew exactly what was going to happen. All I needed to do was convince enough of my fellow travellers of what this rogue was planning, so we could stop him before he made his getaway.

I began by making the case for Secreto during the journey to Epsom, pitching my view to anyone who would listen that he was the one to be on. Usually, I avoided tipping horses, as you were only asking for grief later when they didn't win, but in this case, I had no such concerns. I already knew the result. By the time we reached the course, I'd persuaded a good half-dozen of the lads, including Billy and Chris, to back him, each way if they preferred, given the price. That didn't stop them backing their original fancies, win only, mainly El Gran Senor, or Lester Piggott's mount, Alphabatim, but win and place investments on Secreto made for a nice saver. Even if he came second or third, they would make a profit.

I'd held back from saying anything about John Smith until we were on the course. I needed to pick my moment and choose my words carefully. When I eventually spotted him, not far from where the coach had dropped us, I gathered the lads I wanted on the team. Eddie, Billy, Chris and Sammy huddled in close as I called them over with an urgent tone. We were just yards away from the fake bookmaker's pitch.

The afternoon was glorious. The sun was beaming down from a blue sky, making it the quintessential English summer's day. The hill was a sea of bodies, packed tight with punters, and the whole place pulsed with a frenetic, festival-like energy. It was the kind of day that etched itself into memory, and this time, I was going to make sure those memories would be good ones.

"You see that guy there," I said, trying not to draw attention, though it was doubtful Smith would have noticed, so absorbed was he in taking bets. He was offering El Gran Senor at even money, while every other bookmaker was odds-on.

"Well, he's a wrong 'un," I added quietly. "He's going to do a runner with all the stake money."

"And you know this how?" asked Eddie, rubbing his chin in a way that suggested scepticism.

"Because apparently he did it before, at a point-to-point meeting in the spring," I lied smoothly, hoping it sounded convincing.

"Best we don't bet with him, then," said Billy, now fully recovered from his beating at the hands of the Georgiou brothers, casting his eye around the other bookmakers for a safer alternative.

"On the contrary, that's exactly what we must do," I said. "He can't be allowed to get away with it. You all know how strongly I fancy Secreto, and I'm going in big. If you've got any sense, you'll do the same. Then we make sure he sticks around to pay us out. Simple as that."

Smith wasn't operating alone. He took the bets while a younger clerk recorded the bets behind him. Smith himself was about forty and lacked the natural padding you saw on many of the old-school bookies, despite having all the garb. He no doubt needed to keep fit, given the exit strategy he had in mind. What he hadn't reckoned on, unfortunately for him, was someone rumbling his game – and why would he?

We placed our bets close to the off, mingling with the crowd and approaching him individually, so as not to arouse suspicion. But unlike the rest of the punters, we didn't allow our heads to be turned away by the spectacle of the race. And soon, our little group was bolstered by a couple of other punters we'd seen backing Secreto with Smith. They were big, muscular blokes who would be ideal recruits to the cause.

"Excuse me, did you just bet on Secreto with that guy?" I asked one of them, just as he turned away.

"I did, and why would you want to know?" he asked, somewhat abruptly.

"My name's Nobby," I explained, "and we have good reason to believe this bookie is going to do a runner with all the stake money as soon as the race starts. I was wondering, could I count on your help, uh ..." My speech tailed off as I fished for his name.

"Barry," he said. "So we've got a rogue bookie, eh? Well, me and my mate Steve here are in the army. He's not going to strong-arm us."

"Perfect," I replied. With our newfound military friends, we hovered a while longer, then closed in, forming a loose but effective ring around the charlatan and his clerk just as the final couple of horses were going into the stalls.

"Here, what's your game?" said Smith, flustered at this unexpected disruption to his scheme.

"Just a little insurance," I replied. "To make sure you're around to pay out."

"This is unlawful imprisonment," he said, trying to edge past. "Or kidnapping."

"If you like," I said. "I prefer to call it a citizen's arrest."

"I'll have the Old Bill on you," he snapped, wriggling in vain to try to get through a gap in the circle.

"Not so fast, matey," said Barry, stepping in and easing him firmly back into the middle of our eight-strong group. "Now be a good chap and enjoy the race.

Then you can pay us our winnings, and you'll be free to go on your way."

Smith's face paled as he backed away to his board, realising he had been sussed, with a look of bemusement as to how. There was a flicker of fear in his eyes because he had taken so many bets on the favourite; if El Gran Senor won, it was doubtful he would have the funds to pay everybody out. It had been a long time since a bookmaker was lynched at a racetrack, but there was no knowing what might happen with an angry crowd demanding their winnings.

His face was positively ashen when El Gran Senor surged into the lead at the two-furlong pole, but his bacon was saved by Secreto's late surge to win by a head in a nail-biting photo.

That might have rescued him from any ugly scenes, but he was still going to be heading home empty-handed. Thanks to all our bets on the winner we had effectively cleaned him out, not only of what he'd taken on the other runners, but also of the profits he'd made from earlier races. By the time he'd counted out the wads of tenners and twenty-pound notes to all of us, his satchel was practically empty. I alone walked away with £1,700. I'd put on a hundred this time, not the twenty I had in the original timeline.

The bracelet had no issue with that, because I'd done the right thing. I'd exposed a conman and seen justice served. And I'd already pledged to donate my extra winnings to an animal welfare charity, so it was a fair result all round.

Loaded up with cash as we were, the rest of the day passed in a golden blur of beer, betting, and banter. We even ate the corned beef sandwiches, despite them getting rather warm in the sunshine. There was a real sense of camaraderie about the day, thanks to taking down John Smith, that spilt over into a good old-fashioned singsong on the bus home. Somehow, we had acquired two extra passengers, two young women dressed up to the nines, who Chris and Danny had met on the hill. While they were canoodling on the backseat, the rest of us were belting out everything from 'Roll Out the Barrel' to 'My Old Man's a Dustman'.

It had been a cracking day by anyone's standards, one of those you knew you'd be talking about for years to come. Yet, even as the laughter and singing reverberated around me, a shadow loomed over it all for one simple reason: my father wasn't there.

He would never have missed a Derby outing like this. If he were here now, he'd have a bottle of light ale in his hand and would be singing along with the rest of us. When I'd arrived here in 1984, I had been convinced that setting things right for him was the prime reason I'd been chosen as custodian of the bracelet, and that the way to do that would be made clear to me. Yet here we were, nearly halfway through the year, and he was still banged up in Pentonville.

When I next visited him in mid-June, it marked six months to the day since he'd been locked away. It was only half a year out of a ten-year stretch, but still half a year too long.

I wouldn't go so far as to say he was a broken man. Far from it. My dad was made of tougher stuff than that. But the glint in his eye had dimmed. Not gone, but dulled. And the weight of it all, of being inside for something he didn't do, was starting to show in the lines on his forehead, and the way he stared into space and paused a little too long between words.

There was a key difference between him and most of the others on the wing. He wasn't guilty. He wasn't some career villain who'd been nicked one too many times and knew they were bang to rights. He was a decent man, caught in a trap designed to deliberately ensnare him, and that would chip away at anyone, eventually.

I'd pleaded with the bracelet. Begged it. Asked it for signs, direction, anything. Every time I asked whether I would eventually get him out, it glowed green. But what bloody use was that? I even lost my rag with it one day while wandering out near Camden Lock, resorting to yelling at my wrist like a lunatic.

"Just tell me bloody when!"

A few passers-by looked at me like I was off my rocker. That wouldn't have happened in the modern world, as people would just have assumed I was arguing with someone on a Bluetooth call.

I did my best to lift Dad's spirits on these visits. I told him about everything that had been going on in his absence, such as how Reg and I had seen off the developers, and all the other little deals and scams going on around the manor. I also told him all about our successful day out at Epsom. All these things seemed to cheer him up, and he was especially pleased when I explained to him how well Bud & Bloom was doing.

But there were other things I refrained from telling him. I never once mentioned Frankie, especially not after the visit he'd paid me back in February. If I did, I knew he'd tell me to leave well alone, plus it would be a weight on his mind that he didn't need right now. It seemed that he had accepted his fate and was reduced to wondering how many years he would have to do before he could get out for good behaviour. For now, I had to let him believe that was the case, assuring him that Mum, I, and the business would all still be waiting for him when the time came.

I always felt like his redemption was just around the corner, but time kept ticking by, and it was just more endless waiting. Royal Ascot came and went, the summer solstice passed, and with it came an increasing feeling that the year was beginning to drift away. Wimbledon began with Connors, McEnroe, and all the usual suspects grunting on the telly, and still nothing happened.

Then, just as June was slipping away, I was minding the shop one quiet afternoon when the phone rang. Nine times out of ten, it would be someone calling in to place an order. A funeral wreath, a wedding bouquet, something along those lines. But not this time.

This time, it was the call I'd been waiting for.

"Nobby? It's Molly. I need to see you."

July 1984

"Why are we meeting here?" I asked as I joined Molly, already seated at a table by the window in the Islington branch of Wimpy, on the day after I turned twenty-one.

"Because I don't want anyone we know to see us together in public," she replied, her tone short and curt.

"Are you still that ashamed to be seen with me, even after all this time?" As far as bearing grudges went, she certainly seemed to be milking this one. I didn't want to guilt-trip her, but I didn't think it would do any harm to remind her of my recent good deed.

"How's the minibus that I paid for going?"

"Very well," she said. "They all went to Southend yesterday. Gran loved it and even won a game of bingo in the seaside arcade. She came back with a Frisbee, which was what she chose as her prize. Goodness knows what she's going to do with it."

"I shudder to think," I said, imagining a load of old folk flinging a Frisbee around inside the care home, sending cups of tea and plates of Rich Tea biscuits flying everywhere.

"Anyway, you took what I said the wrong way. I meant that I don't want to be seen in public with you anywhere near home. When you hear what I've got to say, you'll understand why. It's vital neither Frankie nor any of his associates twig there's any connection between the two of us."

"Fair enough," I said, perusing the menu as she spoke. I loved the Wimpy and fancied ordering the

Bender Brunch. Those curled-up frankfurter sausages were a guilty pleasure because I knew they weren't exactly the healthiest of options. Still, my body was young again now, and I was sure it could cope.

"So you've found something out, then?"

"I have," she said.

"Good, because I was starting to think you'd forgotten about it," I said, letting a hint of my impatience seep out.

"That's because I had to be certain before bringing it to you," she said. "Let's order, and I'll tell you all about it. And since I'm the one supplying the information, you can pick up the tab."

I ordered my Bender Brunch, while she opted for a cheeseburger. Then she began to fill me in on what she'd discovered.

"So, I started off working as a waitress…"

"In a cocktail bar?" I quipped.

"Very funny," she replied. "But as you know, what I really enjoy is running the tables, and after a few weeks Frankie took a shine to me, and set me up as a croupier at the top roulette table, the one where the real high rollers play."

"Not too much of a shine, I hope," I said, again unable to contain my jealousy, just as when I'd found out about her and Martin.

"Frankie has all the women he wants. Among his many activities, he's got a high-class escort agency on the go. From what I hear, he has the pick of the girls whenever he feels like it. And he 'auditions' any potential new employees, if you know what I mean."

"The trappings of the gangster lifestyle, eh? And you know this how?"

He hadn't tried it on with her, had he? More jealousy.

"Oh, you'd be surprised what you can find out when you're working on the inside. Me and the other girls, well, we chat from time to time. Things slip out. Anyway, we're wandering off topic. I want to talk about the roulette wheel I run."

"Let me guess, it's bent."

"Nope, nothing like that. As far as I can see, it's perfectly legit. It's more about the people who play, and one guy specifically, by the name of Charles Lane."

"Never heard of him."

"You won't have done. We get plenty of wealthy types in, and they aren't all glamorous movie stars or racing drivers. This guy's just as rich as them and he made his money in the City, playing the financial markets."

"And now he plays the roulette tables."

"Exactly. For high stakes. And he loses most of the time. Not that he seems particularly bothered about that."

"If he's as rich as you say he is, why would he care?"

"Oh, you'd be surprised. People who get rich like to hang on to their money. We get plenty of bad losers, no matter how loaded they are."

"So what's so special about this guy?"

"Well, that's what I've been trying to figure out. It started off with little things I noticed, and over time, I started to put them together. That's why it's taken so long. But now, I've pretty much got it figured out. Shall I tell you what I think's going on?"

"Please do," I said, leaning forward, eager as I was to hear more.

"OK, so Charles comes in three nights a week, as regular as clockwork. Monday, Tuesday, and Thursday. He cashes ten grand's worth of chips before he starts playing, every time. However, just after he sits down, I've noticed he adds a couple more chips, which he slyly slips onto the table from his sleeve before he starts playing."

"Fake ones?"

"No, they're ours alright. And the highest denomination chips we do. Unlike most of them, which are circular, these very high-value chips are different. They're rectangular, black, embossed with gold lettering, and have a face value of a thousand pounds."

"Wow, that is high," I remarked, which it was, for 1984. I wasn't too sure of the laws on casino staking, and if there were any legal limits. Given the shady nature of Nirvana, they might well have been flouting the gaming laws. Anything went when the criminal underworld was involved.

"Don't the cameras pick this up?" I added.

"If they do, no one's ever challenged him on it. At first I thought, perhaps he just takes these chips home with him each night, but it was odd that I never saw him do that, even though I kept a keen eye on him.

Technically, you aren't supposed to take chips out of the casino, though people do. Some have their own lucky chip that they like to hold on to."

"But not in this case?"

"No, because when Charles finishes playing, he always cashes in everything he has. Which is often more than the ten grand he started with, even though most nights, it seemed like he was losing. His profit is all down to those two additional chips."

"So where are those extra chips coming from?" I said, mulling it over. Unlike modern casinos, where chips were electronically tagged so they could be tracked, no such technology existed in 1984. "And you are absolutely sure they aren't forgeries?"

"That was my first thought, but they look the real deal, and besides, if he was adding them in every visit, then they would show up in the audit. At the end of the night, all the chips are taken into the back room to be cashed up, and on the nights that Charles plays, Frankie is always around to oversee the process. That's something he never does on other nights or at any other table. I kept my eye on Frankie too, and then one night, I noticed him slip those two thousand-dollar chips into his pocket."

"You mean Frankie's stealing them? That's crazy. No one steals from Vincent. They wouldn't dare. Not if they want to keep breathing."

I knew that Frankie, despite playing 'the big I am', was very much subservient to Vincent, who owned the club. Frankie was his undisputed and totally trusted second-in-command. Reg had told me that Vincent, with no son of his own, saw Frankie as his natural successor and was grooming him to eventually take over.

"Do you think he's getting greedy?" I asked. "I mean, how old is Vincent now? I've never met him."

"I have, and he must be pushing seventy."

"Perhaps Frankie thinks that the old man is over the hill, and he can get away with pulling a few strokes."

"Thing is, if he were simply stealing, it would show up. The chips are carefully audited before and after play. If two high-denomination ones go missing, the audit would pick it up. But that isn't what's happening here."

"Because he's only removing the extra ones that Charles is bringing into the club." It was all beginning to make sense.

"Exactly. Those chips never show up in the accounts, because to all intents and purposes, they don't exist. They are, for want of a better term, ghost chips."

Our drinks arrived at that moment, tall glasses fizzing and packed with ice, which we eagerly reached for, the cool and refreshing fruity taste of Quatro hitting the spot instantly. It was the perfect drink on a day when London was positively sizzling.

Molly continued, keeping her voice low as if she was still wary of being overheard, even though it was unlikely over the din of traffic and the constant background hum of chatter.

"This is what I think is happening. Each night, after Charles has been at the table, Frankie slips those two chips into his pocket before they're counted. At some point before Charles next visits, he meets with him and gives them back."

"Presumably for some sort of cash payment?"

"Precisely. Let's say, for argument's sake, Charles gives him a grand each time. Charles has just bought two grand's worth at half price, and Frankie pockets that cash. That's a grand each in profit, three times a week, stolen directly from the club. And they've been doing it for months."

"So it's free money for Frankie, and a little bonus to help fund Charles's gambling habit. So even if he's a grand down on the evening, he breaks even. It's a clever little scheme, I'll give them that."

"Seeing is believing," she said. "I've been busy. I found out where Charles lives from the membership book and went to stake out his house one Tuesday morning, keeping well out of sight across the street. Sure enough, just before noon, guess who called round?"

"Frankie?"

"Got it in one. He didn't even go in, just spoke to him on the doorstep, which is presumably where the switch took place."

"But you didn't see it."

"No. That's pretty much all I know. But I was hoping you'd be able to take it further. Maybe get some evidence. Do you think you can?"

I looked at the bracelet, which was glowing green on my wrist. It considered that I could, and with any luck, it would point me in the right direction.

"I believe I can," I said, just as our meals arrived. "But I need some time to think about it."

We ate, chatting about other things like family, music, and stuff going on around the manor. I was encouraged by her markedly friendlier persona compared to when I had last seen her, and wondered if perhaps she had genuinely warmed towards me. The conversation flowed easily, the previous tension gone, and at the end when we parted, she was amenable to the idea of meeting up again, should I need her help any further. She also warned me to be careful, with a look of concern in her eyes, telling me she didn't want any harm to come to me.

Whether the invitation to meet again extended to anything beyond what we had discussed, I couldn't say, but it seemed that the door was at least a little ajar, and I was more than happy to take that for now. Where to go next with the information she had provided, I wasn't sure, but the bracelet knew what to do, prompting me once again to go and see Reg.

After what I'd done to save the café he was more than eager to get involved, but as always, his advice came with a generous helping of caution. Wherever I went, it seemed people were issuing me with warnings. Understandable where Frankie was concerned, but if I was going to get results, there would inevitably be risks.

"If what you say is true, this is dynamite," he said, as we chatted over a cup of coffee the following evening, after the café had closed. "No one, but no one, steals from Vincent and lives to tell the tale. Not even his beloved protégé Frankie. He would see that as the greatest betrayal of all."

"So we've got him?" I asked, hoping Reg would agree. But it seemed there was a long way to go yet.

"You've barely made it to first base, as our American cousins would say. Knowing it is one thing, proving it is quite another."

"Then we get proof," I insisted, confident that the bracelet would help point me in the right direction.

"You, personally, can't do that. You can't be seen anywhere near this," said Reg. "Because if Frankie gets even a hint you're investigating him again, he'll unzip you from your throat to your groin faster than you can say Clarence Birdseye."

"Who's Clarence Birdseye?"

"The man who invented frozen food. That's where the name on your fish fingers comes from."

"Right. What do you suggest, then?"

"We need a professional team on this, the best people we can find. And they don't come cheap, if we can even persuade them to do it. Once they know who the mark is, most will run a mile or demand sky-high fees. Frankie is dangerous, and dangerous equals expensive."

"But you do know people?"

"Oh, I know people. Back from the old days. But can you pay them the sort of money we're talking about? You are going to need thousands."

"I can afford them," I said with confidence. "I've got plenty stashed away. You know how good I am on the horses."

I didn't have thousands stashed away; I had a few hundred, which was nowhere near the amounts Reg was talking about. I would just have to hope that the bracelet would help me with some more bets. This wasn't for charitable purposes, but it was still for a good cause. A glance confirmed the bracelet was on board, and it came to my aid further, as Reg began quizzing me in more detail, putting images in my head to help me answer.

"You say that Molly's seen these chips being introduced into play by Charles, and Frankie pocketing them at the end of the night. If we could get video footage of that, it would help enormously," said Reg.

"How are we going to do that?" I asked. This wasn't 2024, when people could walk around with body cams, recording anything and everything. If such technology existed in 1984, which I doubted, it would surely be so primitive and bulky as to be completely impractical, and certainly not concealable.

"Casinos have CCTV as standard," he said. "I'm sure, with the table you mentioned having the highest stakes in the club, it would be monitored at all times."

This is where the bracelet started kicking in, furnishing me with the details. In my mind, I saw the table through the grainy black-and-white lens of an old CCTV camera, recording every move, including Charles slipping the extra chips into play.

"Yes," I said. "There is. Molly told me."

This was a lie. I seemed to be telling a lot recently, but how else could I explain how I knew?

"I doubt Frankie would be foolish enough to get caught on camera," said Reg.

"I'm not so sure," I said, seeing another vision of Frankie dealing with security at the end of the night. "He's got total power in that club and control over everything, including security. The only person who is going to look at those tapes is him."

By now, the bracelet had put me in the picture. At the end of the night, Frankie took the tape from that table and replaced it with another, later wiping the original to remove all evidence.

I explained all this to Reg, who listened intently, stating that this information was 'gold dust' and that he knew exactly what we needed to do.

We then went over the rest of it, talking about Frankie's visits to Charles's house to exchange the chips for cash, at which point Reg raised the question of where the money went after that. I didn't know, and if the bracelet did, it wasn't letting on, so by the end of the conversation we concluded we needed to hire three people.

First, we needed an inside man, someone who had expertise from working with teams of conmen or robbers, to gain access to the club so we could get our hands on the tape. Next, a private detective, someone to trail Frankie outside the club, particularly when he went to visit Charles. And thirdly, someone who could break in anywhere we needed, to steal any other evidence we could find without leaving a trace.

Reg assured me he knew who to ask, and they were people he trusted, ones who wouldn't snitch on us to Frankie. I left him to get on with that, while I went away to raise the funds.

It was the Eclipse Stakes at Sandown the following Saturday, a race I knew would be won by the legendary stallion Sadler's Wells. Getting hundreds of pounds on in the betting shops was becoming increasingly difficult, so I decided to go to the track, where large bets on one of the season's major races could be placed easily with the on-course bookmakers.

With the bracelet's help in finding a couple of other winners on what was a gloriously hot, sunny day, I headed back to Kentish Town with bulging pockets once again, suitably funded to pay the team Reg had been putting together.

We met at the café, late one evening. It was all very cloak and dagger, with us entering via the kitchen one by one, before assembling in the café, blinds drawn to avoid being seen by any nosy parkers on the street.

I had persuaded Molly to join us, hoping she wouldn't ask too many questions about where the money I was flashing around had come from, or about the dubious nature of some of the characters Reg would no doubt have invited. This was as risky for her as it was for me, and I had thought twice about involving her, but the bracelet had assured me she would be safe. Her inside knowledge of Nirvana could prove invaluable.

She was more than happy to oblige, and as keen to nail Frankie as I was, given what she had learned about him during her time at the club. Along with her and Reg, we were joined by three others. The first, Reg introduced as Jackson, a fixer who was part of a team of grifters. He was middle-aged, with thinning hair, and appeared quiet and unassuming, the sort of person who looked more like a parish councillor than a criminal mastermind. Perhaps that was the point – he didn't attract attention.

The second was a private detective, a young Scottish woman by the name of Deborah Doyle. And the third, an ageing safecracker who went by the moniker of Locksmith Larry, a man whose history stretched right back to working for the government behind enemy lines during the Second World War.

None of these people were from our neck of the woods, because Reg had stressed how vital it was that none of them were known to Frankie. Jackson's crew operated south of the river, and Deborah worked mainly in the City, dealing with financial fraud. Her connection to Reg was courtesy of her father, an old friend of his who had done similar work in the past. As for Larry, most of his nefarious activities had taken place long before Frankie rose to prominence, and he had been semi-retired for many years. But he still liked to keep his eye in with the odd job now and then. Between them, these three had all the skills we needed to take Frankie down.

Molly was able to brief Jackson thoroughly on everything she'd discovered about the club's security setup, as well as bring the others up to speed on Frankie's movements, relating all the details she'd previously shared with me. Armed with this knowledge and backed by a few generous wads of my cash, the team went to work. They warned it would take a few weeks to gather what we needed.

Those weeks seemed to crawl by. We'd agreed to keep communication to an absolute minimum until the operation was complete, which meant I was left in the dark with no updates, no hints, just silence. Then, on another sweltering evening in late July in what was proving to be an extremely hot summer, Reg finally called. The team was reconvening at the café that night, after dark.

As I looked around the room once we were all assembled, I couldn't help but reflect on what a motley crew we were. I'd had my doubts about Larry, who looked every bit of his seventy-odd years, but Reg had sworn he was still razor-sharp. Deborah, youthful and fresh-faced, was a far cry from the image of the grizzled private eye popular in cinematic portrayals. Perhaps that was her strength. She didn't draw attention.

Then there was Jackson, who had turned up wearing a painter and decorator's overalls, for some reason. I didn't know if he was doing up his house, or midway through some grifting job that involved posing as a workman to gain access to somewhere. It was probably best not to ask.

According to Reg, the three of them had worked fantastically together, exceeding even his expectations. Considering I'd shelled out the best part of ten grand to get them this far, that was just as well.

"Let me present Exhibit A," began Jackson, handing me a standard Betamax video cassette, giving a decent impression of a barrister mid-summation. "Plus a little bonus to go with it," he added, presenting a thick sheaf of papers, neatly paper-clipped and numbered.

"You've got Larry to thank for this lot," he added, giving a nod to the older man beside him. "Once I'd got my feet under the table in security, it was easy to smuggle in whoever, and whatever, I wanted."

"How did you get inside?" I asked.

Jackson leaned back in his chair, clasping his hands behind his head, clearly relishing the opportunity to show off his not inconsiderable skills.

"Oh, it wasn't difficult," he said, making it sound as if it were child's play. "My predecessor met with, shall we say, an unexpected illness that kept him away for a few days. When the club phoned the security firm for a replacement, they just happened to come straight through to me. It's amazing what you can do with a few telephone wires, access to the exchange, and the right telephone number, if you know what you're doing. Molly was able to help with that."

"I hope the security guard is alright," said Molly.

One of the things we'd agreed from the outset was that no one was to get hurt.

"Nothing a few days in bed won't cure. Oh, and a few dozen trips to the bathroom. Mild, but effective. Once I was in, I soon had the run of the place. Most of the security is focused on the casino floor and the front entrance. But the booth? Just me. By the second day, I knew the layout like the back of my hand: alarms, camera positions, blind spots, the lot. While I concentrated on compiling this tape, Larry here was digging into the office files, getting details of the nightly takings. They make for fascinating reading when you put them alongside the footage."

Larry had been silent up to that point, but this was his cue to pitch in. "Somehow, even though Charles lost both those big chips, that table barely made a profit that night. And there's no record of those two extra chips in the accounts that evening at all. Or any evening, come to that."

He was animated, using his hands expressively as he spoke, which were wrinkled and marked. Age didn't seem to have dulled his enthusiasm though, as he continued, with plenty more to relate. "I also found a few other things in the accounts while I was at it, which might be of interest if you want any extra ammunition. Let's just say Frankie's little chip fiddle isn't the only stroke he's been pulling."

"That's excellent," I said, my enthusiasm matching his. "What about you, Deborah?"

She leaned forward, youthful eyes gleaming, suggesting she too had plenty to say. Unlike the other two, she radiated professionalism in her smart business suit .and blonde hair, which was pinned up in a bun.

"I spent two weeks on Frankie's tail," she said, in her soft Scottish accent, making me idly wonder what part of the country she was from. Edinburgh, maybe.

"And he didn't spot you?"

"He never suspected a thing. I'm very good at blending into the background. I've got photographs of his meetings with Charles, and recordings too, from where I bugged his porch. There's enough there to incriminate him on that alone, but there's plenty more. Want to know what he's doing with the money?"

"I'm all ears," I said, watching the excitement spark in her expression. She looked like she'd been dying to tell us all what she had been up to. It was one thing all three of them had in common. They all loved what they did. Reg had chosen his team well.

"Right, so once a week, Frankie goes to a jewellery store and gold dealer in Hatton Garden. Not one of the glitzy ones, this one's more of a backstreet type of place where fewer questions are asked, if you know what I'm saying. While he's there he buys gold sovereigns, with cash, which he then takes to a bank about a quarter of a mile away, and stashes in a safety deposit box."

"How did you find all this out?" I asked.

"I tailed him. The shop and bank are public places, so I just posed as another customer. Not on the same day, that might look like more than just a coincidence. The first week, I was browsing the displays in the jeweller's. The second, I made sure I was in the bank, heavily disguised. I was a redhead that day, with thick-rimmed glasses, unrecognisable from the previous week. I knew he was on the way, as I'd followed him to Hatton Garden at precisely the same time the previous week."

"And once we knew about the jeweller," said Larry, "it wasn't hard for me to get inside and pull together the evidence we needed."

"Not difficult?" I raised an eyebrow. "I'd have thought a gold dealer would be locked up as tight as Fort Knox."

Larry laughed at my suggestion. "I've not yet found the place that can keep me out. And I wasn't after the gold, which was well protected. Just the invoices, and they were in a filing cabinet out in the back office. It wasn't even locked. Who would be interested in nicking a few invoices? Not even me, because I just copied them, then put them back. That's the beauty of what I do. It's like I was never there."

"You'll be telling me you got into the bank vault next," I said.

"No need," said Deborah. "I've got the number of the safety deposit box. I was close enough to catch a glimpse of the key when he took it out of his pocket."

"OK, good. So what exactly did you get from the gold dealer, then?" I asked, turning to Larry.

"Records of Frankie's transactions," he replied. "Six months' worth. Three grand in gold, every single week since January. £78,000 in total."

"That's the exact amount he's been making each week from the scam," I said, staring down at the documents Jackson had handed over. "It soon mounts up, doesn't it, as DI Ritchie would say, if he were clever enough to figure something like this out. And all this information is in here?"

"Everything," said Deborah. "Dates, amounts, serial numbers, photographs. You couldn't ask for a clearer-cut trail. Oh, and this," she added, handing over a cassette tape. "That's the audio of Frankie dropping himself and Charles in it on the porch."

"Surely we've got him, then?" I said, scarcely daring to believe it. My father's freedom now seemed tantalisingly close. "Confront him with this, and he's finished."

"Whoa, hold your horses," said Reg, keen to rein in my enthusiasm. "What do you think will happen if you go marching up to Frankie with all this? He'll have your guts for garters."

"What about the police?" asked Molly.

"You must be joking," replied Reg. "We may as well all go and jump off Westminster Bridge right now."

He was right, of course. Facing down Frankie was incredibly dangerous, but there was no avoiding it. My father's liberty was at stake, and I was risking my life to secure it.

"We'll sleep on it for now," I said, needing time to think it through. "And meet back here in a few days."

Confronting Frankie? The stakes were higher than any gamble I had ever taken, but like any bet, I weighed up the odds.

I was convinced they were now in my favour.

August 1984

"Are you crazy? He'll skin you alive!"

There was no mistaking the concern in Molly's eyes as they met mine. It was a response I had hoped to elicit, being almost deliberately foolhardy in my proposed course of action to gauge her reaction. Encouraged by her level of apprehension, I allowed myself to be distracted for a moment, thinking about the two of us rather than the matter at hand.

August had arrived, and the sultry heatwave that had baked London for weeks on end was showing no sign of abating. It was slowing the pace of life for some and fraying tempers for others, with a notable increase in the number of horns sounding in the street, from stressed-out, overheated drivers stuck in London's inevitable jams. It was no coincidence that most riots happened in the summer, and elsewhere in the country, tensions around the miners' strike continued to grow.

For us, in the stifling heat of Reg's café where he'd been frying bacon and sausages all day, it wasn't exactly the most conducive environment for our council of war, which this evening consisted of just me, Reg and Molly. Now that our crack team of experts were all done and dusted, there was no further need for their involvement.

"What do you suggest, then?" I asked, shifting my weight from one leg to the other. The cheap plastic chair I was seated upon had become a torture device in the oppressive heat, my bare thighs adhering to its tacky surface, like skin to a plaster. Every slight movement produced that revolting peeling sensation as sweat-dampened flesh reluctantly separated from the unforgiving surface. I knew it had been a mistake to wear shorts, especially in the 1980s when they lived up to their name, the fashion at this time dictating they be particularly brief. In my efforts to stay smart most of the time, I hardly ever wore the things, but had reluctantly, like everyone else, given in due to the heat.

I tried to snap out of my intrusive fantasy of her and me getting back together, and concentrate. I wasn't exactly obsessive about it, but since we'd been working together on this project, I'd found myself analysing every little word or gesture from her for the tiniest hint that, once this was all over, she might be open to rekindling things between us.

"Molly's right," said Reg. "I told you this the other day. You can't just wander into the club and hand him the evidence. What do you think he's likely to do? He's hardly going to admit you've got him bang to rights and meekly accompany you down the cop shop, is he?"

"I suppose not," I said, looking across at Molly. She looked fantastic in a pale pink cotton top that clung to her in the humid air, paired with white denim shorts that showed off her tanned legs. While I squirmed against the sticky plastic of the café seats, she looked completely at ease, and beneath the wide brim of her straw hat, her loose blonde pigtails were catching the golden shafts of evening sunlight filtering through the café window. And once again, I had to remind myself to focus. There was far too much riding on all this.

"Of course he won't," said Reg. "He didn't get where he is without being cunning and ruthless. Whatever we do, it's got to be completely watertight.

Even the slightest crack in our plans, and we'll be sunk. And I mean all of us, because he'll know you didn't manage to do this all on your own. He'll torture you until you give up our names, and then we'll all be finished."

"He's right," said Molly. "We've both put our necks on the line for you over this. We can't afford for you to screw it up now."

"This needs to be planned with the same sort of precision as if we were organising a bank job," said Reg. "With not a single detail left to chance. Now, here's what I think we should do."

We listened intently as Reg laid out his proposals. When he'd finished I was impressed, but remained more than a little wary. I was still going to be putting myself very much on the line, and at one point, he even offered to do the most dangerous part and confront Frankie himself. I wasn't happy about that, nor was the bracelet.

"Thanks, Reg, but I can't expect you to do that," I said. "This is about my father, and it's my responsibility. I'm probably going to feel a bit like Daniel going into the lion's den, but brave heart and all that."

"Just be careful, and don't underestimate him, Nobby," said Molly. "I see what he's like all the time in the club. Plus, you know what they say about cornered animals. Don't let your guard down for a second."

We talked some more, and then I went home, where I found my mother engrossed in watching *V*, an epic science fiction series that was being shown on ITV over five consecutive nights, in direct competition to the Los Angeles Olympics on BBC1. I sat down with her to watch this memorable show about invading alien lizards who had a penchant for swallowing rodents whole. I hadn't seen it since the original broadcast, when I had been blown away by the special effects. Now, they didn't quite live up to the level in my memory, but the rest of the story remained entertaining, despite being a little cheesy in places.

I didn't say a word to her about what we had planned. Why worry her? If all went well, she would get a pleasant surprise later in the month, with none of the angst that I was shouldering in the meantime.

Just under two weeks later, the day our plans would come to fruition arrived, and to say I was bricking it was putting it mildly. Despite us having put together what seemed like a foolproof plan, and with reassurance from the bracelet, I still barely slept a wink the night before.

When I did briefly drift off, I slipped into nightmarish visions of giant fish having their stomachs ripped open by Frankie, who was laughing manically every time his oversized knife sank in, sending blood splattering in all directions. It wasn't the ideal preparation, and I don't know why the bracelet didn't spare me from it. Perhaps it was just keeping me on my toes, warning me not to become complacent.

Friday was the day when Frankie went to buy and deposit his gold, at the same time every week. He rarely went anywhere without a heavy or two by his side, but this trip was an exception. Presumably, this was to ensure as few people as possible knew what he was up to. Even the most trusted henchman was still a security risk, so it was a rare opportunity to get Frankie on his own.

Reg had recruited some new people for this final stage in the plan, and with the fresh team members all in place, all I had to do was confront Frankie after he left the bank and convince him to do my bidding.

Despite everything we had on him, it was still a tall order. Would he even engage with me? If he wouldn't, then what? We could still give Vincent the evidence, but that wouldn't get my dad out of prison. I was only going to get one shot at this, and if I failed, our whole plan would fall apart.

The hot weather had persisted into the second half of August, which didn't help matters. I'd dressed smartly, wanting to look business-like, but could already feel sweat gathering under my collar as I waited outside the bank, which was baking on the sunny side of the street.

I'd seen Frankie go in the tall, five-storey building, and was now positioned directly in front of the door, so he couldn't fail to spot me when he came out. When he did, sharp as he was, he clocked me straight away.

"Well, well, if it isn't the jailbird's son. Didn't I warn you to stay away from me?" he said, patting his side as if to suggest he still had the knife on him that he'd flashed at me before. But the bracelet told me otherwise. That made sense, I suppose. Perhaps he only carried it when he was going to threaten someone, and it was too risky to carry it the rest of the time.

"Can I have a word?"

"With me? I've got a business empire to run. I don't have time to waste on kids."

With that, he turned and began to walk away, but I had something to say that ought to stop him in his tracks.

"You wouldn't say that if you knew your life depended on it."

Now I had his attention. He stopped and slowly turned around.

"That sounds like a threat," he said. "It's been a while since anyone dared to threaten me."

"I'm sure it has."

"I'd say you could ask the last person who did how that worked out for him. However, I doubt that standing in the fast lane of the M25 at this time of day, trying to get him to hear you from ten feet below the tarmac, would be a worthwhile use of your time."

"It's not a threat. It's a warning. If you don't listen to what I've got to say, you won't see another dawn."

It was an incredibly audacious thing to say, and I saw a murderous look spread across his face, eyes laced with disbelief that some young pipsqueak like me could dare to be so bold.

"Go on, then," he said. "Indulge me. But if you're fucking me about, you're a dead man."

"Not here," I said, gesturing across the street to an upmarket coffee shop. "Over there."

"You've got ten minutes," he said. "And one coffee. And this had better be good. It had better be bloody good."

The place was bustling, lively, and full of affluent city types. We were still a year or two away from the dawn of the yuppie era, but I could already spot a few candidates in here, sipping cappuccinos and lattes. One even had a Filofax, soon to become an essential tool for the aspirational.

I tried not to let my nervousness show. Even though we were in a busy public place, and I'd been assured he didn't have his chef's knife on him, I still felt vulnerable.

"Right, what's this about, then?" he demanded, as soon as we were seated.

"It's about you, Frankie. And your future. If you have one."

"The sheer gall of you," he exclaimed. "You've got more balls than your old man, I'll give you that."

Inside, I was quaking, but I persisted. I didn't want to launch into a lengthy explanation. The longer I talked, the greater the chance I'd lose my cool, so I gave it to him in bullet points.

"You see, I know what you've been up to. Thousand-dollar chips. Charles Lane. Gold sovereigns. Safety deposit box 8672. With me so far?"

The aggressive look on his face remained, but it shifted. Now there was an element of fear, and the confidence was waning. I had his full attention now. Was I about to see the cornered animal that Molly had warned me to look out for?

"I'm listening," he said.

"Oh, you can do more than listen," I said, reaching inside my jacket and pulling out an envelope containing some of the incriminating evidence, mainly photographs and receipts. "You can look too. And that's just the photo evidence. We've got you on audio talking to Charles and video of you both at the club, too. Oh, and I'm sure it goes without saying, we've got plenty of copies."

I watched as he sifted through the contents before looking up and fixing his gaze on me.

"So what do you have to say to that lot?" I asked.

"I say... have you ever heard the expression 'dead men don't talk?' You just signed your own death warrant."

"What are you going to do, stab me in front of all these people?"

"I don't need to. We'll leave together, and then we'll take a little walk."

"I don't think so, Frankie. If anyone's dead, it's you, unless you do exactly what I tell you."

"Me, take orders from you? You're deluded."

"Oh, I'm not deluded, and nor is anyone else on my team. You don't think I did all this myself, do you? Now let me explain what's going to happen."

I took a glance at my Casio wristwatch, which I had purchased after the fake Cartier one I had got off Eddie gave up the ghost. "It's twenty past eleven now. In five minutes, you and I are going to leave here, and you are going to accompany me back to Camden, where you'll hand yourself in at the local nick."

"You're having a laugh!" he protested, but I could see he was on the back foot. He was far weaker than I expected. Perhaps he'd been getting his way so long, he wasn't used to a scenario where he was holding the losing hand.

"And don't even think about trying to nobble me on the way, because we've got someone watching the station. If we don't arrive together by half past twelve, then there's a courier ready to deliver everything in that envelope, and more, straight to Vincent at the gentlemen's club he frequents every Friday lunchtime."

"And what's to stop me from taking you at gunpoint to this courier and destroying the evidence before he can deliver it?" he replied, patting his left shoulder pocket to try to suggest he had a gun on him.

"Please. You think we haven't thought of that? We've got three others lined up, independently, all carrying copies of the same stuff. Even I don't know who they are. It's how the French Resistance used to operate. If you don't know anyone beyond the next cell, you can't incriminate them. And I've got a man on the inside at the police station. He's waiting for you to confess to the Camden bank job, and will contact me once you have. You've got until midnight to sign it to allow for any internal delays. And if anything goes wrong after that, we've got a final guy holding on to another set of copies until my dad's out of prison."

"Like that's likely to happen!"

"Oh, it's very likely. Because you're not only going to tell the police that he had nothing to do with it, but you're going to sign this note I've written on your behalf to give to Des. It's about that night when he could have given my dad an alibi, and will instruct him to miraculously recover from his amnesia."

He looked at me in utter disbelief, but he wasn't quite ready to throw in the towel yet.

"How do I know you're not bluffing?" he said. "All this talk of couriers, video evidence. You could be making it all up."

"I could. But can you afford to take that risk? The way I see it, you've got two choices. You can go to the police, confess all, and get a ten-stretch, just like you fixed up for my dad. With good behaviour, you might be out in seven. Harsh, but you'll still be alive. Or you can decide I'm bullshitting and risk the wrath of Vincent. And you know what that will mean. Seems like a clear-cut choice to me."

He leaned back in his chair, took a sip of his coffee, and mulled it over. I had him, and he knew it.

"If I go down, it won't be for life, kid, just remember that. And Vincent isn't going to live forever, either. He's no spring chicken."

"And that's why you got greedy, wasn't it? You thought he was past it, and you could skim a nice little income off his profits every week. But you got careless, and now you've paid the price."

"For now, maybe," he said. "But you'll be watching your back for the rest of your life. Once Vincent's gone, you'll have nothing on me. Then there won't be a place on this planet you can hide; not you, or anyone else that's important to you."

"You know, I thought you might say something like that, and you aren't doing yourself any favours. Because if I suspect you're even considering something along those lines, then there's nothing stopping me from giving Vincent the information anyway, once my dad is free. And then you'll be cowering in your cell every night waiting for the inevitable. I could make it happen, just like that, as the late, great Tommy Cooper used to say."

Frankie said nothing, just sat there, scarcely able to believe what was happening to him. All those years at the top, all those enemies he'd crushed, and now he'd been brought down by a twenty-one-year-old whom he had never seen coming.

"So here's the deal," I continued. "You go along with this, and give me your word there'll be no comeback in the future. That's the only way you get to survive this. In return, I won't tell anyone about your gold, or anything else you've got stashed away. It'll all be waiting for you when you get out. All you've got to do is confess to the robbery and clear my dad. And then, give me your solemn word that you'll never come near me, my friends, or my family, ever again."

"It seems I have no choice," he said.

"You don't."

Was he going to meekly comply? Did his word mean anything? Those were the questions I directed to the bracelet, and I got the green glow in response. Perhaps, despite all his other faults, Frankie was a man of his word.

We left and travelled back to the police station in Camden in a black cab, as there was no way I was letting him out of my sight. I remained nervous throughout the journey, in case he tried to pull some last-minute desperate stunt, but all was well, and as I watched him trek, shoulders slumped, up the steps and into the station, I could scarcely believe I'd done it.

I had just taken down Frankie the Fillet in a battle of wills more satisfying than any poker hand I had ever played, including the one when I had cleaned out Theo.

None of what I'd told him had been bullshit. We really had covered all the angles. But I had still put my life on the line, there was no denying that, and the relief now washing over me came in waves. I needed a livener, so I headed for The Salisbury.

Friday lunchtime was always busy, and it took a while to get served among the general hubbub, as Des tended to attend to his more favoured patrons first, and one of them, I most certainly was not.

"Double brandy," I said eventually, hoping it would do the trick, remembering that people were often given it to steady their nerves.

"Medicinal?" asked Des.

"Too right," I said.

"Why, what's wrong with you? Flowers in the shop giving you hay fever? You look perfectly fine to me."

"I've just had a bit of a shock, that's all."

"Has someone died?"

"No," I replied, aware that if anyone had been at risk of dying today, it had been me.

"Well, man up, then, you big girl's blouse. I don't know what the world's coming to. Fucking pub's full of pansies these days."

He went off to serve someone else, but I wasn't finished with him yet. I waited until he rang the bell at half past two, bellowing in his usual customer-friendly fashion that it was "fuck off home time."

"That applies to you as well, Petunia," he said, once he'd herded out the stragglers. He'd developed this irritating habit lately of calling me by the names of flowers, presumably because he thought it was funny, given my occupation. I just thought it was lame.

"Not just yet," I said. "I've got a bit of business to discuss with you."

"I'm not having flowers in here, if that's what you're driving at," he said. "It'll make the place look poofy."

"On the contrary, I think they'd brighten things up a bit," I said, glancing round at the dreary striped wallpaper, in various shades of orange and brown. "But that's not the kind of business I'm talking about."

"Well, it can wait until later," he said. "I'm off for my afternoon kip. Piss off for a few hours and come back at half five."

"Not until you read this," I said, handing him the letter from Frankie.

"What the fuck's this?"

"Just read it," I added. "You can read, I presume?"

"Are you asking to get barred?" he said, but took the letter anyway.

"How do I know this is genuine?" he said once he'd looked through it. "You could've faked it and forged Frankie's signature. Do you know what he'll do to me if that's the case?"

"He won't be able to, from where he is. And that's genuine alright, as you'll find out later when DC Ashe comes calling."

Ashe was my inside man at the station. As coppers went, he wasn't half bad. He even came into The Salisbury sometimes while off duty. While the regulars still viewed him with a degree of suspicion, it was generally accepted that he was alright so long as Ritchie wasn't around and would turn a blind eye to the slightly suspect dealings that went on all around him.

I'd tipped him off the previous day that someone would be coming into the police station to confess to a major crime, and the approximate time that would happen, so I knew he would be there, and probably involved with it right now.

He had agreed to pop into the pub in the early evening with an update, so I made sure I was back when the pub reopened for the second session. Sure enough, he wandered in around six and confirmed what I'd been hoping to hear. Not only had Frankie made a full confession, but he'd also told them my old man had nothing to do with the robbery, and to speak to Des again regarding the alibi.

"Yes, now I come to think of it, he was in here that night," said Des. "We had a couple of drinks after hours. No money changing hands, mind, just a purely private arrangement. So no licensing laws were broken."

"And we can have that on record, can we?" asked Ashe.

"I'd be delighted," said Des. "You know me, always happy to help our boys in blue!"

After that little exchange we moved away from the scrum at the bar, where a group of thirsty bricklayers had just come in, clutching their bulging pay packets. At a small table next to the fruit machines, Ashe brought me up to speed on what had been going on back at the station.

"You should've seen Ritchie's face earlier," he said. "Proper fuming he was, when he realised he'd sent down the wrong man."

"I can imagine. How long will it take to get my dad out?" I said, raising my voice as the fruit machine next to us suddenly started spewing out twenty-pence tokens, those odd little copper discs with grooves in them that they used to pay out instead of proper money.

"Get in, you beauty," yelled the lad playing it, punching the air as the machine clattered away. He'd probably pumped in twice what he'd won, but that didn't seem to matter to him now.

Ashe waited until the noise had abated before answering.

"A few days. It's the weekend now, and there's paperwork and other legal stuff to sort. But the main thing is, he's going to be free. I always knew he didn't do it. But Ritchie wouldn't listen to me, as is usually the case."

"You should have his job."

"The way things are going, that might well happen. I'm putting in for my sergeant's exams, and I'm not sure Ritchie's going to be around much longer. I sometimes think he's verging on the edge of a breakdown."

"I notice he hasn't been in here lately."

"It's not good for his blood pressure. He gets terribly stressed every time he visits this place. Now, I'm curious. How did you get Frankie to confess?"

"I'd rather keep that to myself, for the sake of the others who were involved. Let's just say we did our homework and gave him an offer he couldn't refuse."

Our conversation came to an end, and I was left in a celebratory mood. When Billy and Chris came in, I was tempted to share the good news and get stuck into a proper sesh. But there was someone else I needed to talk to first.

My mother had been completely in the dark about my activities, and with news sure to travel fast around the manor, I was determined to get home and tell her myself before she heard it from someone else.

When I got in, she was sitting in her usual spot on the sofa, watching *Winner Takes All* with Jimmy Tarbuck on ITV. She looked surprised to see me because she knew I usually had a few drinks with the lads on a Friday night. These days she rarely went out, spending most evenings glued to the telly. She hadn't been like that before Dad was sent down, and I was looking forward to sharing the good news that all that was about to change.

I'd brought back a couple of bottles of light ale from the pub, so I cracked them open and sat down beside her. Then I told her everything, the entire tale, right back to when Frankie had come to threaten me in the shop. As I spoke, I watched her expression shift from fear to disbelief, and then amazement as I laid out all that I and the others had done.

"You could have been killed, Robin!" she said, pulling me towards her in a tight embrace, more out of relief than anything else.

"I could, but it was a risk I had to take. I couldn't just leave Dad to rot in jail."

I didn't mention the bracelet, of course. But I was proud of how much I had achieved without its intervention. Sure, it had helped get me started, but after those first chats with Molly and Reg, we had figured out most of the rest ourselves, and I was immensely proud of that.

"So, he's really coming home?"

"He is," I said, with complete confidence.

A week later, I stood outside Pentonville and watched the gate slide open. Out stepped my father, straight into my mother's arms. It was a moment I'd feared I might never see.

Tommy Clarke was free.

And now, I was free to try to mend things with Molly.

September 1984

"You've done an amazing job, Robin. I'm seriously impressed!"

After a few days enjoying his freedom, my father was back in the room we used as an office behind the shop, going over the figures for the months he had been away.

"He's got a real knack for dealing with those sharks at the market," remarked my mother, who had just popped in from the front of the shop to put the kettle on. "He always gets the best blooms at the best prices."

"I'll say," said Dad, as he turned another page, scrutinising the columns of figures. "I mean, this is shaping up to be the best year we've ever had. I should go away more often."

"Please, don't say that," replied Mum. "We've had enough miscarriages of justice in this family for one lifetime. I couldn't bear it if I lost you again."

It was so comforting to have the two of them back together again. Mum had been completely revitalised by Dad's homecoming, and the two of them had been out and about over the weekend, almost like young lovers. They spent the whole of Sunday picnicking in the park, following a hero's welcome in The Salisbury on Saturday night. It was lovely to see, and it was my hope that I could emulate them by reigniting things with Molly.

"So what happens now?" I asked. "You'll be wanting to come back full-time, I presume?"

"Well, yes, but look, the way things are going, there's plenty of work for the three of us," said my father. "What I'd like you to do is to continue doing all the buying because you've clearly got a real talent for that. And to be honest, I'm more than happy to forgo those early mornings. It means your mother and I can have a few lie-ins while you're down at the market."

He gave her a flirtatious look, and she smiled back, making it obvious exactly what he meant by lie-ins. Ordinarily, hearing such a thing from one's parents would gross a person out, but I was happy to cut them a little slack, given what they had both been through.

"Sure," I replied, which was fine in the short term, but he was unaware that my clever dealing was largely courtesy of the bracelet, which I only had possession of for a year. How would I manage once it was gone, or more accurately, how would the version of me I left behind here cope, without that assistance?

Possibly, I might still do well, if not perhaps quite up to the current standard. Although I'd had the bracelet to guide me all this time, I had been going to the market two or three times a week for over eight months. By now, I had learnt the ins and outs of how the place operated and all the quirks of the individual traders. I knew what made them tick, and I knew the price of beans, to quote a phrase I often heard Eddie use when people were trying to sell him stuff in the pub. Perhaps with all this experience, I could manage on my own merits.

Whatever happened, the business was in good shape and seemed unlikely to fold now, like it had in the old timeline. With the family's security safe for the time being, it was time to think about my own needs.

Despite all the upheaval at Nirvana following Frankie's hasty departure, the club remained open, and Molly retained her job, having successfully kept her role in what had gone on under wraps. I left it a few days to give her a bit of space, then gave her a call to ask her if she would like to come out to dinner. She accepted, and we made a date for the following Saturday night, at a restaurant in Camden.

That Saturday was the date of the St Leger, so I popped into Big Mick's intending to have a small bet, nothing serious. I never pulled off any of my betting coups in there, as Mick was a friend, and the old phrase 'never shit on your own doorstep' sprang to mind. However, Mick was becoming all too aware of my activities elsewhere, and when I came in, Brenda, who was rushed off her feet taking bets on the morning dogs at Hackney and Crayford, called me over to the counter.

"Mick wants a word," she said, gesturing behind the counter and hopping up from her stool to open the hatch at the side of the counter. "Out the back."

For most customers, this instruction usually spelt bad news. The most common reason for being summoned into the back room was to receive a bollocking for exceeding one's credit limit, which in the case of Mick meant no more bets until it was cleared. Thankfully, I had never found myself in this sorry predicament, and I wasn't in it now, so he must have some other reason for wanting to see me. Even so, the other punters, several of whom had taken this walk of shame themselves in the past, assumed otherwise and gave an ironic cheer as I walked through, curious to know what this was all about.

"Ah, Nobby, just the man," he began, beaming away, which was a promising start. It didn't seem as if I was in trouble. "Come and sit down."

"You wanted to see me?" I asked, which was a rather unimaginative question, but I couldn't think of anything else.

"Yes, now look, something's been brought to my attention that I think you ought to know about."

This sounded ominous. "It's not bad, is it?"

"Well, it's not the worst problem you could ever have. But it's still a problem. Take a look at this."

He handed me an A3 photocopied sheet of paper with black and white photographs of twelve men on it. It looked like one of those old Wild West 'Wanted Dead or Alive' posters, and my eyes were immediately drawn to my own face, looking back at me from the end of the top row.

"What's this?" I asked, slightly perturbed at seeing my mug plastered on a poster like this.

"We call it the rogues' gallery. We bookies all talk to each other, as I'm sure you know, and share information, particularly about any problem customers operating in the area. Every few months, this poster is updated, and that came through the door this morning. In short, you're becoming a marked man."

"Why? I haven't done anything wrong."

"Oh, I quite agree. Don't worry. No one's accusing you of anything untoward. Not like some of these on here. See that guy there?"

He pointed to a guy in the middle row, with a chubby face and a wild crop of curly black hair.

"That's Freddie 'Slow Count' Taylor. So-called, because he's got this scam where he goes to the tills just as the bell's ringing for the start of a dog race, with a betting slip for twenty quid on the favourite. As soon as his slip is time-stamped, he opens his wallet and then begins to painfully slowly count out single pound notes onto the counter, all the time listening to the commentary from the speaker. By this time, the race has started, and then one of two things happens. If the favourite breaks in front, he rapidly hands over the rest of the cash for the bet, figuring it's likely to win."

"And if it doesn't break first?"

"He scoops the money back up, saying he's changed his mind, and scarpers. So he is banned from every shop in the district."

I looked over the rest of the faces to see if there were any more I knew, and spotted a most familiar one on the bottom row.

"Why is Eddie on here? He doesn't even bet that often."

"He doesn't. But he upset Ken, up at Arthur Prince, by selling him five thousand inkless biros."

"Why on earth would anyone buy inkless biros?"

"He didn't know they were inkless when he bought them. Completely dry they were, the whole lot. He was furious, so he stuck Eddie's face on the poster for revenge."

"Why did he buy so many? Surely no one needs five thousand biros."

"Oh, you'd be surprised how many we get through in here, every week. Dozens, if not hundreds of them. People nick them, just like they do those little pencils in Argos. Brenda suggested I put chains on them at one time, like they do in the banks, but it's not worth the effort. And it makes the punters feel better."

"How so?"

"If they steal a pen off me that's worth about 2p, after they've done all their dough, then I'm not complaining. They probably think they've got one over on me, even if that pen's cost them a tenner. It's all psychological, and keeps them coming back."

"Fascinating," I said, keen to draw this riveting line of conversation to a close. "But you didn't call me in here to talk about pens. I'm more interested in why my face has been stuck on here, with the rest of this motley crew."

"Right, well, the thing is, you've been winning too much. Far too much. It's like you've got the Midas touch."

"I've been on a bit of a winning streak of late, I'll admit that." I had feared something like this happening, and was trying my best to justify it. "All punters get lucky spells, but you know most of us give it back in the end."

"This is more than just a lucky run, mate. For months now, you've been systematically fleecing every bookmaker in the district. Singles, multiples, even mug bets like forecasts, your luck's too good to be true."

"I haven't done it to you."

"No, and I'm grateful for that. But as far as all the others around here go, you're now effectively barred. Every single one of them will have a copy of that poster pinned up behind the counter and be on the lookout for you."

This wasn't good. I'd run into this sort of thing a lot in the future with internet accounts, when freezing out winning punters was all part of the bookmaking industry's modus operandi. I had hoped to get through my year here without this happening, especially given that I still had my big end-of-year heist to look forward to. One of the first things I did when I got back to 1984 was to write down that list of winners I'd memorised from my formbook before I'd left. But I wouldn't be able to do what I had in mind if I couldn't get any bets on.

"What are my options?" I asked. "Are you banning me too?"

"No," he said. "But I am very interested in where you're getting your information from. Care to share it with me?"

"There is no information," I insisted. "I'm just good at form study, and lucky, I guess."

"Well, if I were you, I would be extremely careful from now on. If you're not willing to reveal your sources, I'll respect that. But there are plenty of unscrupulous types around here who might also be curious about your success, and they might not be so willing to take no for an answer. Take it from me, you need to rein it in before you find yourself in a sticky situation."

"So I can still bet here, then?"

"Yes, but if you want any decent-sized bets, discuss them with me first, and I'll lay them off. And you shouldn't have any problem getting on at the track."

"I'm glad you said that, because I did come in to back a horse today. I want twenty quid in the St Leger on Commanche Run. You've got it at 7/4. Ladbrokes are going 2/1, so you can lay it off with them for a profit."

"And how confident are you?"

"Very," I said, which I was. "You should cut your price. After I've backed it, obviously."

I knew it would win, and this time I was betting for my own benefit with no restriction from the bracelet. I had fancied this horse, ridden by the great Lester Piggott, the first time around and backed it then. Since I was only repeating the bet I had made forty years before, I wasn't breaking any rules.

"You're on," he said, so the bet was placed, and later that afternoon, I returned to collect my winnings, getting accosted by Jinxy Jack in the process, who was keen to tell me about his latest system. This one involved only betting on Arabian-owned horses with long, unpronounceable names, the theory being that they were difficult to spell, so punters would be far less likely to want to write them on their betting slips. As a result, so the theory went, they would be bigger odds than they should be.

Once I'd finished listening to this latest piece of nonsense, which he had bought from another dubious tipster in the back of *The Sporting Life Weekender,* I collected my winnings, which with my stake amounted to £55. At 1984 prices, this was more than enough to pay for my night out with Molly.

We'd booked a table at Andy's Greek Taverna, a legendary local haunt where Reg had gone for his meal with Pollock and Morland a few months before. I believe that it is still going strong in the twenty-first century. I put on my best suit and tie, keen to impress, and Molly looked stunning in an elegant, knee-length black dress, which was by far the most glamorous garment I had ever seen her in. She was putting just as much effort into this as I was, and I could see she had been to the hairdresser too, her blonde hair newly styled in a shorter, bob-like cut.

We greeted each other with a kiss, well, more of a peck really, outside Andy's, beneath the blue and white awning in the colours of Greece's national flag. Inside, it was as busy as ever, the tables packed with diners enjoying the traditional dishes on offer, surrounded by whitewashed walls and blue panels, giving the place a real Aegean theme.

We ordered some mixed olives and feta cheese in garlic and olive oil, with warm, fluffy pitta bread to begin, and a bottle of retsina to share while we waited for our main courses, both choosing souvlaki.

To begin with it was mostly small talk, before we moved on to revisiting our recent success at taking down Frankie and toasting my father's freedom. I didn't want to spoil the atmosphere by coming across as too pushy by talking about our relationship too soon, and had half-hoped the bracelet might give me some pointers, but it remained inert all evening. I assumed this was its way of telling me I was on my own with this one. As the year had gone on, it seemed to be intervening in my life less. Perhaps it assumed that the longer this went on, the more proficient I would become at managing this strange, double life, where my past and future personas combined.

I had rehearsed the conversation I wanted to have with her countless times in my head, especially the sixty-four-thousand-dollar question, and in the end, I just blurted it out while I was easing a perfectly grilled piece of lamb off a wooden skewer.

"So, how do you feel about the two of us getting back together?"

She looked across at me, saying nothing to begin with, instead lifting her tumbler-shaped wine glass to her lips and taking a sip, meeting my eager gaze as if she were weighing up whether I was worthy of her.

"I can't say I haven't thought about it," she said, after an uncomfortably long pause. "I wouldn't be here tonight if I weren't considering it."

"But you're only considering it?"

"For the moment, yes. Because there are still one or two things I'm not too happy about."

"Like what?" I asked, as if I didn't already know.

"Your betting, mainly. I don't like it, and never have."

"Even though these days it's all in a good cause?" I replied, wondering if I should bring up the minibus again. On reflection I decided not to, as I'd probably milked that cow enough already.

"Which is all very well when you're getting lucky, but what about when you get unlucky? Imagine you and I started living together, like we talked about last year. How can I be sure I'm not going to come home one day and find the bailiffs at the door because you've spunked all the rent money up the wall on a horse?"

"I would never do that," I said, and it was true. In all my years of betting, I'd never once failed to pay any sort of bill because of gambling. Rent, mortgage, gas bill, you name it, those things always came first. Right now, though, I had no way of proving that.

I poured some more of the wine, taking a sip of its slightly unusual, earthy flavour, and then she dropped the bombshell.

"OK, cards on the table," she said. "Which is rather an appropriate expression for you, don't you think? I will get back together with you, but you've got to promise to give up gambling."

I had been expecting something along these lines, and had already been toying with how to respond in my head. The thing was, when it came to betting, with the bracelet's help, I had already achieved most of what I had set out to do. Almost everything anyway, because I wasn't quite done yet, but when I was, I'd be more than happy never to have a bet again, especially if the prize was keeping her.

"I will," I declared confidently.

"You will, or you have?" she asked. "If you want me back, you have to stop as of now."

Now what was I going to say? For a moment, I was almost tempted to tell her about the bracelet, but I resisted. The only upside lay in the slim possibility she would believe me, with the more likely negative responses including her thinking I was lying, mentally unstable, or both. As someone who had spent a lifetime weighing up odds, it wasn't a good bet.

Alternatively, I could lie, but that was also a very bad idea. She wouldn't tolerate that if I got caught out, and why should she?

"I am going to stop," I vowed. "Very soon. But before I do, I've got one last big wager lined up, and it's by far the most ambitious I've ever attempted to pull off. The granddaddy of all betting coups, you could say."

"If that's more important than getting back with me, then go for it," she said, gaze unwavering as she took another bite of the delicious souvlaki. "But you'll be doing it without me by your side."

"Nothing's more important than you and me," I insisted. "But this thing I've got planned, it's about far more than just me. This is something that's going to benefit the whole world. It's going to save lives, for heaven's sake. I can't abandon that now, knowing that people will die if I do."

Again, the unblinking gaze as she sized me up.

"I've no doubt that you're sincere about what you're saying," she said. "But how can you be so sure you'll succeed? What's it all about?"

"You'll know soon enough. It's only a couple of months away. For now, I'm just going to have to ask you to trust me. I swear, once this year is over, that's it. I'll never be placing another bet as long as I live."

She mulled it over, as the Greek bouzouki music played in the background, then said, "Alright. I'm willing to believe you have honest intentions, so here's what I propose. I do want to be with you, you know that, and every beat of my heart yearns for us to get back together. But for now, we're going to take it slowly. You get whatever it is you've got to do out of your system, and once that's over, we'll talk properly about the future."

"But we do have a future?"

"That depends on you. I'm not making any commitments until then. And I am serious. If, after this big gamble you've got lined up, you still carry on, then you can forget about me for good. And the same goes for if you let me down again. When you left me standing at the tube station that day because you couldn't drag yourself out of the betting shop, you broke my heart. And then you went and did it again, two weeks later, on New Year's Eve, of all nights."

"I won't do that again."

"You had better not."

"So, can we still see each other for now? Get back together – sort of?"

"We'll see."

'We'll see' was better than no, so I decided not to push things any further, and change the subject, talking about the excellent food and my past visits to Greece.

"I didn't realise you'd been to Greece before," she said, after I related a tale of a lovely place I had once stayed in Crete. "When was this?"

"Oh, years ago," I said, realising I had slightly put my foot in it, as it had not been in the past, but at least a decade in the future, sometime around 1995. "But honestly, it's so beautiful. I mean, sitting here in Andy's, eating this amazing food, is as close to Greece as you can get here in London, but nothing compares to being there."

"Gosh, I would so love to go," she said. "All I can think about sitting here looking at the décor is sun-drenched islands and whitewashed cottages. I've been wanting to go ever since I saw a thing about Crete on that holiday programme with Judith Chalmers."

"Well, why don't we then?" I suggested. "How long have you been at Nirvana now?"

"About six months."

"And have you had any leave yet?"

"Not really, only a couple of days at Easter."

"Well, there you go then. You must be due some time off. And now my dad's back, he can take care of the shop. There's absolutely nothing to stop us. It's still hot out there at this time of year, and quieter now the kids are back at school. It's the perfect time."

"Didn't I just say I wanted to take things slow? And now here you are, trying to whisk me off to some tropical island?"

"We can just go as friends, if you want," I said. "These places always have twin beds, so we don't even have to sleep together. And it will be a chance to spend some time together properly, away from here, to reacquaint ourselves. What do you say?"

"Why not?" she said, with barely a pause. "We'll do it. But just as friends, mind."

On Monday morning we went straight down to Lunn Poly to book it, and less than two weeks later, flew out of Gatwick to Crete, where we'd booked a week in what the brochure called a pension, which meant a one-bedroom apartment.

The heat hit us the moment we stepped off the plane at Chania, a dry, dusty warmth so different from the humid, sticky air that had enveloped London for much of the summer. Molly had referred to it as a tropical island, which wasn't strictly geographically true, but it certainly felt like it, and I was filled with promise for the week ahead as we made our way across the shimmering tarmac towards the low terminal building. There, our suitcases would hopefully, eventually, trundle around on the sole operating carousel. This slumbering, almost deserted airport was a stark contrast to the bustling hive of the Gatwick terminal we had left behind.

Luggage retrieved, we headed outside and boarded a battered old blue bus, even more ancient than the one Eddie had hired to take us to Epsom. Soon we were heading along the coast road to Georgioupoli, a sleepy village well away from the bustle of the main resorts. The journey was a slow one, winding past olive groves and low, whitewashed houses where flowers spilt from cracked clay pots and chickens pecked about in the dust outside. The sky was a deep, endless blue, and from time to time, we caught glimpses of the sea glinting through the gnarled, twisted branches of the olive trees. A more idyllic scene was hard to imagine, and when my hand instinctively found Molly's, she didn't pull hers away.

When we arrived, the pension turned out to be better than expected. I had memories of staying in some decidedly ropey apartments on my early visits to Greece, but this was a simple, spotless place, with tiled floors and wooden shutters, painted blue on the outside, which we were certainly going to need, as despite it being nearly the end of September the temperatures were still well into the eighties in Fahrenheit, a scale which many people still used back in 1984.

What the room did not have was twin beds, as I had assured Molly it would, but as I looked across at her for a negative reaction on seeing only a double, there was none.

It was teatime when we arrived, so we unpacked, took showers, and headed out for the evening, exploring the sun-baked village streets, catching wafts of grilled meat laced with herbs emanating from the scattered collection of tavernas, many of which seemed little more than private houses with a couple of tables thrown up outside. This part of Crete was still mostly unspoilt by mass tourism, and even I was stunned when the bill for our evening meal, which consisted of starters, freshly caught fish, dessert, and a bottle of the local wine, came to less than a fiver.

Later, after dark, we held hands as we walked back beneath a sky brilliant with stars, brighter than Molly had ever seen after so many years living under the lights of London. And later, in the apartment, as we finally rediscovered each other, it felt as if the flames were burning more brightly than ever, fuelled in no small part, I'm sure, by the beautiful place we were in. The double bed had turned out to be a blessing, not a mistake.

The week slipped by in a haze of sun, sea, and, to put it bluntly, sex. We spent our mornings on the beach or by the private pool allocated to our small cluster of apartments. It was so hot by midday that we would return to the apartment for lunch, then enjoy what we jokingly referred to as our siesta, even though we weren't in Spain. It's fair to say, not a lot of sleeping went on.

Later, we would head out walking, working up an appetite for dinner, which was invariably fantastic, wherever we chose to eat. The only thing I passed on was the ouzo. I can't stand the stuff, but Molly drank quite enough for both of us.

Our time away was everything I could have wished for and more. Just two people falling in love, with the grime, gamblers, and gangsters of London a million miles away. For that one special week in Crete, the rest of the world simply didn't exist.

October 1984

When I got back from Greece, it was to the news that Harry 'Tinker' Bell had died. I can't say I shed many tears over him, not after the way he had humiliated me at New Year. It wasn't the losing that had hurt so much, because the blame for that could clearly be laid at my door. It was the way he had belittled me afterwards that had stuck in my craw, and I had hoped for the chance of a rematch before the year was out. That wasn't going to happen now.

The funeral had taken place late in the afternoon on the very day I returned, and according to my father, it had been sparsely attended. He hadn't taken a single order for flowers through the shop, as it seemed Harry was estranged from most of his family. Of the few friends he could still lay claim to, most had gathered in The Salisbury at evening opening time for an unofficial wake. I wasn't aware of this until I turned up, keen to show off my tan and catch up on the latest gossip.

I was completely out of the loop, given that the village where we'd stayed in Crete had been all but cut off from the outside world. It had only a single telephone capable of making overseas calls in the local post office. The price of that, in drachma, was ruinously expensive, especially given how cheap everything else had been on the island.

As well as being a greyhound trainer, Harry had also been a boxing promoter back in his day, and among the rather paltry collection of mourners in the pub, I recognised one of his former charges, Mickey 'Mad

Dog' Malone. Back in the sixties he'd been hugely successful in North London, and at one time had been talked of as a potential world champion. He'd never quite scaled those heights, being rather too fond of the ale to achieve the level of fitness required, but still made a decent living in his time.

He was long retired from boxing now, and in his late forties still retained a solid, heavyset physique that spoke of the power he'd once possessed, but the craggy nature of his deeply lined face gave away the passage of time.

I should have been delighted to see this local hero right here in The Salisbury, but that was not the case, and with good reason.

Why wasn't I pleased to see him? Because I knew this man's destiny, and it was not a happy one. I had mostly forgotten about it until now, but seeing him, in the flesh, chatting to Eddie, brought it all back. And the flashing red jewel on my wrist confirmed the role I was going to be required to play. This man's fate was in the balance, and I had to ensure I tipped the scales the right way.

What had transpired, back in the old timeline, was that around this time Mickey had come back onto the scene, and for whatever reason, probably financial, had decided to make a comeback. It wasn't unheard of for boxers his age to do this, with George Foreman and Mike Tyson being notable examples, but in Mickey's case, it proved fatal.

I was at the fight and remembered that despite retaining his ferocious, rapid punches, which had earned him his nickname along with his formidable drinking habits, he was sent crashing to the canvas in the eighth round, and hadn't got up again. It was a massive blow to the chest that had knocked him down, but that alone wasn't enough to kill him. He had suffered a massive coronary from a previously undiagnosed heart condition, and that was what had ultimately done for him.

There was an outcry afterwards, including questions over how this could have happened, given that all boxers were meant to be given medical checks before fights, but since this was an unlicensed event, not sanctioned by the governing bodies, it seemed corners had been cut. And given the identity of the man who was behind organising the fight, that was no surprise at all.

I got a pint off the ever-charming Des, who made a derogatory comment about my tan that was bordering on racist, and sidled over close to where Eddie and Mickey were deep in conversation, hoping I could eavesdrop without making it too obvious. Perhaps I might be able to intervene when the conversation turned to boxing, which surely it would.

"Just dropped me, just like that, he did," said Mickey in his broad Northern Irish accent, taking a swig from his pint of bitter as he spoke. "Said I was too old. Well, I'm not. I can still handle myself."

"Didn't you tell them who you were?" asked Eddie.

"He said he'd never heard of me. Can you believe it? The bloke can't have been over thirty. I said, it'll be your funeral on match day when the West Ham fans come in smashing the place up if they lose to Leicester."

He put down his pint and picked up his whisky chaser, which he necked in one go, allowing me to intervene.

"I've heard of you, Mr Malone. My dad talks about you all the time. You're a legend in these parts."

"Here, maybe, but not in the East End."

"That's where he's been working the last few years," explained Eddie. "Bouncing, minding, that sort of thing."

"But these days work's hard to come by," said Mickey. "People see this old boat and think I'm over the hill."

He ran his palm across his weathered and lined features as he spoke. I loved the way people back in 1984 still used so much of the old cockney rhyming slang, in this case, boat, as in boat race – face. Mickey hadn't even been born in these parts, but he'd still adopted the lingo after moving here from Belfast as a teenager.

"Perhaps it's time you came back home, then," said Eddie. "You're better known around here. I don't know why you felt the need to move out east in the first place."

"Well, let's just say there was a woman involved. But she's long gone now, so perhaps you're right. I don't suppose you need any hired muscle, do you? I mean, you're always getting into scrapes, aren't you, with all that dodgy gear you sell. No offence."

"None taken. I've got all the help I need with Danny and Chris over there," replied Eddie, gesturing at the lads on the other side of the room, who were at least two decades Mickey's junior.

"You see what I mean? It's all youth, these days. Everyone thinks I'm past it. And I'm skint. If I can't get some cash together by the weekend, my landlord's going to kick me out of my flat in Forest Gate."

Eddie gave Mickey that pensive look he always had when he was dreaming up his latest scheme, before a beaming smile broke out. I knew what he was thinking and what was coming next.

"Perhaps you're not as past it as you think," said Eddie, eyeing up Mickey's still formidable frame. "You used to draw a huge crowd in your day. Come home to Camden, and you can do so again."

"You mean box?"

"Why not? Imagine the headlines. Local legend returns home for big comeback fight. You're still up to it, aren't you?"

"Well, I look after myself. I can handle myself in a scrap, but I haven't fought in the ring for over a decade."

"You've still got it, son, believe me. And think of the money. The box office on this will be gold dust. I've got just the man for you to fight, plus I know where we can get our hands on the perfect venue."

I didn't need the bracelet to tell me to intervene. I needed to try to nip this in the bud right now.

"How do you know he's still got it?" I asked.

"Just look at him," replied Eddie. "Would you want to come up against that down a dark alley? It would be like coming across Thing from The Fantastic Four."

"He hasn't fought for ten years. How do you know he's up to it? It could be dangerous."

"There's nothing wrong with me," said Mickey. "Never been sick a day in my life and not had to see a doctor since before my last big fight."

"Exactly," I said. "You don't know. You could have some sort of undiagnosed heart condition. I wouldn't agree to anything until you've had a full medical, blood pressure, ECG, the lot."

"He doesn't need any of that," said Eddie, lighting up a Park Drive. "He's fit as a fiddle, he said so himself. Smoke?"

He offered us the pack, which I declined, though Mickey eagerly reached for one, which was another bad sign.

"I thought boxers had to go through strict medical checks before a fight?" I asked.

"If it's licensed," said Eddie. "But this is going to be off the record, just for show, if you like. We'll present it as an exhibition match and we'll hold it at the Roundhouse."

"I thought that closed down ages ago," I said.

"The building's still there, though, isn't it? The council's taken control of it for the time being while they decide what to do with it. I'll pull a few strings and see if we can't get it opened up for the night. We can squeeze a couple of thousand in there, no bother."

"This sounds distinctly dodgy to me," I said.

"It'll be fine," insisted Eddie. "And you'll never guess who I've got in mind for you to fight."

"Who?" asked Mickey.

"Only Bobby Bennett himself."

"The Belsize Bruiser?" I asked.

"The very same," said Eddie. "He retired from boxing in '79, and runs a second-hand car dealership in

Primrose Hill. Only the other day, when I was selling him a lovely second-hand Dolomite Sprint, he was telling me how badly he got burned in the recession and how he was struggling to recover."

"Buying cars off you can't have helped," I said.

"That's a bit harsh," replied Eddie. "There was nothing wrong with that Triumph that a new gearbox, engine and chassis wouldn't have cured. Anyway, the point is, he could once draw a crowd around here as big as you could, Mickey. Though I don't think you ever fought each other, did you?"

"No, he was coming through just as I was winding down," said Mickey.

"There you go, then. Two of the biggest names in Camden boxing history, one night only. Trust me, we'll be quids in. All your money worries will be over, and people round here will be falling over to employ you."

"Yeah," said Mickey, a smile breaking out across his face for the first time since I had arrived, making the lines around his eyes crinkle up ever deeper. Eddie was right, he did look a bit like Thing out of the Fantastic Four. "Let's do this."

I thought about trying to dissuade him some more, but he was so enthusiastic, not to mention the worse for wear from the alcohol he was copiously knocking back, that I decided to leave it for the time being. The fight would take some time to organise, and once I knew more about exactly what was planned, perhaps I could find another way to scupper it.

The first thing I needed to do was talk to Eddie again. After all, he was the one organising the whole thing. So after the weekend, I went round to see him at his Emporium, where I had some difficulty fighting my way through to his office due to a large array of exotic potted plants which were taking up most of the floor space.

"What's all this lot?" I asked. "I thought you said you weren't into the floral trade."

"Bankrupt stock," he explained. "From that garden centre that went bust on Leighton Road. Quality stuff, this lot. Very upmarket, perfect for the conservatories of the well-heeled."

"And the well-heeled shop here, do they?" I asked, looking around at the usual collection of mostly downmarket tat poking out from between the leaves. While I was doing so, my eye was drawn to a poster on the wall, advertising the fight as taking place on Saturday, the 27th of October. He hadn't wasted any time.

"We go to them," explained Eddie. "The full service and a free bottle of Baby Bio with every order. You can have a few for your shop if you want. It could be a whole new line for Bud & Bloom. I've got tons more out the back and I need to shift them sharpish before the first frosts come. They're not used to our climate and won't survive in the winter outside."

"I'll pass, thanks."

"Shame, because I think you're missing a real opportunity. Anyway, since you haven't come about the plants, what can I do you for?"

"It's about this fight. It's not on, you know."

"Oh, not this again. I had enough of you trying to put the mockers on it the other night. Well, forget it, it's a done deal. I've secured the venue, got the posters done over the weekend, and got both my guys signed up."

"You can't go ahead with this. Mickey's not up to it."

"So you keep saying, but where's your evidence? And I'm too deep into this to back down now. It's shaping up to be a lovely little earner. I've got two thousand tickets printed, at a tenner a ticket, that's twenty grand."

"That building has been mothballed for months, if not years," I protested. "What about health and safety? How have you even managed to get access to the place?"

"You don't need to know about any of that," he replied, tapping his nose as he spoke. "It's all perfectly legit. It's not what you know, it's who you know. You did me a favour when you got rid of that cretin Pollock. The new planning officer is far more amenable to my ... suggestions, shall we say?"

"Is that so? Well, I doubt that the British Boxing Board would approve."

"We don't need their endorsement. This is an unsanctioned exhibition match, just for entertainment. I don't see what your problem is. They both need the money, the punters get to see two of their past heroes battling it out, I make a nice wedge, and everyone goes home happy."

"Except Mickey," I said. "How much are you paying him?"

"I can't tell you that, it's confidential. The businessman's code."

"I bet it's peanuts. You're just taking advantage of him."

"We agreed a fair price, it's all above board."

"But he's not a young man anymore. This could be dangerous for him. Can't you see that?"

"Do you know what, Nobby, you're beginning to sound like a right old woman. Now this fight is going ahead, whether you like it or not, so unless you're willing to help me out with the organising, I reckon it's time you ran along and let me get on with it."

I was getting no joy here. Eddie had only pound signs in his eyes, as was usually the case, so I decided to go and state my case to Mickey instead, who was now living back in the area. He had been thrown out of his flat in the East End and had taken up temporary residence in one of Eddie's run-down flats. I found this out from the regulars one lunchtime in The Salisbury. He had been drinking heavily there every night since moving back, all on Eddie's tab.

He explained, when I called to see him the next morning, that he was living rent-free until after the fight. Going by the state of the place, that was just as well, as my eyes were drawn to an ugly black stain in the kitchen where mould was spreading across the wall above the kettle, one of many signs of neglect from Eddie, who wasn't the most diligent of landlords when it came to maintaining his properties.

"It's just another way he's got a hold over you," I said, as he passed me a cup of tea in a chipped mug from the Queen's 1977 Silver Jubilee celebrations. "How long do you think he would let you stay here for free if you backed out of the fight?"

"All the more reason why I can't," he said. "But I don't want to back out. I'm looking forward to it."

"How much are you getting for this bout?" I asked, hoping he wouldn't be as reticent as Eddie about revealing the numbers.

"Two grand," he replied.

"Is that all?"

I should have been stunned, but it wasn't that surprising, knowing Eddie as I did. If he was paying Bobby the same, then even after all the expenses, he was going to be raking it in.

"He's ripping you off," I said. "Two grand is an insult."

"I need the money."

"And how long's that going to last? A couple of months or so? Then what? You'll be back at square one."

"It's not just about the money, though, is it?"

"Isn't it? Tell you what, then, how about this? What if I give you five grand not to fight?"

"Where are you going to get five grand?"

"Oh, I can get it, believe me."

"I told you already, it's not just about the money. This is about so much more. Do you know how crap the last few years have been for me? This is a chance to be someone again, to have a crowd cheering me on, with all the light, the noise, and the buzz it all brings. Eddie says that once I've done this, people will see I'm no back number, and they'll be falling over themselves to employ me. I've got to do it, can't you see that?"

I didn't have a lot I could say in response, and the bracelet wasn't helping at all. So I tried another tack.

"At least get yourself checked out, then. Go and see a doctor and get certified fit. Your life could depend on it."

"You said all this the other day, and I told you that I don't need doctors. Now I'm going ahead with this fight and that's that. Nothing you can say will persuade me otherwise."

He glanced at his watch and then added, "It's nearly opening time. Do you fancy going down The Salisbury for a couple of pints?"

"No, I don't, and you shouldn't either. Why not stick to orange juice until after the fight? You want to be in tip-top shape on the night, don't you?"

"Soft drinks are for kids. Grown men drink beer and whisky. I've always thrived on it."

I left his flat feeling equally as deflated as when I'd left Eddie's the previous day, annoyed that not only was I getting nowhere, but the bracelet had been of no help whatsoever. That night, however, the entire fight played out in my dreams, right up to Mickey's knockout, and by the following morning, I had figured out what I needed to do. There was one more person involved in this whom I had not approached yet, so I needed to pay a visit to Primrose Hill.

I was confident that this time it would be third time lucky, but I could not go there right away as I needed some cash upfront for what I had in mind. At the bracelet's behest, I took a trip up to Newmarket on Saturday to back a horse in the Cesarewitch, one of those grand old flat handicaps with a massive field, and an even more massive-priced 40/1 winner by the name of Tom Sharp. This conveniently provided the war chest for my next little operation.

I had been granted a stay of execution by Molly on the quitting betting front, at least until after my big end-of-year coup, though I very much had the impression Molly was expecting me to do only that, and nothing in the interim. I doubt my outing to Newmarket would have met with her approval, but fortunately she was working at Nirvana that day, and I would not be seeing her until the evening. The train was late getting back, and I was worried about missing our date to go and see *Purple Rain* at the cinema, but I made it just in time, after stopping to drop off the winnings at home first. Walking around with large amounts of cash on my person always made me uncomfortable.

On Monday, with just five days to go until the fight, I made my way over to Bobby's car showroom, knowing this was probably my last chance to do something to avert Mickey's fate.

'Showroom' was perhaps overstating it. It was little more than a crumbling forecourt behind a pair of rusty iron gates, on a patch of land that had once been a bomb site, much like the land next to Reg's café. The cars on display formed an uninspiring line-up of ageing British Leyland models, mostly Marinas, Allegros and Princesses, in a dreary palette of browns, greens and beiges.

A sign proclaiming, 'QUALITY USED CARS' was a blatant offence under the Trade Descriptions Act, and right at the front stood a P registration, mustard-coloured Triumph Dolomite Sprint, proudly highlighted as 'CAR OF THE WEEK'. It bore the outrageous price of £1,295. This had to be the dodgy motor that Eddie had sold him.

The showroom itself was little more than a glorified Portacabin, from which Radio One was blasting out 'Freedom', Wham!'s latest chart-topper. Bobby was lounging back, feet on the desk, leafing through one of the tabloids when I stepped inside. He leapt up at once, as if startled to see an actual customer. Business must have been bad.

"Morning," I said. "Are you Bobby?"

I knew he was because I'd seen him on the posters, but we'd never met, so he didn't know me.

"I am," he said, grabbing my hand with enthusiastic force and pumping it in a handshake that made me wince. He certainly had the physique of a boxer.

He went straight into salesman mode, trying to size me up and firing off the usual patter, which went on for a couple of minutes before I managed to steer the conversation to the real reason I was there.

"Look, I'm not here for a car," I said. "It's about this fight on Saturday. You can't go through with it."

"I have to," he said. "I need the readies. I haven't sold a car in almost a month, and I'm desperate."

"How much is Eddie paying you?" I said, the sense of déjà vu growing stronger. "Let me guess. Two grand."

"How did you know?"

"Because I've already had this same conversation with Mickey."

I went on to offer him five to stand down, the same offer I had given Mickey, but he shook his head.

"I'm telling you, if you do this, you'll kill the poor bastard. How old are you?"

"Thirty-three."

"Exactly. He's nearly fifty. Do you want his death on your conscience for the rest of your life?"

"Of course not. Mickey was one of my heroes growing up, but I've already given Eddie my word. Did you see that big sign outside the office? 'MY WORD IS MY BOND?' I can't go back on that."

He was proving a tough nut to crack, so I tried another approach, which also was not initially well-received.

"Throw the fight?" he said, staring at me as if I'd just suggested stealing the Crown Jewels. "I couldn't possibly countenance doing something like that."

"Well, that's very interesting, Bobby," I said, bracing myself in case he decided to live up to his nickname and give me a thumping. "Because I happen to know you did exactly that against Jack 'Two Jabs' Jarvis in 1976. And again when you fought Bertie 'Brickhouse' Briggs in '77. Need I go on?"

How did I know this? The bracelet had done its homework and furnished me with the information. And as I saw a flicker of guilt cross his face, I knew I had him.

"I didn't think anyone knew. Vincent assured me it would stay a secret. And he uses very persuasive methods to get people to cooperate."

"I'm sure he does," I said, wondering exactly what form of coercion Vincent had used on him. Was that why he'd quit the ring so young? "Just do it again for me, and you'll have five grand in your pocket on Saturday night."

"That's not good enough. I need something upfront now."

I'd come with a decent wedge, half expecting this, and was about to offer him an advance when he came up with another suggestion.

"Tell you what," he said. "You see that Triumph out there? Buy that right now, in cash, at the marked price. Then give me another four grand on Saturday, and you've got yourself a deal."

I didn't need a car because I had the use of Bud & Bloom's van, but I didn't have much choice. So I briefed him carefully on exactly what I wanted him to do on Saturday, then bought the car, driving it away as it popped, banged, and belched out smoke. Halfway home, the exhaust pipe fell off and I spluttered to a halt.

I'd never live this down if anyone back home found out I'd bought this heap of shit, so I left it smoking by the side of the road, found the nearest phone box, and called a scrapyard to come and collect it. Bobby must indeed have been desperate to have bought it off Eddie in the first place. Still, with the money he'd soon be pocketing from both the fight and from me, perhaps he could finally turn his ailing business around.

I visited Eddie once more, insisting that he ensure there was a proper doctor on hand, because I couldn't trust him not to cut that vital corner. At least then, if anything went wrong, there would be someone there to help immediately. After that, there was little more I could do except wait for Saturday to roll around.

The disused venue, brought back to life for this one night only, echoed with noise, packed to the rafters with punters jostling for space. A makeshift ring had been assembled, its ropes sagging slightly, the canvas scuffed and stained. Trust Eddie to do it on the cheap. Tickets were being handed in rapidly at the door, the event having completely sold out, and as more filtered in, the noise from all the excited voices grew steadily louder in eager anticipation.

I half expected the Old Bill to turn up mob-handed, given the dubious nature of reopening this place just for one night, but whoever Eddie's inside man at the council was, he'd done his job. I even spotted Ashe in the crowd at one point, enjoying himself as much as everyone else. Of Ritchie, there was no sign. I'd heard a rumour he had gone on long-term sick leave.

Pretty much everyone I knew was there, including all the regulars from the pub, my family, and by my side, Molly. With her in tow, I was precluded from having a bet with any of the undercover local bookies who were inevitably in attendance, though I did hear on the grapevine that Bobby was favourite at 1/3, with Mickey at 5/2. As far as they were concerned, this fight was straight. Only I knew differently, and since I wasn't attempting to profit from it, it didn't matter.

The fight was scintillating, everything the crowd had hoped it would be. I was ringside, watching closely as Mickey climbed through the ropes, a look of sheer joy on his face at being back in the spotlight after so long away. Bobby followed moments later, full of confidence, acknowledging the cheers with a cheeky wave to the audience. Both were crowd favourites, and I don't think anyone, unless they'd had a lumpy bet, would begrudge either of them the victory.

The referee gave his instructions, the fighters touched gloves, and the bell rang to a massive cheer from the packed house. What followed didn't come across like an exhibition match, with both men coming out hard, trading punches with ferocity and purpose, neither willing to give an inch. The atmosphere was electric, and the crowd were gripped by every exchange, swept up in this wonderful spectacle of these two seasoned gladiators giving their all.

I was worried for a moment that Bobby might be so caught up in the heat of battle that he would forget my instructions, but those fears were allayed, as in the fifth round he let Mickey get the upper hand without making it look too obvious, eventually leaving himself wide open to be knocked down, failing to rise as the referee counted him out.

It was over. Mickey stood in the centre of the ring, drenched in sweat, chest heaving, his face a mask of weary triumph as the referee raised his arm to declare him the winner. Around us, the crowd roared their approval, swept up in the thrill of a fight that had delivered everything they'd hoped for, even if it had only gone five rounds.

Then I saw it, a flicker of pain across Mickey's face, a hand clutching at his chest.

No. Not now. This couldn't be happening, not after everything I'd done to prevent it. This wasn't how it was meant to be. In the original timeline, he'd collapsed in the eighth round after a severe blow to the chest. This had ended in the fifth. Why was it still happening? Had the excitement of the victory pushed his heart too far anyway?

"Get the doctor!" I shouted, my voice cutting through the noise as Mickey staggered, sinking onto the dirty canvas, his breathing ragged. Help arrived swiftly, as Mickey rolled onto his back, the doctor's hands moving swiftly into position, beginning chest compressions, counting, pressing, fighting to keep him alive.

This wasn't supposed to happen.

Not like this.

November 1984

"You don't get rid of me that easily," said Mickey, putting a brave face on things, though his voice was weak, almost croaky.

"Don't joke about it," I said. "You're lucky to be alive. If that fight had gone on any longer, you'd have been a goner for sure."

I stood beside his hospital bed, taking in the sorry state of him, pale and worn out, with wires and tubes protruding from everywhere. Unlike Billy, who'd been in a shared ward, Mickey had been allocated a private room, given the level of monitoring and care he needed. It was four days after the fight, visiting hours were limited, and this was the first time I had been allowed to see him.

I sat down on the chair in front of the machines monitoring him, as he managed a faint smile.

"I won, though, didn't I?" he said. "That's the most important thing."

"Important enough to risk your life for?"

"I didn't know about my heart, did I? Though I do appreciate you trying to warn me. I suppose I should have listened, but you know how I was fixed."

"So what happens now?"

"I've got to have a bypass operation, it seems. But after that, provided I do as I'm told, I should make a full recovery."

"No more fighting, then?"

"I've no need. I proved myself and had my one last moment of glory. That was all I wanted, and it was enough for me. I'm more bothered about the doctors saying I've got to knock the drinking and the smoking on the head. That's not going to be easy."

"Probably not, but it's better than being dead."

The door opened, and in walked Eddie, carrying a bunch of grapes.

"Here he is, the man of the moment," announced Eddie. "You're the talk of the town!"

"I don't feel like the man of the moment," replied Mickey. "Look at the state of me."

"Oh, give it a few weeks, you'll be right as rain," said Eddie breezily. "I've already got a fantastic new opponent lined up for you, and I reckon if I pull a few strings, I might even be able to get us into the Albert Hall for the next one!"

"Are you for real?" I asked, astounded by Eddie's brazen proposal. "This is incredibly insensitive, even by your low standards. The man has just had a heart attack. He's not going to be boxing again. Ever."

"I'm afraid so," said Mickey, as Eddie looked to him for confirmation. "My fighting days are over."

"Oh well, I suppose it was good while it lasted," said Eddie, admitting defeat. "Quit while you're ahead, as they say. Which, incidentally, I am, because I had a nice little tickle on you at 5/2, which was a bit of a Brucie bonus."

"I trust you'll be passing some of that good fortune on to Mickey here?" I asked.

"I'll see you alright, don't you worry," said Eddie. "There'll be a nice drink in it for you, down at The Salisbury when you're back on your feet."

"He can't drink anymore," I said.

"That's what the doctors say," said Mickey.

"Doctors, what do they know?" scoffed Eddie.

"If you really want to help me, Eddie, you can put the word around the manor that I'll be looking for a job when I get out of here, and I don't mean bouncing or minding."

"I'm sure we'll be able to sort something," replied Eddie, just as the sister who'd let me in earlier, with strict instructions to keep it brief, came bustling in. She looked every inch the ward matron: late forties, no-nonsense, with tightly permed hair and a starched blue uniform with white trim.

"Who are you?" she asked Eddie sharply. "What are you doing in here?" Then, turning to me: "Didn't I tell you it was strictly one visitor at a time?"

"Oh, sorry," said Eddie. "I didn't realise. Here, have a grape."

"What I want to know is how you got past the front desk without me seeing you?" she demanded, ignoring the bunch of grapes he had just thrust under her nose.

"I'm not sure. I must have just slipped through the net."

"Well, you can slip right back out again, because no one gets in here without my say-so. That goes for both of you. Mr Malone here is still very weak, and he doesn't need the likes of you two overexciting him."

We were ushered out of the room, and that was that. Mickey was in a bad way, no doubt about it, but he was alive, and that, I reckoned, was the best thing the bracelet had helped me achieve so far. It had saved a life.

And if I had anything to say about it, it was going to save a good many more before the year was out.

Over the past month, while I'd been caught up in the business of the fight, two major events had dominated the news. The first was the Brighton hotel bombing, something I hadn't seen coming. I remembered that it had happened, but I had forgotten exactly when, and preoccupied with the fight, I hadn't paid any attention to the autumn party conference season. As for the bracelet, it hadn't given me so much as a nudge in its direction. That had got me thinking.

All year long, I'd noticed how the bracelet seemed mostly concerned with the lives of ordinary folk and the small, local happenings that impacted their lives, rather than major national or international events. I often found myself wondering who had designed it, and why it focused on these seemingly small things, rather than things that could change the entire course of history for the better.

For the lives it touched, it changed everything. In Mickey's case, it had meant the difference between life and death.

The second news story to break was the spark that ignited one of the greatest phenomena of the 1980s. By late October, reports were coming out of Africa about the famine there, and Michael Buerk's shocking broadcasts from Ethiopia had gripped the nation's attention. Most notably, they had inspired Bob Geldof of

Boomtown Rats fame, and he immediately got on the phone to fellow musicians, determined to do something about it.

By mid-November, the wheels were well in motion, preparing for the recording of the million-selling single that would become the Christmas number one. Once again, the bracelet didn't seem particularly interested in getting me involved. But on that front, I was already a step ahead. From the moment I'd known I was coming back to 1984, my thoughts had turned to Band Aid, and that was the reason I had gone up into the loft to fetch my old Chaseform annuals, before memorising the results from one specific day at the end of November.

I'd chosen that day for a reason. Across the three meetings that took place, a surprising number of outsiders had come in. There were six double-priced winners, including one at 66/1. This was ideal for my purposes. On my first day back in January, I had scribbled these results down and kept them safe until now.

I planned to back these horses in various combinations of accumulator bets, spread across different betting shops. This approach was far less likely to draw attention than putting on large bets on a single horse. The stakes were small, and the bets themselves were the kind bookmakers encouraged, aimed at what they considered to be their mug punters because of the high profit margins they made on this type of bet.

Punters loved these so-called exotic bets for the chance of a big win from a string of winners. What most didn't realise, though, was that with every extra selection, the bookmakers' advantage multiplied against them, like compound interest working the wrong way.

For me, these bets were the perfect way to get my money on, assuming that I could place them at all, given my face was still on the rogues' gallery in every local shop. But that was far from the only problem.

Simply by placing these bets, I'd be altering the timeline, in this case without being specifically guided by the bracelet. Why? Because if the early legs of a multiple bet won at big odds, the bookmakers would be sitting on huge potential losses for the last leg. In that situation, they'd be forced to hedge by sending money to the racecourse bookmakers, which would inevitably drive down the odds on that last horse. It would also become a major talking point on what would, in normal circumstances, be just another race.

A famous example of this was Frankie Dettori's legendary 'Magnificent Seven' at Ascot in 1996. With so many punters having backed his mounts in accumulators, bookies were left with fortunes riding on his final ride, Fujiyama Crest. That horse had been 14/1 in the morning but was hammered into 2/1 favourite by the off, because of the sheer weight of this money. For some of the on-course bookmakers, notably the legendary Gary Wiltshire who was happy to take on all-comers at the shortened odds, this was bad news indeed.

That was exactly what I needed to avoid. If I lumped on accumulators at starting price, there was no way my selection in the last race at Chepstow, due off at 3.40, would start at 66/1, which was the price it had been according to my old Chaseform annual. Its odds would collapse, slashing my winnings if I had to settle for the starting price.

It even crossed my mind that with so much money at stake, someone might interfere with the result. The jockey could be bribed to lose, or the trainer persuaded to withdraw the horse. This was unlikely, but such things were not unheard of. What was in my favour was the tight timing of the last two races. My penultimate selection ran in the 3.30 at Sandown, leaving little time for any last-minute skulduggery.

Thankfully, both these races were big-field handicaps, which meant they were offered as early-price races. Unlike in the 2020s, when you can take a price on any horse first thing in the morning, back in 1984 only a handful of races each day were priced up early in this way. It was perfect for me as it meant I could lock in the generous odds on my final two selections, safe from any late market moves caused by money sent back to the course.

But there were still other hurdles to clear, almost as many as would be jumped in that final handicap hurdle at Chepstow. All bookmakers displayed a long list of rules on the shop wall, full of small print that had tripped up many an unwary punter.

First came the payout limits. Every bookmaker capped the maximum they'd pay on a winning bet. The major chains like Ladbrokes and William Hill usually offered six-figure limits. But there were strings attached, such as lower limits on evening racing after shops closed, not a worry in November, or on smaller dog tracks. The smaller chains and independents were trickier. Some capped their payouts as low as £10,000.

Some also had restrictions on so-called 'across-the-card' bets where selections came from meetings running close together, time-wise. That could potentially affect my final two races. Not every chain enforced this rule, but I would have to factor it in when deciding where and how much to bet.

All of this meant that I couldn't simply waltz into one single shop, place a big accumulator, then go home and put my feet up while I waited for the horses to romp home. This was going to take serious legwork.

My target was to win a million pounds for the famine relief fund, while staying within the rules and the limits. I'd worked out that I needed to spread my bets across at least fifteen shops, all belonging to different companies. Yet another rule barred punters from placing multiple bets across branches of the same chain to get around the limits. In these cases, they could refuse to pay out at all. So, in the run-up to the big day, I toured the district, picking my targets carefully.

Ideally, I'd have gone many miles from home to reduce the risk of being recognised, perhaps even out of London, where I would be out of range of the rogues' gallery. But with so many outlets to hit in so little time, that wasn't an option.

The shops opened at 10am. With the short November days, racing started around midday, and my first selection was in the 12.30 at Chepstow. To get everything on, I'd have only about ten minutes per shop. That was just about doable in my area, which I knew like the back of my hand, enabling me to take the best route, but probably not further afield.

I toyed with the idea of bringing in an accomplice to share the work, but turned that down. There wasn't anyone I trusted enough to get this right, or not to blab and blow the whole thing. It was down to me, and me alone.

I'd lined up all the big names: Ladbrokes, Coral, William Hill, Mecca, Tote, plus some smaller operators like Surrey Racing and Arthur Prince, and a handful of local chains. But not Big Mick. I might need him as a potential ally if anyone tried to wriggle out of paying, which was always a worry. So now, the only thing left to do was ensure I could physically get the bets on, which required me to go incognito.

Here was where I needed to enlist some help. With Reg's assistance, I got back in touch with Deborah Doyle to see if she could lend me her expertise about going undercover. I needed some decent disguises, not cheap wigs or false beards and glasses from a joke shop, which would look ridiculous and be a red flag to the betting shop staff.

I was steering clear of the shops I used most regularly, where I knew there were staff who might recognise me even through a disguise. But there was still the poster with my mugshot on it to worry about, which could be in any or all of the other shops on my list, so this had to be done properly. I remembered what Deborah had said about changing her appearance when she'd been trailing Frankie. She was the ideal person to consult.

She knew a man in Soho, an old hand from the theatre world who'd done work for TV and, occasionally, the police. For a sizeable fee, which was well worth it given what was at stake, he agreed to kit me out.

Since I was normally well groomed, it made sense to dress down for this operation. A fair chunk of any betting shop's clientele consisted of local workmen popping in for a quick flutter, so it seemed wise to go down the uniform or overalls route, with some added facial extras to cover my features.

By the time we'd finished, I had three distinct looks: a bearded milkman, a decorator in paint-spattered overalls with a curly wig and a moustache that wouldn't have looked out of place in the Liverpool football team, and a postman complete with large, NHS-style glasses.

I was more than happy with the results and felt confident I'd be able to wander in and out of as many shops as I liked without anyone suspecting a thing. Milkman and postman were good choices, as I often saw them in betting shops, with most of them finishing work for the day by lunchtime.

I'd divided the day into three chunks of five shops each, with the van parked nearby so I could change outfits in the back after each stint. It was vital that I didn't get recognised, not in a single shop, because even in this era, word would soon get around if there was so much as a hint of someone trying to pull off a betting sting.

But the disguises held up well, as did my policy of keeping stakes low and mixing up the bets. Although I had six horses to play with, I only needed to include four in my preferred choice of bet, the Yankee, which aroused no suspicion at all, given that it required a stake of only £11 per slip, plus the ubiquitous 10% betting tax that prevailed in the 1980s. For shops I'd identified as having across-the-card limits, I made sure not to include the 3.30 and 3.40 on the same slips, so I was confident I wouldn't fall foul of that rule, though it did run the risk of the alarm bells sounding earlier.

It was a madcap dash across a rain-soaked North London, starting in Islington and finishing in Primrose Hill, following the exact route I had planned, with military precision. The van had a full tank of petrol, and I was in milkman mode to begin with, keeping the other disguises in the back, as I raced around the first five shops without incident.

After that, now in my decorator's overalls, I started to run into problems with the traffic, from delivery lorries blocking narrow side streets, to lengthy queues at traffic lights. My impatience at crawling along was shared by other irritated drivers beeping their horns, and the incessant hammering of rain on the van roof didn't help, either.

Just as I'd cleared one set of lights that had held me up for a good five minutes, I hit a set of roadworks that had sprung up out of nowhere since I mapped the route the previous week.

By the time I reached Primrose Hill for the final stop, disguised now as a postman, it was almost 1pm, half an hour after the first horse had run, and won, but that wasn't an issue. Figuring time might be tight, I had left that early runner out of the bets lined up for the last few shops, just in case of delays. This had proved to be a wise move. So that was it, all fifteen shops done, fifteen bets placed, and all I had to do now was wait.

I was curious to see what effect my bets would have on the prices of the horses running later, especially the last one, so I changed back into my normal attire and went to Big Mick's to while away the afternoon with the usual suspects. While I was there, Jinxy Jack told me about his new system, which was to back the horse in each race that had had the longest break since its last run, because that meant, in his words, "it would have had a nice rest." It didn't seem to be going too well, as he hadn't backed any winners.

Mine, on the other hand, were all winning as expected, and it was only when it got to the last couple that I started to notice the weight of my money in the prices.

I'd done something I would not ordinarily have done, by taking the poor-value early morning prices of 25/1 and 33/1 about my runner in the last race, even though that was half or less of the starting price from the Chaseform annual.

But I knew it wasn't going to be 66/1 this time around, and sure enough, it was not. This was no Dettori-inspired Fujiyama Crest moment, but even so, the money that my bets had racked up on this horse led to it going off at a greatly reduced starting price of 7/1.

I couldn't contain my excitement as I listened to it take the lead at the last on the Extel speaker, cheering it home, something that didn't go unnoticed, and shortly after, Brenda called me over, indicating that I was once again required in the back room.

"This was you, wasn't it?" asked Mick.

"What was me?" I said, feigning innocence.

"You know very well. What's gone down this afternoon. My phone's been ringing for the past hour. Word has got around."

"Yeah, it was me," I admitted. "Alright, so you sussed me. Does anyone else know it was me?"

"Not as far as I can tell. I've got reports of a milkman, a postman, and a builder. Were they all you?"

"Actually, the last one was a painter, but two out of three ain't bad. The old bookies' telegraph has been busy today, then, eh?"

"I'll say. Now look, why didn't you tell me about this, or cut me in? I could have helped."

"I couldn't take the risk," I replied. "I had to keep this under wraps. I didn't even tell the bloke I got the disguises off what they were for."

The only person who knew the truth was Deborah, but since there was no way of tracing her connection to me, that wasn't a problem.

"Yes, but I'm out of pocket now, aren't I? Because I took a few bets from other bookies desperate to lay off, and by the time I tried to lay them off myself, the price had collapsed. Your little scheme has cost me nearly five grand."

"That's a trifling amount compared to what I've won today. As soon as I've collected, I'll see you alright. How does double what you lost sound? For the inconvenience."

"That sounds most agreeable. If you collect, that is."

He was voicing something I had feared all along, but the bracelet had given me no indication that there was any danger of not being paid out. Mind you, it had been practically dormant throughout this entire operation, seemingly having washed its hands of any involvement.

"There's no reason to think I won't get paid," I replied. "I haven't broken any rules. I was extremely careful."

"Maybe you were," he said. "But I've had some pretty upset people on the phone today. Don't expect any of them to be welcoming you with open arms when you go to collect. I should leave it for a few days, if I were you. And after this, I'd stay out of the game for good. You simply won't be allowed to pull a stunt like this again."

"Don't worry, I intend to," I replied, remembering my pledge to Molly.

"What are you going to do with your winnings?" he asked. "Going by the calls I've had today, you've probably got enough to retire on, haven't you?"

"I'm not keeping a penny of it. It's all going to Band Aid, to the relief fund."

"An admirable cause," he said. "Tell you what, just square me the five grand I dropped, and chuck the other five you were going to give me in the charity pot. I'm not going to try and profit out of this when there are lives at stake."

"Nice one," I replied. He was a decent sort, and I was sorry he'd got stung today because of me. But at least he would get his money back, hopefully.

I decided to follow his advice and leave it until after the weekend for things to blow over before I went and collected. Mick was right. I needed to let the dust settle.

But it seemed I didn't leave it long enough, because on Tuesday, my luck finally ran out.

December 1984

"Get in the car!"

It all happened so quickly, I barely had time to register what was going on. One minute I was walking out of a betting shop in Primrose Hill, and the next, I'd been grabbed off the street and bundled into a dark Ford Granada with tinted windows. The instruction had been barked at me by one of two blokes, both thickset, thuggish types, squeezed into suits a size or two too small for them.

I didn't have time to absorb any other details, as the waves of fear coursing through me and the suddenness of it all left little space for rational thought.

As for the interior of the car, I barely had time to catch a glimpse, as the second I was shoved inside, a strip of tape was slapped across my mouth, and a coarse straw sack was thrown over my head. Then, my face was pushed down abruptly against the seat. Why they felt the need to do that, given the windows were already tinted, I couldn't say. Maybe it was just to add to the general air of intimidation. If so, it was working. I was terrified, and I genuinely thought this might be the end. I couldn't even check the bracelet, with the bag over my head.

I had seen enough films where this sort of thing went on to know I was facing one of two possibilities. Either I was being driven somewhere to be bumped off, or I was being taken to see someone who wasn't too happy with me, for one reason or another. It wasn't hard to guess what that might be, given what I'd recently been up to.

Big Mick had tried to warn me, but I had brushed it off. Now I was paying the price.

All I could do was pray it was the latter, which, weighing up the odds, seemed the more likely option. My thinking, fractured as it was by my predicament, was that if they were planning to kill me, there'd be no need to stop me seeing where we were going. Dead men don't tell tales, and all that.

That was the single crumb of comfort I clung to as the car sped through the streets, my restricted vision and growing discomfort disorientating me. The minutes passed, and nobody spoke. I could hear the hustle and bustle of London all around me; the odd horn, engines revving, and the stop-start rhythm of the journey as we negotiated the traffic.

Eventually we came to a halt, and I heard what sounded like a large garage door slamming behind us.

"Get up!" barked the same voice as before, the first words I'd heard since the initial instruction. Not that I had much say in the matter, as I felt myself being roughly manhandled out of the car. Then the bag was whipped off, taking my glasses with it and sending them clattering to the floor, not that this mattered. I had been wearing my bespectacled postman disguise, and the lenses were just plain glass. Finally, I could see that the bracelet was red. Well, it was a bit late to start warning me now. Where was it half an hour ago when I needed it?

We were inside a large, mostly empty space, either a sizeable garage or a small warehouse, where the sound of the car doors echoed sharply as they were slammed shut. Other than a couple of bags of what looked like cement or concrete, a cement mixer, and a few large builder's buckets, there was very little else in there.

A metal staircase zig-zagged up one wall, leading to a mezzanine level above, where I could see a sealed-off area behind a plain wooden door. This, I assumed, must be some sort of office.

There were three of my captors altogether, most likely the two who had grabbed me, plus the driver. One of them looked vaguely familiar, and I tried to recall where I had seen him before. Then I remembered him as one of the heavies Frankie had brought into the shop earlier in the year, called Lenny or something along those lines.

I looked around, but there was no way out, and it was pointless even thinking about escape. I was just going to have to face whatever was coming to me. They marched me up the stairs, shoes clanging on the metal steps, then one of them rapped on the door.

"Enter," came a calm and level voice from inside. It wasn't aggressive or threatening in any way, but even so, I felt my stomach tighten.

The door opened, and I was ushered into a largely featureless office space. It had stark concrete walls, no windows, and a single, naked lightbulb hanging from the ceiling. The air was thick with cigar smoke. There was a battered filing cabinet in one corner, two chairs, and a plain wooden desk. It was little more than a cell, or, as I began to suspect, an interrogation room.

Behind the desk sat a large man, aged roughly in his late sixties or early seventies, in an expensive grey suit, and with immaculately coiffed white hair. He didn't rise to greet me, but just sat there, arms resting on the arms of the chair, a cigar smouldering in one hand, eyes fixed on me. His appearance screamed criminal mastermind, like something out of James Bond. All he was missing was the cat.

I had never seen this man before in my life, but had already guessed his identity before he spoke.

"Allow me to introduce myself," he began. "My name is Vincent Maddox. Please sit down."

"I'm…" I began, taking a seat opposite him.

"I know who you are, Nobby. Or should I call you Robin? You were brought to my attention a while ago, and after your little visit to my establishment this morning, I thought it was time I had you in for a little chat. You must forgive the office, by the way. It is rather basic. Ordinarily, I reside in more luxurious surroundings, but this place, shall we say, has its uses."

He oozed charm, but with each sentence, I felt the threat level ratcheting up another notch. I had heard psychopaths often used this tactic – sweet-talking you before they flashed the steel. The implication in his words was obvious. This was the place he came to do his dirty work.

I peeked at the bracelet and wished I hadn't, as it continued to pulse red. Whether that was a warning that I was in trouble, which was stating the obvious, or an admonishment for what I had been up to over the past few days, I couldn't say. But there was no doubt I was up to my neck in it here, and what I said and did over the next few minutes was likely to have a serious impact on my life expectancy.

I decided to try to adopt a light-hearted approach, even though I was petrified with fear. Perhaps I could bluff it out. I was good at doing that, playing poker, maybe I could apply the same techniques here.

"Well, it was lovely of you to bring me here, Mr Maddox, but you needn't have gone to so much trouble. I'd have been happy to pop in for a chat. You only had to give me a call."

And then it came, a harsh, stinging slap around the face from one of the goons.

"Ow! What the hell was that for?"

"Don't disrespect Mr Maddox," snapped the same guy from earlier, seemingly the only one with a tongue in his mouth, and even then, he was a man of few words.

"Please, Ivan, we don't need to get all heavy-handed," said Vincent. "Not yet anyway. Nobby here has just popped in to answer a few questions, haven't you? I'm sure he's going to be co-operative, and if he isn't, well…"

He let the sentence tail off, so I intervened, noting the disappointed look on Ivan's face.

"What sort of questions?"

"Oh, nothing too taxing. Quite easy, really. More like *Blankety Blank* than *University Challenge*. Like this, for instance. I understand that you work as a florist. So could you explain to me why, when you were apprehended leaving my betting shop this morning, you were, and indeed still are, dressed as a postman?"

My decision to adopt my disguises again when I went to collect had, in hindsight, probably been a mistake. They knew who to look out for.

"Your betting shop?" I asked.

"Yes. BetterBet Racing is my chain, all twelve shops. But I'm guessing you didn't know that."

It was news to me. I wouldn't have gone anywhere near it if I had known. It seemed the supposedly all-seeing bracelet hadn't known about that either. Or had decided to let me dig my own grave.

"No, Mr Maddox, if I had known, I would have gone elsewhere. Honestly."

"You did go elsewhere. At least a dozen other places. And in every single one, you landed a string of miracle bets. And not for the first time. The fact that you also saw fit to adopt various aliases arouses further suspicion. I suggest you knew exactly what you were doing and planned all this in meticulous detail."

"I just got lucky," I said, not expecting him to buy it, and I was right.

"No one's that lucky," he said, echoing what Mick had said to me before. "You've been getting information from somewhere, and with it, you've cleaned my flagship shop out of twenty-five grand."

"Well, it should have been thirty, but I went over the shop limit," I said. "But look, there's no need for any hard feelings, so why don't I just give you back the money and we'll call it quits?"

I reached into my pocket, took out the cheque, which I'd asked the shop to make out to the relief fund, and handed it to him.

"Oxfam," he said, reading it. "We're a proper little good Samaritan, aren't we?"

"I just like to do my bit for charity," I said.

"Charity begins at home," he said, tearing the cheque in half.

"OK, fair enough. Can I go then? I'm sorry about this little misunderstanding, but you've got your money back now. I promise it won't happen again."

"Not so fast," said Vincent, not to my great surprise. I'd have been deluding myself if I'd believed it was going to be that easy.

"I want to know where you're getting your tips from."

"There aren't any," I said. "It's all form study."

"I'm sorry, I don't buy it. One of those horses had never even raced before. Another was pulled up on its last three starts. There's nothing in the formbook whatsoever to say those horses had any chance at all. So, let's try again. Where are you getting your information from?"

"I don't have any, honestly."

"Ivan!" he said, and I saw a grin break out on the big guy's face as he punched me squarely on the jaw, causing me to almost fall backwards off the chair.

"That was a warning," said Vincent. "Now, I don't know how far I have to go to loosen your tongue, but you are going to give me the information I want. Someone is supplying you with it, and you are going to tell me who it is."

"I can't tell you what I don't know," I protested.

Another blow, this time to the stomach, causing me to gasp for breath.

"Perhaps I can persuade you another way," he said. "Do you know where this old warehouse is?"

"No, it was a bit difficult to keep my bearings with a bag over my head," I said, struggling to get the words out in my winded state.

"It's directly beside the Thames," he replied. "There are gates out the back that practically open onto the river. They used to ship goods directly out of the rear doors from here, back in the day."

"That's handy," I said.

"It's very handy, I agree. Ivan, go and fire up the cement mixer."

"With pleasure, boss."

"The cement mixer?" And then I remembered noticing it when I came in. I hadn't given it much thought at the time, assuming this had just been some builder's place, but now it had taken on a whole new grisly significance.

"Yes. I understand that I have a nickname. Do you know what it is?"

I knew what he was driving at, and could barely bring myself to say it, given the implications.

"It's Boots," I murmured. Both Reg and my father had told me, and why, months ago.

"Ten out of ten. You see, I said it wasn't *University Challenge*. And do you know how I got that name?"

"Is it because of your impressive collection of footwear?" I asked. It was amazing how, even under these dire circumstances, I could still manage to muster a joke. What was it they called that, gallows humour?

"No, it's because of your new pair of shoes, which Ivan and Lenny downstairs are going to mix up for you. It's quite a simple process. You stand in a couple of buckets, we fill them up with concrete, wait a few hours for it to set, and then chuck you in the river."

"Well, thank you for clarifying that," I replied. "In broad daylight?"

"Oh, we'll wait until after dark. But that won't be long. These short December days slip by so quickly, don't they?"

"They certainly do," I said, thinking about Molly. I had promised to meet her in The Salisbury today, at 1pm for a drink, before taking a trip to Oxford Street to do some early Christmas shopping. It was a carbon copy of what we'd had planned a year ago, the day things had all started to unravel, and all I could think about was her words when we'd got back together.

Don't let me down again…

This was crazy. Here I was worrying about missing a date, when I'd just been told I was to be executed after both the sun and my new pair of shoes had set. But I couldn't stop thinking about her. I'd worked so hard to win her back, and I couldn't risk losing her again now, assuming I got out of this alive.

"Unless, of course, your memory miraculously returns all of a sudden."

"I can't tell you what I don't know," I insisted, looking him straight in the eye. "There is no source of information. I truly did it all myself."

"And you'd rather die than tell the truth? Who are you protecting?"

"I am telling you the truth, and I'm not protecting anyone. Think about it. If there were people out there with that sort of info, why would they give it to me? Especially given that, as you've seen, the money's all going to charity. Do you think it was all done out of the goodness of their hearts?"

I heard the rumble of the cement mixer begin downstairs, as Vincent scrutinised me, trying to weigh me up.

"Do you know how many men I've given a new pair of boots to over the years?" he asked.

"I don't know," I said. "Dozens, probably."

"Surprisingly, only three in thirty years of running the firm. Dozens, perhaps hundreds, have sat in that chair for a variety of reasons. How to bypass security systems, safe combinations, agreeing to fix a boxing match, finding out who grassed to the filth, it's amazing what people will tell you under duress. Most of them had a lot more at stake than you, as well. But faced with imminent death, almost all of them buckled and told me what I wanted to know. And these were hard men for the most part, as tough as nails. Not some kid who works in a flower shop."

"You believe me, then?"

"I'm not sure. But I don't believe you'd throw your life away just to protect the identity of a bent trainer or two."

"Does that mean you are going to let me go, after all?"

"I'm not going to just cold-bloodedly murder you without giving you the chance to prove yourself," he said. "I'm not totally evil, whatever you may have heard. It's just business, that's all. I thought once you heard the mixer going, you'd crack, but it appears not. So perhaps we need to try a different approach."

"Like what?"

"Like this. I'm still not fully convinced you're not lying to me, so here's what we're going to do."

He reached into the drawer and brought out something that sent a chill right through me. It was a small revolver, short-barrelled, black, the kind you'd see in any old 70s or 80s action show. He opened the cylinder with practised ease, dropped in a single bullet, and gave it a casual spin. Then he placed it carefully on the desk.

"You're a gambling man, so I'm going to give you the wager of your life – quite literally. You claim you've got nothing you want to tell me, even with the threat of the cement mixer hanging over you, so I'm going to put your fate squarely in your own hands."

"What… what are you going to do?" I said, fighting a nauseous desire to vomit at the prospect of what might be coming next. It had been one shock after another, and my resilience could only stretch so far. The threat of concrete boots was one thing, but now there was a loaded gun on the table right in front of me. It made the danger all the more immediate, particularly after I'd thought I was out of the woods just a few minutes earlier when he'd led me to believe he wasn't going to kill me. Perhaps that was all part of the tactic to wear me down – give me hope and then dash it again.

"It's not what I'm going to do, it's what you're going to do. Ever heard of Russian roulette?"

"Of course I have," I replied, fear levels ramping up ever higher. "You're not suggesting we play that, are you?"

"Certainly not," he said. "Why would I want to do that? I've no need to risk my life. You, however, that's a different matter. Go on, pick it up."

He slid the gun across the desk towards me. I looked at it, scared to touch it, thinking about the implications of what he was proposing.

"Come on, it won't bite you," he said.

Being bitten by it was the least of my worries, but I grasped it anyway in my right hand, surprised by how heavy it felt. A solid, cold lump of metal that could end my life with a single squeeze of my finger.

"You're not seriously suggesting I point this at my head and pull the trigger, are you?"

"That's exactly what I'm suggesting," he said. "It seems the threat of swimming with the fishes isn't enough to make you part with the information I want, so perhaps something more immediate, and at your own hand, will encourage you. So here are the rules of the game. There is a single bullet in that gun, and five empty chambers. So, you know the odds."

"Five to one," I replied.

"Precisely. So you're going to point that at your head, spin the barrel, and take a single shot. If you survive, you go free. If you don't – well, you killed yourself. It's not down to me."

"And if I refuse?"

"Then it's a few hours standing in concrete, and then you take up scuba diving, sadly without any equipment. I know which option I'd take. I'm a gambling man, too. Of course, if you tell me what I want to know, you won't need to do either."

"Like I've said about six times, there is nothing to tell."

"The gun it is, then," he replied, sitting back in his chair and taking a puff on his cigar. "Whenever you're ready."

I turned the gun over in my hands, weighing up my options. I could, if I wanted to, shoot Vincent there and then, but that would be a distinctly unwise move, given the presence of the one remaining goon who had stayed in the room. I, however, had only one bullet and no idea which chamber it was in.

I looked at the bracelet to see it glowing green, suggesting I had nothing to fear. That was easy for it to say. It wasn't the one about to potentially shoot itself. Presumably it was telling me to go ahead, and that I would survive, but who would cheerfully do that, even with all the guarantees in the world? We were talking about holding a loaded gun to my head and pulling the trigger here.

I knew I had no choice. Slowly, I raised the weapon.

I closed my eyes, shaking, and pressed the cold metal to the side of my head. My finger trembled on the trigger. Every fibre of my being was screaming 'no' at me.

And then I pulled.

Click.

Nothing.

I opened one eye, then the other, heart going nineteen to the dozen, and exhaled deeply, realising I had been holding it for several seconds. The bracelet was still glowing green, as if to say, 'told you so'.

Vincent studied me for a long moment, then gave a smile of approval.

"You've got guts," he said. "And I'm satisfied now that you were telling the truth. You would never have put yourself through that if you weren't."

"So I really can go now?"

"Yes. I'll get the boys to run you back to where they found you. But just one thing, Nobby."

"Yes?"

"If you ever set foot in one of my betting shops again, I'll have you back here and we'll play this game again. But next time, there will be four bullets in the gun. Understand?"

"Yes," I replied, relieved at the ordeal finally being over. If Ivan and the others got their skates on, I might not even be late for my date with Molly, though that meant I wouldn't have time to go home and get changed, which would be something I'd have to explain.

It was in fact ten past one when I arrived at The Salisbury, courtesy of Ivan and the gang, who were kind enough to drive me straight there. Now that I was no longer in trouble, they had proven to be quite amenable in the car on the way back. Even so, I still had to wear the bag for the first part of the journey, to protect the location of Vincent's warehouse.

"Sorry about knocking you about earlier," Ivan had said. "I was just doing my job."

"Don't worry about it," I replied, though his earlier attentions had given me cause for concern, because when I caught a glimpse of myself in the Granada's rear view mirror, there was a puffy, dark patch on my jaw where I'd been punched, which would doubtless develop into a full bruise as the day went on. I also had a slight cut to the corner of my mouth, which had oozed a little blood onto my chin. I hadn't noticed this at the time due to the all-consuming fear, but Molly certainly would. So that was another thing I was going to have to explain.

"Someone's been in the wars," announced Des, clocking my injuries as I entered the pub, which seemed even more dark and dismal than usual. "Moonlighting for the Post Office now, are we? What happened? Did you get bitten by a dog?"

Molly, sitting at the bar, looked up and frowned, possibly initially at my late arrival, but that was soon replaced by concern as she took in the swelling on my jaw.

"Nobby, what on earth have you been up to? And why are you dressed as a postman?"

"I got mugged," I replied. "Coming out of a betting shop, would you believe?"

It wasn't the right thing to say. She had been working over the weekend, and I hadn't told her about the details of my big heist yet. I had planned to do it this afternoon, now that it was all over.

"I thought you said that would be finished by the end of November," she said, examining me with concern. "Are you all right?"

"A bit sore, but I'll live. I could do with a beer, though."

"Bottled beer only, today, I'm afraid," said Des. "All the electrics are fucked and the pumps are off. There's some bloke down in the cellar trying to fix them right now. Bloody Eddie, I'll swing for him."

"Let's go over there where we can talk," I said to Molly, as Des handed me a bottle of Holsten Pils.

We took a seat by a rather forlorn-looking Christmas tree, all decorated but not lit up.

"What's Eddie done?" I asked.

"He sold Des some dodgy Albanian Christmas tree lights. When he put the tree up this morning and switched them on, they blew the whole fuse board and half the sockets in the pub. But never mind that. I want to know what you've been up to."

So I told her the whole story, focusing on how I'd studied and planned the whole thing, always keeping the emphasis on how it had all been for the famine effort. The only things I didn't mention were the bracelet and my trip to see Vincent. I wasn't going to be telling anybody about that. The mugging story wasn't a complete lie in any case, I had been jumped and had the cheque taken from me, I just didn't elaborate.

"But you told me you were planning this months ago, before we even knew about the situation in Ethiopia," she said.

"Before the media got hold of it," I said. "The crisis in Africa has been an ongoing situation for over a year. The charities have been aware of it, but there wasn't a lot of press coverage until Michael Buerk's report. But I got wind of it months ago, when I got chatting to a woman in an Oxfam shop."

"So, how much have you made?"

"A lot," I said, pulling the four remaining cheques I had collected that morning out of my pocket. This was the second day I had been around collecting, and Vincent's shop had thankfully been the final one on my list.

"My God, Nobby, there's over two hundred thousand pounds here."

"And plenty more where that came from," I added. "All collected yesterday, and safely stashed away at home."

I had twelve cheques in total, out of the fifteen. Two had refused to pay out, and Vincent had taken his back, but in total, I was looking at around three-quarters of a million pounds. Not the million I had aimed for, but most satisfactory, nonetheless.

"And now," I said, pausing for dramatic effect, "That's it. I quit. I've placed my final bet."

I meant it. All desire to ever bet again had gone. All I'd ever been interested in was beating the odds, and with this charity haul, I had landed something that could never be bettered, especially given that I'd no longer have the bracelet after the end of the year. Not only that, but I'd also faced down the ultimate gamble through the barrel of a gun, and come out the other side.

Even after I went back to 2024, I couldn't imagine ever being tempted into a bookie's again. What would be the point? I could honestly say I had well and truly got it out of my system.

All that was left to do now was enjoy my remaining time in 1984 and think about what might come next. For today, it was all about spending the day with Molly, doing what we should have done a year ago. Then tomorrow, I would be visiting Oxfam to donate my winnings. I hadn't heard 'Do They Know It's Christmas?' on the radio yet, but within a few days it was everywhere, and my donation even made the news, with reports of a mysterious benefactor and their generous contribution to the fund.

The charity was as good as their word and did not reveal my identity, even when tabloid journalists went sniffing around, though Mick informed me it had become common knowledge among the bookmaking fraternity when I ran into him one morning in Reg's. This didn't bother me since I had no intention of ever setting foot in any of their premises again, so it wasn't going to be an issue.

Relaxed and happy with the way the year had turned out, I was able to enjoy the run-up to Christmas, unencumbered by any worries, bar one. I was unsure about exactly what was going to happen to me at the end of the year, only that this version of me was going back to the future. As for the part of me left here, I couldn't say. Jenna had briefly mentioned something about temporary amnesia, but I hadn't fully grasped what she meant. All I knew was that while I had my wits about me and was still here, I needed to do all I could to secure my future.

December 1984 felt more Christmassy than any other I could remember. For a start, the charts were stacked with Christmas songs that year, with Band Aid and Wham! locked in at the top, and numerous other festive offerings in the Top 40. It was also the year that the BBC broadcast the marvellous *Box of Delights*, which I remembered watching the first time around, even though it was on children's television.

On Christmas Eve, I took Molly into Central London to enjoy the lights. In an ideal world, it would have been snowing, but that only happens in Christmas movies. Even so, it was the most romantic setting I could think of as I proposed to her after dark, beneath the lights of the Christmas tree in Trafalgar Square.

To my delight, she accepted right away, with none of that 'it's a big step' or 'I need time to think' bollocks. We kissed under the lights, then walked hand in hand through the streets. It might not have snowed, but I had ticked off another romantic Christmas film trope. I got the girl at the end.

With the money I had saved up, getting married and buying a first home was still a realistic prospect in London in 1984, and a good investment too, given the property price boom which I knew was on the way. So we agreed to start looking in the New Year.

I cherished every moment of Christmas Day with my family, one that had been very different before, with Dad languishing in Pentonville. Then, in my final few days, I spent as much time with my friends as I possibly could. Billy, Reg, Eddie with his dodgy deals, even the cantankerous, foul-mouthed Des, I was going to miss them all.

As the countdown to midnight began in The Salisbury, I couldn't help wondering how different my life might be in the future. Would it work out with me and Molly? Would my life be better?

I was about to find out.

January 2024

"Give us a kiss, darling!"

I watched, horrified, as Andy lunged forward off his stool, attempting to grapple with Lauren over the bar, while cries of 'Happy New Year' rang out all around me.

My horror did not stem from the sight of a dishevelled man in his forties foisting his unwanted attentions on a girl half his age, unpalatable as that was. In any case, I knew Lauren was more than capable of fending off his advances, she'd had enough practice, and sure enough, a sharp slap across the chops proved more than sufficient to have him sinking back onto his stool.

No, my dismay was triggered by the discovery that I was right back where I had started, before Jenna had whisked me away to tell me of the adventure I was about to undertake. What about all the changes I had made, my vows to build a better life, and my efforts to repair my relationship with Molly? Had none of that made any difference whatsoever? If it had, surely I wouldn't have landed back here, as if none of it had ever happened?

I looked down at my arm, where the jewel in the bracelet was happily glowing away in all its green glory. There were times when it felt like that thing was taking the absolute piss.

Then my eyes were drawn to my hand. Perhaps it did know what it was doing after all. It had taken me a second or two to register, but now I was focused on the gold wedding band on my finger. And just as I was getting my head around that, I heard a soft voice behind me.

"Where's my kiss?"

I turned, and there she was, my Molly. Forty years older, yes, but unmistakably her. The lines time had etched into her face had done nothing to dull the warmth in her eyes, or the way she looked at me, just as she had that night I had proposed to her beneath the Christmas tree in Trafalgar Square. That was a week ago for me, yet four decades had passed for her. But those timescales were immaterial. We were in love then, and it seemed like we still were now.

I obliged her request, indulging her in a long, passionate kiss, exhilarated to find that we were still together, even if I had no idea how we had ended up here, back in the same town. It would have made more sense if we had still been in London.

"Wow!" she said when I broke it off. "It's a long time since you've kissed me like that."

Perhaps that was the case. I don't know how many people keep the passion levels high for forty years, but she seemed happy, which inspired me to make the most of the moment, so I kissed her again.

Without a clue about what was going on right now, or at any time in the past forty years, the last thing I needed was too much conversation. Full of desire, I suggested we go home, with just one thought in mind, one that would require few words. Later, we would sleep, and perhaps tomorrow, things might be a little clearer.

I made my first mistake the second we walked out of the pub, turning right instead of left, instinctively heading for my old place. This led her to rightly ask where we were going. It seemed I didn't live in my old place anymore, so I made a joke about going to the kebab van, before we turned back the other way. As we did so, I took hold of her hand. This wasn't just me being romantic. Since I didn't have a clue where we were going, by doing this I could let her lead and guide me to my, as yet, unknown new home.

We walked just a short distance, into the heart of the market square, before I saw it right in front of us, an impressive, three-storey building, the ground floor of which was taken up by a florist called none other than Bud & Bloom. That hadn't been there in the old timeline; it had been a nail bar. But now here it was, even painted in the same colours as our old shop in Kentish Town. It seemed that in this altered reality, I had decided to come to this town, just as I had before, but this time, I had brought both Molly and the business with me.

It was a sizeable building, and as I was later to find out, unlike most of the shops in the town centre we owned the freehold and lived on the two floors above. So, we can't have been doing too badly for ourselves.

The sex that night was incredible, with Molly at one point commending me on my energy and remarking that it was "like I was twenty-one again." If only she had known.

The next morning, when I woke up, I still couldn't remember anything about the missing forty years, and wondered how long this would persist. I could bluff it out for a day or two, but if it lasted longer than that, I wasn't sure what I was going to do.

I wondered again if I should have come clean with her, just as I'd considered doing in the past, but I remained reluctant. I just couldn't think of any way of expressing myself that wouldn't sound insane. So instead, after breakfast, I fired up the laptop in the office at the back of the shop and got onto the internet. Social media, something I hadn't been overly keen on in the past, was hopefully going to be my friend today and fill in some gaps.

My memory wasn't completely shot, because the laptop wanted a PIN when I opened it, and without hesitation, I typed in the code, only realising afterwards that the number, 2305, meant nothing to me – not at that point, anyway. I later discovered it was my younger daughter's date of birth.

Speaking of which, I soon found out, unsurprisingly given that I had been married for nearly forty years, that I had two grown-up children. Neither lived with us, but both were still local. Hopefully, by the time I saw them, my temporary amnesia would be gone, because it was going to be decidedly weird if they seemed like strangers, both for them and for me. How could I act like the old dad they had always known, and hopefully loved, if I had no idea who that person now was?

It would be like opening the door one day to a thirty-year-old, who would then announce that they were a long-lost daughter, as a result of an over-exuberant Club 18–30 holiday sometime back in the 90s. We would be total strangers.

My trawl through Facebook helped, with certain pictures triggering snippets of memory here and there. Details of the new timeline I had created after 1984 were beginning to come back, just bits at first, but anything I couldn't remember, I could do my best to find out. As well as social media, I had years of emails, photographs, and all manner of other documentation to draw on.

I was also quite canny in my conversation with Molly over lunch that day, going down the reminiscing route, in a way that allowed me to ask questions indirectly, in the way that people do when they're chatting about old times.

"I must admit, I miss the old London, but I don't regret moving out this way," I began. "How long have we been out here now? I can't remember exactly."

"It was the year after your mum died, so it must have been 2001," she said. "I remember, because that was the year Bethany started primary school just a few days before 9/11."

"Of course," I said. "The old memory's not what it was."

I suppose it had been too much to hope that my parents might both still be alive, even though they had been together in the new timeline, but I was still saddened that they had gone so early – Dad in '99, and Mum a year later. Both had only been in their sixties. At least I'd had the chance to spend another year with them, and had a chance to say goodbye properly.

Bethany was the youngest of our two girls, the other being Tiffany. For a moment, I felt cheated. I had missed their entire time growing up, but thankfully, within a couple of days, those feelings went away.

By the following morning, when we reopened the shop, the memories were beginning to flood back in torrents. I saw our wedding day, in the summer of 1985, and our first home, a tiny flat in Kentish Town, close to

The Golden Dragon, where I'd had my fingers burnt at seven-card stud by Harry 'Tinker' Bell. I saw the old shop, booming, and us opening a second, which Molly and I ran. Then, in the 1990s, the births of both our daughters.

I saw friends, old and new, come and go, and then our move here, selling our business in London and bringing Bud & Bloom out to the shires. I watched the girls grow up, and our holidays abroad, with the comfortable lifestyle our thriving business brought us. And nowhere in that was there so much as a hoof-beat or the turn of a card. I'd made Molly a promise in 1984, and stuck to it.

And now, a week on? I remember it all, though strangely, not so much about my old life, the one I lived before. It's odd, but that world feels distant now, as if it happened to someone else entirely. If I could see it, it would be like watching an actor on television portraying an alternative version of me that no longer exists.

The bracelet was still with me, though dormant, perhaps storing up its energy for the next life it was destined to change. I wouldn't know who that was until the end of the year, but whoever they were, they had an amazing experience ahead of them. Like me, when it was over, they would have effectively lived two different lives.

My year in the past might not have all been plain sailing. Moments like that trip to Vincent's warehouse would have been enough to traumatise some folk for life.

But the rest of it? The people, the places, and the moments I thought I would never get the chance to see again. I wouldn't have missed it for the world.

THE END…but you can meet the next recipient of the bracelet in *1985: A Year in the Life of Robbie James.*

Also by Jason Ayres

A Year in the Life

Travel back in time and relive the 1980s in this stunning collection of humorous and nostalgic tales.

- 1980: A Year in the Life of Keith Diamond
- 1981: A Year in the Life of Nick Taylor
- 1982: A Year in the Life of Wendy Wood
- 1983: A Year in the Life of Jenna Rae
- 1984: A Year in the Life of Nobby Clarke
- 1985: A Year in the Life of Robbie James

Each book in this anthology series follows a different character in a different setting, and all of them can be enjoyed standalone.

The Time Bubble Collection

The Time Bubble is a complete fifteen book series, following a rich cast of characters from youth to old age, their lives intertwining across decades, alternate realities, and the very fabric of time.

1) The Time Bubble
2) Global Cooling
3) Man Out of Time
4) Splinters in Time
5) Class of '92
6) Vanishing Point
7) Midlife Crisis
8) Rock Bottom
9) My Tomorrow, Your Yesterday
10) Happy New Year
11) Return to Tomorrow
12) Cause of Death
13) Lauren's Odyssey
14) Gone to the Rapture
15) Closing Time

The Ronnie and Bernard Adventures

The Ronnie and Bernard Adventures are a pair of humorous novels with mild science fiction and horror elements set in the 1970s. The stories follow the fortunes of two actors from very different backgrounds.

Together they tackle mysteries, travel in time, and negotiate the rocky path of life as jobbing actors, from daytime soaps to panto.

Anyone who remembers the 1970s will love these nostalgic stories looking back at a time when life was simpler, and the world didn't take itself too seriously. Packed with period detail, humour, and references to the era, they are the perfect antidote to modern living.

1) The Crooked Line
2) The Haunted Theatre

Follow the Author

To ensure you never miss a release, or to be informed of special deals on Amazon, sign up to follow me on my author page which can be found here:

https://www.amazon.co.uk/stores/Jason-Ayres/author/B00CQO4XJC

For exclusive content from me, regular newsletters and occasional freebies and offers, sign up to my mailing list here:

https://www.jasonayres.co.uk/contact/ or email me directly: jason.ayres@btinternet.com

And of course, there is Facebook, X, and YouTube!

https://www.facebook.com/TheTimeBubble/

https://twitter.com/TheTimeBubble/

https://www.youtube.com/channel/UCg13jmfTUTFCqWWZrPmXqJQ

Finally, if you loved this book and have the time to leave a star rating or review on Amazon, it is always hugely appreciated!

Printed in Dunstable, United Kingdom